The Two Lives
of Maddie Meadows

OCTOBER HOUSE BOOKS

Copyright © Sharley Scott 2020

Sharley Scott asserts her right under the Copyright, Designs and
Patents Act 1988 to be identified as the author of this work. This
novel is a work of fiction. The characters portrayed within it are
the work of the author's imagination. Any resemblance to actual
persons, living or dead, is entirely coincidental.

Cover © Sharley Scott
Cover design: More Visual Ltd

All rights reserved. No part of this publication may be
reproduced, stored in a retrieval system or transmitted in any
form or by any means, mechanical, electronic, photocopying,
recording or otherwise, without the prior written permission of
the author.

ISBN: 9798656409667

To our lovely dad,
Rod Pengelly

*As you look upon a flower and admire its simplicity –
remember me.*

Margaret Mead, 'Remember Me'.

Chap

CW00400551

I BIT MY LIP TO MASK A SMILE as I'd been reading it and re-reading it all day and couldn't wait to see Rachel's reaction. Once I'd unfolded the sheet, I ironed out the creases on my lap before dangling it in front of her. Her brow furrowed in confusion. Then, like a sprung letterbox, she snatched it from my fingers, her grin widening as she scanned each line, until she flung her arms around me and hauled me into a bear hug. The arm of her glasses dug into my cheek as she enveloped me in the stench of cheap perfume – one of the ways she tried to hide her smoking habit from her partner, Kieran. The other was spearmint gum, which she now chewed inches from my ear.

"You've only gone and done it! A manager! How posh are you now?"

"Posh?" I laughed.

"I've heard you talking. 'Is that Charles? Fetch me my corgis.'"

I stuck my tongue out. Unlike her excellent impersonation, I couldn't sound like the Queen if I tried. Her imitation was apt: Rachel lived in the Windsor House block, while I was stuck in Stuart House at the rear of the Court Place estate. All the blocks were named after royal houses. I've always thought it strange that the crummiest estates have the poshest names. All our blocks had their downsides. Mine overlooked the train line, whereas outside Rachel's flat was a huge leylandii hedge which hid the offices behind (and the sun).

"When have I ever spoken like that?"

"Whenever you're at work. Or on the phone. I should call you

Hyacinth Bucket."

Nothing she called me could dampen my excitement. This would be a great year, I could tell. Just ten days into 2014 and my life was on an upwards curve. I folded the letter back into its envelope and tucked it into my bag. After I'd clipped the flap in place to ensure my prize couldn't escape – it was more cherished than a love letter, offering more opportunity for taking me places than any man could – I looked up to find that Rachel had got to her feet.

"Celebratory cup of tea?"

I checked my watch. Just forty minutes until I needed to collect Josh from my cousin's house.

"If we're quick."

I followed her through to the kitchen, with its white melamine units and beige countertop identical to mine, except my walls and fridge were covered with Josh's paintings while a pack of dinosaur figures encircled our biscuit tin, protecting his favourite jammy dodgers.

She raised her voice over the whirr of the washing machine. "Bog-standard Tetley – or is it now Earl Grey?"

"The usual."

She bustled around the kitchen, clanging cupboard doors and wiping the sides while she waited for the kettle to boil. I nosed at her calendar, which showed busy days ahead: her nan's birthday, a dental appointment for Kieran and – this looked interesting – a night out at bingo.

"Who're you going to bingo with?"

Her mouth twitched and she tapped her nose. "You hate bingo."

"So do you!"

She tossed a teabag into each cup. "But it's at the football club."

When I gave her a blank look, she spoke in a voice that said I should know better. "Leah fancies Aaron and he's working behind the bar that night."

Leah made the third corner of our friendship triangle. While Rachel smoked like a puffing billy when she wasn't on the patches, Leah consumed men – unsuccessfully – and alcohol – with a lot more success. The idea of them gossiping together about going out to hook Aaron rankled. Why hadn't they asked me? But I knew the answer. I was the fallen angel who never went out on a school night. Not that I was ever angelic. Just that there were three Charlie's Angels and three of us girls. I was the brunette who'd met the man of her dreams, got pregnant and watched him walk away because he felt he was too young to have a child. But not to create one. Perhaps us girls should have styled ourselves after *Sex in the City*, which would have been more fitting, except there were four of them. And they were a lot posher than us – and I include myself in that statement, no matter what Rachel said.

A dark object shot past the window. With the glass being obscured by the floral nets, I couldn't tell what it was. When a crash reverberated through the building, Rachel slammed the kettle onto the worktop and shot out. I joined Rachel on the concrete walkway, to find the Flying Scotsman shouting above us.

"Load of junk. That salesman's going to get a right earful." A small white strip plummeted to the ground: the butt of a roll-up, joining the multitude that had gone before it. "I'll tell ya, he's in for it."

A door banged shut and the estate fell silent, apart from the clatter of a train on one side and the drone of passing cars on the other.

Rachel gripped the balcony railings to check he'd gone before turning to survey the wreckage below. I'd thought I'd seen something black fly past the window, but what was left of a silver-framed TV lay embedded in the muddy grass and tyre tracks below. The recent spell of heavy rain hadn't done the verges any good, especially with the parking issues on the estate but, luckily, whoever had taken to parking there had moved their car.

She gave a drawn-out sigh. "They'll have to do something about him. It's a miracle he's not killed anyone yet."

"Or burned them with his cigarette ends."

Whoever had given him his nickname – the Flying Scotsman – hadn't looked far for inspiration: he liked to throw things – usually empty cans or the butts of roll-ups. Also, his surname was Scott and he enjoyed a dram – or ten – of Scotch at the pub. Apart from the occasional colourful rant, he'd have been harmless if he'd been housed on the ground floor, but his flat was on the third floor – all the homes above the ground floor were maisonettes, but we called them flats – and he'd become a scourge to anyone passing below.

I moved away from the railing, brushing off the flecks of green paint that smattered my palm and the front of my jumper.

"Forget the tea. I don't want to be late for Josh."

Rachel pulled a pack of cigarettes from her pocket. "I'll walk with you. I could do with the fresh air."

◆

Emma, my new boss at Holdenwell Council had a core of steel, but – unlike my old boss – she didn't show it by raising her voice or bullying her staff. Her jacket hung across the back of her chair, ready for meetings, while she sported a casual look for the office: black cotton trousers and a collarless top. I'd been in my new post for a few days when I mentioned how well the staff reacted to her assertive but calm demeanour. She pursed her lips and her gaze stole across to David.

"Your job will be hard enough without me making it worse. Think of me as your support column."

I'd heard about David from several colleagues, who'd hinted that he'd wanted my job but his ego had outstretched his ability. It wasn't the only thing he stretched. While an iron wasn't a friend of his, his paunch helped to smooth the creases of his shirt. Between the row of buttons holding on for dear life, his shirt gaped, revealing a white T-shirt. Phone planted to his ear, he leaned back in his chair and rubbed his balding head while he chatted. He'd made it clear that he didn't like me much. When his eyes locked with mine, I was the first to look away.

Emma's words served to add more worry to my pile of woe, which now included the post-it note stuck to the centre of my computer screen. 'Please call the nursery.'

Seriously? Not today, please. Then I felt guilty. Even if it was my first week, work shouldn't come before Josh.

I dialled the nursery's number. Angie, the manager, answered.

"I got a message to call you," I said. "Is Josh okay?"

"He fell and bumped his head. He's been a bit tearful. We think it's best that he goes home."

I bit my lip. Why today? Why not tomorrow, when I'd arranged for Chelsea, my cousin, to pick Josh up from nursery while I attended my first evening meeting? Or any other day when Chelsea didn't have a hospital appointment? The last time I'd been called to fetch Josh from nursery, she'd collected him for me and reported that he was bouncing around within five minutes of being home, begging to go back.

"I understand," I said. "I'll be there as soon as possible."

What would Emma say when I told her I had to leave early on my third day? Especially when we'd just discussed preparing for another meeting in the morning? But I did have to work late tomorrow night, so perhaps she wouldn't mind.

Even though her desk was beside mine, I didn't want other people to overhear, so I crouched beside her chair to whisper to her. "The nursery has phoned and asked me to collect Josh. Do you mind if I prepare for the meeting at home? This won't happen often."

Absorbed in her work, it took a moment for her to register my words. Her fingers hovered over the keyboard until she turned to me with a concerned expression.

"Of course not. If you can't make tomorrow's meeting, let me know."

"He's just bumped his head. He'll be fine."

♦

Never were truer words spoken. Josh squealed, "Nooooo!" when he saw me. He'd been separated from the other children and given a wooden train set to play with by himself. For a two-year-old, this was the equivalent of being given a whole cake without having to share. And now Mummy was taking him away from the train.

As he staged an angry lie-in on the train track, I tried coercion,

10

then bribery – "If you're good, I'll take you to the playground" – but Angie's frown told me this was Not A Good Idea. Looking at the blue lump above Josh's eyebrow, I could see her point. I stroked his silky blond hair, so like his dad's.

"Darling, you've hurt your head and I need to take you home. How about we stop off for a Happy Meal on the way?" Angie's expression told me I'd managed to add more points to my hall of parenting shame.

With a shake of his head that told me Thomas the Tank Engine trumped McDonald's, Josh turned back to the train track.

"You can come back to nursery tomorrow," Angie cooed.

"No!"

I'd had enough. At this rate, I'd be here all afternoon. No longer caring what Angie thought, I wrestled his writhing, furious body into my arms and strode past a dozen open-mouthed little children, their paint brushes and sponges held in mid-air. Angie held open the door and waved us goodbye with a shrug of commiseration.

Once I'd struggled to get a screeching Josh into the car, he opted for the inverted-crescent trick, which involved him sticking his belly out and becoming more rigid than stone. His refusal to sit in his car seat left me one option: the knee-in-stomach manoeuvre, which sounds a lot worse than it is. My knee became my third hand, holding him down while I clipped him into the seat.

With Josh hollering in the back of the car, I dived into the driver's seat and turned the key in the ignition. When a DJ's voice blasted out, I tapped the CD button and pulled away to the sound of 'The Wheels on the Bus', his favourite song. Josh's tears quietened into a sulk, but when the song ended, he called, "Again!"

Moments later, I spotted his arms in the rear-view mirror,

waving along to the wipers going swish-swish-swish. My relief was cut short by the sudden realisation that I'd left my laptop at work. Without it, I couldn't prepare for tomorrow's meeting. I had no choice but to take Josh into the office to collect it. To the sound of snorting – we'd reached the pig in 'Old MacDonald had a Farm' – I pulled into an empty space outside the Holdenwell Council offices. My first bit of luck. Hopefully, Josh would behave for the few minutes it would take to retrieve the laptop.

The four-storey brick building nestled beside an ugly 1970s flat-roofed leisure complex. Even an abundance of trees didn't soften the harsh lines. When we reached the top step, the doors whirred open, and I carried Josh through the bustling reception area and down the warren of corridors to the second floor, where our team was based. Luckily, we were the first four rows by the door, so I didn't have to walk past dozens of enquiring stares. I doubted many people brought their children into work here, especially on day three.

David's chair sat empty, his desk cleared of all his belongings. This office ran a clear-desk policy at the end of every day – and I'd broken it, leaving my laptop, mug and papers strewn across the desk. Thank goodness I'd had to return.

"I thought you'd be back." Emma swivelled around in her chair and caught sight of Josh. "Hello, little one! That's a nasty bump."

Josh rewarded her with a vacant stare.

"Actually, while you're around, do you mind if I check a few things with you ahead of your meeting tomorrow?"

"If it's not a problem with Josh being here."

She shrugged. "He looks a lovely, quiet boy."

I didn't mention the earlier episode, but popped him on the floor with a pen and a sheet of paper.

"After you left, I had a phone call. It turns out the group's chairman won't be at the meeting. The new person who's chairing it is one to watch. I've tried to shuffle my diary around so I could attend, but I can't."

While Emma ran through the list of queries she needed me to raise, I kept a watchful eye on Josh, who seemed subdued after his outburst.

When she reached the end of the list, she laid down her pen. "You've handled tough sales meetings and dealt with politics at the charity you worked at before. This will be a doddle."

I stifled a grimace. Nothing I'd done before sounded as challenging as all the politics – big and small 'p' – that seemed to be at play here. But I needed her to think I was professional and capable, so I gave her a confident smile. Then I noticed that Josh had disappeared, leaving pens and a few scribbled sheets on the floor. I jumped up in panic – where was he? – and rushed into the centre of the office to scan the corridor between the rows of desks, before dropping to my knees to check beneath them. Nothing but legs, bags and bins.

Emma came over, her voice calm. "He can't have gone far."

As she spoke, a man laughed. "That's a picture!"

On the other side of the office, people by the filing cabinets had turned to where he pointed. It must be Josh, I knew it. What on earth had he done now? As I rushed over, a grinning woman took a photo on her mobile phone. Chuckling, she showed it to her companion.

Josh sat on the carpet beside the open drawer of a filing cabinet, sucking a strange blue object, which he pulled from his mouth to show me. My hands shot to my burning face. *No, it couldn't be!* It looked just like a blue dildo. It even had balls, although they were flat at the bottom.

Beside me, Emma laughed. "He's found the teenage pregnancy drawer, I see."

"The *what?*"

A woman stepped forward to take the object from Josh, but he stuck it behind his back. "*My* lolly."

"Bless him," she said.

She wouldn't think that if she'd seen him earlier. If he wouldn't give up Thomas without a fight, how would I wrestle this blue thing from him without causing a scene? I knelt on the carpet and held out my hand.

"Give it to Mummy, please."

He shook his head then clamped the thing in his mouth, leaving me stymied. I really didn't fancy dragging a screaming child from my workplace.

The woman joined me on the floor beside Josh. "We take these out to teach young people about safe sex." She took a green one from the cabinet and placed it on the floor, out of Josh's reach. The flat bottom enabled it to stand upright. "We've got them in a range of colours. It stops them from looking quite the real thing."

Emma rested a hand on my shoulder. "If you don't mind, I can swap it for a real lollipop. The drug and alcohol team have a stock of them."

My eyes widened. "What sort of lollipops would they have?"

She laughed. "Normal ones. The street teams take them out at night on their patrols. I'll introduce you to Simon and he can tell you more about the work they do." She nodded towards Josh. "But

14

let's get that off him first."

Five minutes later, Josh and I hurried out with my laptop. He'd picked a red lollipop – the colour of my face. But one positive had come from this – if you could call it that. I was no longer quite so scared about tomorrow's meeting. Instead, I was dreading coming back to the office to face everyone again.

Chapter 2

I SURVIVED BOTH MEETINGS. Facing my colleagues in the office wasn't too bad either. In fact, I seemed to have made a few new friends, thanks to Josh and his blue 'lollipop', as people came up to me in the kitchen and asked about him. When I packed up my desk on Thursday, I found myself looking forward to work the following week.

"You're taking tomorrow afternoon in lieu after doing the evening meeting, aren't you, Madeleine?" Emma looked me in the eye. "In this job, you need to look after yourself and ensure you take the time you're owed."

"Compared to my last position, this has been a breeze."

The unspoken words 'so far' hung in the air between us. I had been warned at the interview that this job would have its moments: good and bad. But didn't all jobs?

Frowning, Emma changed the subject. "Going anywhere nice this weekend?"

"It's a typical weekend. Washing, ironing, shopping and family. I hope yours is better."

She shrugged. "Mine won't be much different."

After giving my colleagues a wave goodbye, I left to collect Josh from nursery. Dark rain clouds loomed, and I wished I'd brought an umbrella. I didn't fancy taking a soaked child around to Dad's place. Thankfully, we made it into the car outside nursery moments before a rumble of thunder signalled a deluge. For most of the journey, my windscreen wipers couldn't keep up and the headlights wouldn't pierce the deepening nightfall. I thought about going home but my brother, Will, wouldn't be happy. He was struggling to deal with a computer issue which, his dozen text messages told me, couldn't wait until I saw them both on Saturday.

Unlike mine, Dad's flat was on a housing estate, where everyone had a good-sized garden. He'd lived in our old family house until his cancer diagnosis several years before, when he and my brother had been moved to a ground-floor flat in the next road. It freed up a family-sized home and meant Dad no longer had to deal with stairs.

Like on my estate, finding a parking space could be hard work, even though many of the front lawns had been turned over to concrete driveways and the grass verges had long since been tarmacked. Cars lined both sides of the road and I found myself breathing in as I squeezed the car between two Transit vans, swearing under my breath when a car drove towards me, forcing me to reverse past the vans again until I found a gap outside someone's driveway. At least the stair-rod rain of earlier had stopped, so I could see. My spirits brightened when I reached Dad's house and found a dry rectangle outside, surrounded by black tarmac that shimmered in my car headlights. That car must have just vacated the spot.

Josh had fallen asleep in his car seat. He squealed and shook his head when I tried to wake him. I sighed, not wanting to take a flailing child to Dad's.

"Will's home. You can play on his computer."

Too late, I remembered it wasn't working, but I'd come to that bridge soon enough. One eye opened to assess his surroundings, then he stretched out both arms and allowed me to lift him from the car. Fingers crossed that Will was in a mood to share. He wasn't always.

As Josh wound his arms around my neck and tucked his hot body into mine, I covered his head with his coat, grabbed my bag and kicked the car door shut. With Josh bouncing in my arms, I dashed down the pathway to the shelter of the porch. When I pressed the bell, it didn't ring – had the batteries gone again? – so I pulled the letterbox flap, which sprang back against the metal.

From inside, I heard Will mutter, "Hold on to your horses."

The door juddered open and Will scowled at us. Then he registered Josh. Grinning, he held out his hands. "Come to your uncle, little man."

Josh slipped into his arms, knocking against his glasses, which Will straightened before whisking him off.

"Hello, Will!" I called to his departing back. "Don't you need me to sort your computer?"

He paused by his bedroom door. "I forgot to tell you. Tariq got it working."

The house smelled of fatty meat. Probably burgers, knowing Will. Woe betide anything green landing on his plate. He'd been known to squirrel vegetables away when Dad turned his back – a habit he'd started as a child when we used to have TV dinners in the lounge. Each teatime Dad would put a mound of tinned peas on our plates, and Will stuffed handfuls of them down the side of the settee when Dad wasn't looking. With our attention taken by the TV, neither Dad or I noticed. In fact, we didn't find out for years – and by the time we did, they'd become grizzled pellets. We might never have known how they'd got there, had Will not been so truthful when presented with the evidence. He'd held the object between finger and thumb, sticking his tongue out as he scrutinised it.

"That looks like one of my old peas."

He didn't use the settee as a dumping ground now, but somehow vegetables found their way to the kitchen waste bin – or the outside bin – and Dad sighed with exasperation whenever he lifted the lid to find an empty cereal box or similar filled with broccoli or cauliflower. (With the start of the new century, Dad had expanded his vegetable repertoire.) Recycling was damned, thanks to Will.

I strolled through to the lounge, where I found Dad snoring in his armchair, the news blaring on the TV. Although this flat was smaller than his previous house, he'd insisted on bringing all the furniture with him, which meant the settee jostled with the armchair, a sideboard and a glass display unit, while the TV stood in front of the old fireplace – which was no longer in use since the council had installed central heating years before. A coffee table stood in the middle of the room, an obstacle that punished inattentiveness with grazed legs or stubbed toes. The fact that this lounge was smaller had been a blessing, as we'd been able to bring Dad's old carpet here and cut it down to size, but it had become threadbare by his feet.

I turned down the sound and nudged Dad's leg. He woke with a start and gazed around, bleary-eyed. Spotting me, he picked up his mug.

"If you're making one, I wouldn't say no."

On the way to the kitchen, I poked my head into Will's bedroom. He and Josh sat on his bed, watching *The Simpsons*. Was that appropriate for a two-year-old? I'd never seen a whole episode.

Giggling, Josh tapped Will and pointed at the TV. "Stupid cat."

Will nodded and his gaze slid back to the screen. The programme looked harmless enough – anyhow, the humour would go over Josh's head. Before leaving, I asked if either wanted a drink but, in unison, they shook their heads.

Mugs in hand, I went back to the lounge where Dad had put on a lamp. It cast a warm glow over his side of the room. As I bent to put our drinks on the coffee table, I spotted a letter. The flap lay open, revealing the letterhead: Holdenwell & Chartley Hospital Trust. Curious, I picked it up. It was an appointment for a scan next week, followed by an appointment with the consultant almost a fortnight later. A feeling of dread ran through me. Dad had been given the all-clear last year, so why did they want to see him?

"Nosey!" Dad chuckled. He scratched his face, his fingers rasping through several days' worth of stubble.

"You didn't exactly hide it."

He must have wanted me to notice it. Mum died when I was a toddler, and he'd brought my brother and me up. Will was two years younger than me and had Down syndrome. Until the end of his cancer treatment, Dad had been stoic. He'd been an indomitable force when we were children. If he'd been upset by Mum's death or by the loneliness of bringing up two children alone, he hadn't shown it. But he'd reached a point where he needed to lean on someone else for a bit. Who could blame him? To be honest, though, sometimes I wished he had someone other than me to offload his worries about Will. No doubt every parent with a disabled child feared for their future once they were gone, especially with the cutbacks in social care. Would Will be able to find a supported-living place in the future? I hoped so.

The settee creaked as I sat down. "Why have they called you in for a scan?"

"It's just a standard check-up. Nothing to worry about."

But of course we would. The grim cloak of cancer draped over everything we said or did. He could try to sweep away the worries, but they hung like a cloud of dust, ready to settle over us again.

"How will you get there?"

"June is going to drive me to the scan. But she can't find anyone to take me to the appointment with the consultant, so that'll have to be a taxi."

June must be one of the people in the doctor's surgery car scheme, who helped when patients couldn't get to the hospital.

"You can't go alone. I'll…" I hesitated. I'd left work early the other day. Would Emma mind if I asked for a few hours off to take Dad to hospital? It was a fortnight away and I could make up the time, but that meant asking my cousin to look after Josh for longer.

"I'll see what I can do. No promises, mind."

"I didn't ask for help." With a trembling hand, he picked up the letter to fold it back into the envelope. I gazed at him. Was this appointment just the usual check-up or was there more to it? Please let it be the former. I couldn't bear to go back to the terrible period when we'd been told he had a fifty-fifty chance of him making it. Thank goodness he'd survived.

No matter what work said, I'd made up my mind. I would take him to the hospital.

♦

The following week, I asked for time off to attend Dad's appointment. I'd dreaded asking, but Emma waved my worries away. Moments later, she appeared beside my desk, wafting the sweet scent of perfume. "I've put a meeting into your diary for this afternoon. You'll get to meet Derek Hamilton, who is in charge of our portfolio. He'll be one of the councillors you'll be working alongside in future."

I still hadn't got my head around all the different names within the council. Portfolio, I knew, was a group of linked services. The councillors led the council and were classed as 'very important people' and 'ones who should be obeyed'. Like MPs, they had ranks. The political party with the most councillors awarded the top jobs to their own people; these were chosen by the leader. Those not in a prime position were like back-bench MPs. Councillors of all political persuasions took part in committees, where they would assess services and also see where cuts could be made.

As Portfolio Holder, Derek was a very, very important person. He even had an OBE. Someone once told me it stood for 'Other Buggers' Effort', while MBE meant 'My Bloody Effort', but I had no idea. I'd not met anyone with either before. I wished Emma had given me a bit more notice, because I would have worn a jacket to meet him. Maybe I should keep one in the office, just in case, like she did.

After lunch, Emma arrived at my desk clutching a folder to her chest. She stood to attention. "Ready?"

My heart thudded like the drumbeat for a prisoner marching to their doom, and I wiped my damp palms on my trousers. People like me didn't get to meet titled people. Was an OBE a title? I had no idea. But it was something I would never have, unless a miracle happened.

"There's no need to worry." Emma held open the door in such a way that I had to duck beneath her arm to get past. "This is just a typical catch-up meeting about what's going on in the service. But I'm also introducing you, as you'll be expected to assist Derek at council-related public meetings or when he needs your help in his patch."

She led the way down the stairs, asking me how I felt my first week had gone, and whether there was anything I needed to know. I assured her everything had been good so far. There it was again. So far. Anyone would think I expected things to go wrong.

We'd reached the ground floor. From here we had to go down a corridor, past reception and through to the other side of the building. Emma checked her watch and quickened her pace.

"He doesn't like people to be late," she hissed. "But the one to watch is Margery Arscott. Never, ever be late for her. No matter what."

We arrived with a minute to spare. In the corner, an older woman looked up from where she sat at a desk and nodded hello. The chair next to her was empty but whoever sat there couldn't have gone far, as they'd left their laptop open and a handbag on the desk. The office had the same blue carpet tiles and beige paint as the rest of the building. Apart from its crest on the wall and a large map, labelled 'Holdenwell Borough', this room could have been anywhere. Would the rooms that lay behind the two doors on either side be more impressive? I didn't have long to find out as Emma led me to the door on the right and knocked.

"Come in," a man called. So we did.

I'd been expecting wood panelling and a moustached gentleman sitting at an impressive desk with bookshelves behind it, but Derek's office was no different from the one outside. It was a boring municipal space with a dozen or so pictures on the wall and three chairs surrounding his desk which was in the same style as every desk in the building – except his desk had a side section and presumably he wouldn't have to clear it every day.

While Emma shook his hand, I wiped mine – again – on my trousers, so his first impression of me wouldn't be a clammy handshake. I stood up straight, determined to give a positive impression. When he spoke, his accent hinted at an upper middle-class upbringing.

"This must be…"

"Madeleine Meadows." Using my sales training, I gave him a firm handshake – but not a crippling one – while praying I'd dried my hand well.

Through his glasses, his watery blue eyes met mine. He didn't have a moustache but a network of thread veins that travelled across his cheeks and over his craggy nose. His hair was grey.

He settled back into his seat and tugged at his collar. "Right, let's get started."

I'd once attended training at my first job – a charity for people with sight issues – where the tutor told us that, at any one point in the session, thirty per cent of people in the room would have zoned out. By this, she meant started daydreaming. When Emma brought out the service area budget figures, I remembered the tutor's words and tried to keep focused, but my jobs for the night encroached on my thoughts – Josh's tea, phone Dad, check that my cousin Chelsea could look after Josh for an extra couple of hours later in the week – until I heard Emma say my name.

"Madeleine will organise that meeting for you. She can liaise with the residents' committee too."

Frantically, I rewound the conversation, relieved to find that my mind had somehow filtered snatches of their earlier discussion. They'd been talking about Hadfield Green – where I lived.

I cleared my throat and made sure I enunciated each word clearly. "Hadfield Green is your area?"

Derek frowned. I'd made a basic error by not checking the boundaries to his electoral ward.

"I'm just trying to get a feel for which areas are in your ward and which are not. The boundaries changed a few years ago, so I'm not sure if yours was one of those affected."

Thank goodness I'd read that. He smiled. "Yes, that's right. I lost a bit of Petersfield but gained more of Hadfield Green. Sadly."

"Sadly?"

He raised his eyes to the ceiling. "I ended up with the Court Place estate. Do you know it?"

Like the back of my hand.

When I gave him a nod, he sighed. "Place is full of thieves and drug dealers. Single-mum city, they call it. Scum, I say."

That was *my* home. *I* was a single parent. Did he include me in the term 'scum'?

I didn't mean to let them slip – especially when I'd worked so hard to mask my true self – but the words shot out. "*I* live there."

Emma glanced across at me and pursed her lips. But Derek slapped his desk and burst into laughter. "We've got a joker in the team, have we? You nearly got me there."

He thought I was joking? It was anything but a laugh living there. If Court Place had too many of the wrong type of people, the blame lay with him. It was up to the people within his Portfolio to decide who was housed and where. But I didn't say that. I needed this job, needed the money. Instead I gave him a thin-lipped smile and clenched my fists in impotent fury. I moved to safer ground. "What about the Roundel Way estate? Is that still in your area?"

He shook his head. "I lost that one, thankfully. Maurice wasn't pleased to inherit that. He calls it Downtown Beirut."

My mouth fell open. Roundel Way was my childhood estate – and it was lovely. The roads didn't even have the pretentious names they'd given our estate, just normal ones, and the houses were airy family homes. Even Dad's ground-floor flat wasn't a bad size, and he had front and back lawns. Some of the gardens might be a bit messy and one or two families might not be the perfect neighbours, but you got that everywhere.

Again, my anger overrode pretence. "My dad lives there."

Laughing, Derek threw back his head and clapped his hands. "You should go in for stand-up comedy. You're gold, I tell you."

Emma flashed me a sympathetic look and her voice turned to ice. "Let's move on, shall we?"

Derek dabbed the corners of his eyes. Chuckling, he said, "I'll tell my colleagues to keep an eye out for you. You'll be wrapping them in knots with that humour."

Right then I wished I had a knot for him – with a bloody noose at the end. But my angry vibes flew over his head. I didn't concentrate for the rest of the meeting. I couldn't. Indignation rose in wave after furious wave. Who on earth did he think he was, speaking like that about my home? An OBE recipient, in charge of community services for Holdenwell Council, that's who. How could he look after the community if he despised and looked down on part of it? And why had he thought I was joking?

Because he'd met Madeleine, not Maddie, who I'd left in Court Place. At work I was Madeleine, where I spoke and behaved differently. Did that mean I was denying my friends and family? Or did other people do the same? I had no idea. But I could hardly enter a meeting and say, "All right, mate!", could I? Not that my friends would say that. They'd modify their tone and language, just not in the drastic way I had.

When Emma and I stood up to leave, Derek gave me a hearty handshake. "I'm looking forward to working with you. You'll be a breath of fresh air."

I gave him a weak smile and followed Emma out of the door in silence. Passing through reception, I caught a glimpse of myself reflected in the glass panels that fronted the building: my flushed cheeks, my hair pulled into a bun, the cotton trousers I'd bought from a charity shop, knowing they'd have cost a week's wages when new.

We moved into the corridor and on to the homeward stretch. Just the stairs to go.

Emma cleared her throat. "I'm sorry you had to go through that. But his attitude will be replicated over and over in certain quarters. You'll have to judge which battles to fight and which to leave."

Instead of turning towards the stairs, she went in the other direction, gesturing for me to follow her. "But there are some excellent councillors. I'm going on to meet Dana Orwell, who's leading a youth project in her neighbourhood. Why don't you join us?"

Chapter 3

I COULDN'T WAIT to tell my friends about my conversation with Derek but, with everything going on at work, I almost forgot until they came around on the Friday night and something Leah said rekindled my memory.

"Flaming cheek!" Rachel said after I'd told them. "What wouldn't I do to have a house on your dad's estate. I'm just lucky to have my place."

I didn't know what to say. Rachel had been allocated her flat on the Court Place estate when she was seven months pregnant, but the baby had died a fortnight later. It had been a terrible time for her and Kieran. None of us would ever forget their grief. The grooves that etched her face had never faded, although life had returned to her barren eyes. The following year they'd decided to try again, but nothing had happened yet. I hoped it would. I'd felt awful when I fell pregnant so easily – and unexpectedly – with Josh.

Leah narrowed her eyes. "What I don't get is why he didn't believe you lived here. You don't look any different to us."

Rachel laughed. "Keep up with the times! Maddie's gone all posh on us. Or should I say, Madeleine?"

Leah turned to me. "Madeleine? Why did you choose that?"

"Because it's my name. Mad-e-leine."

Shaking her head in wonder, she said, "You learn something every day." She picked up the wine bottle. "Well, I do."

Rachel's eyes widened as the wine glugged into Leah's glass. "Oi! Don't take it all. That cost me a fiver. Drink that pink crap you brought." Then she glanced at me and lowered her voice. "Sorry, Maddie. I hope I didn't wake Josh."

The baby monitor sat on the mantelpiece. Not a peep could be heard. Like me, they held their breaths while listening for the creak of the bedroom door or Josh padding down the stairs.

"Perhaps we'll close the door while we play Jenga."

"Can our Friday nights get any wilder?" Rachel grinned. "Talking about wild, has Leah told you about Aaron yet?"

Leah covered her eyes, her blonde fringe draping over her hands. "Oh gawd! Don't tell her about that." She looked up, to reveal cheeks the colour of her cerise nails. Resting one hand on the mahogany table, which had been my grandmother's, she reached for her wine glass. I rarely saw Leah without a glass of wine or Prosecco in the evenings.

She gave me a shrug. "It wasn't my finest night. Go on then, Rach. Get it over with."

I settled back to hear the long tale of unrequited love, as told by Rachel, with modifications from Leah. Not only had Aaron spurned Leah's advances, which included several offers to buy him a drink with her bingo winnings, the chance to go to the cinema the next evening or to go clubbing at the weekend, but he'd ended up telling her that whatever she asked, his answer would be no. She'd countered this by offering sex.

"It was a joke! Shame it didn't come across that way, but I'd had a bit too much drink." Leah picked up her wine and swigged it like beer.

"Going for the rollover?" Rachel moved her bottle to the other side of the table. "You need a night off. I've given up the ciggies." She rolled up her sleeve to reveal a nicotine patch.

"You're getting into double figures with all your attempts." Leah got to her feet and smoothed down her skirt. "I need to borrow your toilet."

"Make sure you bring it back," Rachel said.

I had the best friends – ones who would give up a Friday night on the town so I had a bit of company. Not that I stayed in every night. From now on, I'd be going out a lot more for work, and I saw Dad at least one evening a week and on Saturday mornings, and I went around friends' houses. A single parent with little spare cash couldn't wish for more.

"Now, about that Jenga." Rachel went out to get the carrier bag she'd left in the hallway. She pointed towards the front door. "Something's happening outside."

A blue glow flashed through the glass – either the police or an ambulance. I followed Rachel through to the kitchen, where she switched off the light. The flashing lights coming from the road below transformed the white appliances and the teeth of the dinosaurs guarding the biscuit tin from dark to a luminous blue. We hoisted ourselves onto the worktop and lifted the net curtain over our heads, cupping our hands around our faces to peer out. The edge of the draining board poked into my knee so I shifted along, squashing myself against Rachel.

"It looks like your neighbour." Rachel pressed her face closer to the window. Her skin was a strange hue in the gloom, her eyes reflecting the scene playing out beside us.

Two policemen stood feet away on the balcony, their backs to us, while a policewoman came towards them talking into her radio. Snatches of words filtered through the glass, but I had no idea what was taking place. Another police car appeared in the car park below, its lights flashing – but no siren, thank goodness. I didn't need them to wake Josh. It had been hard enough getting him to sleep earlier. Upstairs, the toilet flushed. I rolled my eyes. Usually, it wouldn't be a bother but it added to the commotion outside. I couldn't believe Josh hadn't woken yet.

"What d'you think is going on?" Rachel whispered.

My neighbour appeared to our left, writhing and squirming, a policeman gripping his tattooed arms. Suddenly, light flooded the kitchen and, like a flash photograph, the scene became imprinted in my mind. My neighbour's angry gaze collided with mine. Our eyes couldn't have met for more than a second before they dragged him away, wearing a vest and jogging bottoms, but it felt like minutes. What would he say the next time he bumped into me? Frantically, I tugged the net down, even though it was too late.

"Turn off that sodding light!" I hissed.

"Wha…?" Leah's mouth gaped open.

"Turn. It. Off!" Rachel jabbed her finger towards the switch.

Plunged back into darkness, Rachel and I knelt in shamefaced silence until we heard the rattle of the front door opening. A chill breeze swept into the room. I hadn't noticed Leah leave the kitchen.

"What's she doing now?" Sounding irritated, Rachel slipped down from the side and hurried out to investigate.

I followed, praying Leah wouldn't do anything further to embarrass us. We found her leaning over the railings of the walkway, watching my neighbour being escorted across the car park. The police didn't seem bothered about Leah or the other dozen or so residents who milled around the car park or outside their front doors on the adjacent blocks. Probably used to having

31

an audience, particularly on this estate.

Leah chuckled. "Well, your posh boss bloke wasn't far wrong about this place. You do have your fair share of scummy people."

♦

Although I'd seen Dad at the weekend, I'd forgotten to tell him what the councillor, Derek, had said about his estate. As we sat in the hospital waiting room, hoping it wouldn't be long before the consultant called him in, I decided to recount the tale.

"Damn cheek," he said, echoing Rachel's passionate response.

I shrugged and went on to tell him about the police and my neighbour.

"And what about the ninety per cent of good people on that estate? Like you, for instance?"

I linked my arm through his, feeling the extra layer around his middle. Something to be thankful for. During chemotherapy, he'd lost too much weight.

Beside us, Will banged his feet against the metal chair legs. No doubt the sugar hit had kicked in. He'd downed the dregs of the hot chocolate I'd bought and had tucked the empty paper cup between his thighs. Any other weekday, he'd be working off his energy at his part-time job at the cottage hospital – an annexe of this larger one – but he had Wednesdays off. Later, he'd see his friends at Samson's, a café that ran a fortnightly session for young adults with disabilities but, for now, he was stuck with us.

Opposite us hung the TV on the wall, its sound muted, a tickertape of news headlines rolling across the screen. We'd been here so long I could reel them off word for word. When Dad plucked at a woollen thread dangling from his sleeve, I sighed. If I'd known he'd come out wearing a threadbare jumper, I would have told him to keep his coat on. But then I took in his pinched expression and the way he frowned when his gaze strayed to the consultant's door. He had more to worry about than a stupid hole or two. We all did.

A nurse walked past, followed by a woman in a low-cut top.

Will grinned. "She's got boobies."

"Will, you shouldn't say that," I hissed.

Dad groaned. "It's his new phase."

Will pointed at the woman and clapped his hand over his mouth, sniggering.

"Yes, Will, she has got boobies. So has every woman – and some men too." I pointed towards Dad, whose hands were buried between the mound of his stomach and his chest. "But in his case they're called moobs – or moobies to you."

"Thanks a lot," Dad said. "I have a feeling I'll live to regret you teaching him that."

"Moobies!" Will snorted, while Dad sighed.

A woman stepped from one of the consulting rooms, holding a folder, and called for Alan Meadows. She turned in our direction when she spotted Dad pushing himself to his feet.

"Do you want me to come with you?" I asked. Oddly, we hadn't discussed it before now. I'd just worried about the logistics of leaving work in time to pick them both up.

He shook his head, his face pale. "Just keep an eye on the boobie king."

We both knew that Will didn't need monitoring in a waiting room. He'd become more independent in the past few years and made the short bus ride to work and back alone. If he couldn't get a lift, he took the bus with his friends to Samson's Café, although I picked them up as there wasn't an evening bus back.

I gave Dad's arm a squeeze and whispered, "Good luck."

Dad wanted me to go with him, I could tell, but he didn't want Will to hear possible bad news without having the opportunity to soften the blow. I blinked away the sting of welling tears and clasped my hands together, hoping, praying, that he wouldn't have to face bad news in there alone.

"Is Dad okay?" Chocolate arced the corners of Will's mouth. His blue eyes widened through his thick glasses. "Is he sick again?"

I took the cup from him and tossed it into the bin. It gave me a moment to frame my thoughts.

"I think he's okay. But they're just checking him over." Then I changed the subject. Cowardly, I know, but his words had raised fears I didn't wish to express. Not just about Dad, but about Will too. "It's Samson's Café tonight. Am I picking you up at the same time as usual?"

As he chattered about his plans for the evening, seeing his best buddies, Tariq and Erin, his happiness washed over me, helping me to forget what could be taking place behind the blank white door. Then it creaked open. Will stopped in mid-sentence. Dad walked out, throwing us a tight smile – relief or worry, I couldn't tell. My heart thumped. *Please, please let him be okay.*

Will stood up, then froze. As Dad came towards us, I rested my hand on Will's trembling shoulder. I hadn't realised how worried he must have been about this appointment. But, of course, he would. None of us could forget what Dad's visits to hospital had once involved.

Dad ruffled Will's hair. "Don't look so worried. It's all clear again."

♦

Josh enjoyed our Wednesday evening outing to pick up Will from Samson's. Often the café ran a bit late, so we waited inside where people made a fuss of him and gave him cookies. Tonight, Will's friend, Erin, had perched him on her knee beside a crumb-littered Formica table. Across the table, Will's mooning gaze told the world that he wished he could take Josh's place. Later, when we got into the car, Will would talk about Erin all the way home and I'd sit there smiling to myself.

I could see why he liked her. Tonight, she wore a dab of lipstick, a smear of blue eyeshadow – not meticulously applied, but who cared, as it made her eyes sparkle – and she'd curled her brown hair into ringlets that fell onto her shoulders. As Josh sat on her lap, he twiddled a strand through his fingers, his giggles echoing through the room each time he pulled them and made a 'boing' noise. When Will reached out to touch one too, Erin laughed and tapped his hand away. Although she and Will were in their mid-twenties, she seemed older than him. Maybe it had always been that way.

In the two decades they'd been friends, she'd always been the leader and he her follower. She worked at the local supermarket, which Josh made a beeline for whenever we went past the parade of shops – looking for a cuddle and a sweet. It was the only time she'd stop work for a moment, as she was a stickler for keeping the supermarket rules.

"Right, guys." Harry, who ran Samson's Café, stood centre place in the room. "Everything's been put away – well done. Remember your wellies for the next session as we're doing Pooh sticks in the park. Bet I win."

To calls of, "Bet you won't!" he shouted, "See you then. Goodnight."

The sound of scraping chairs filled the room, and I turned to Will and Erin. "You ready? Where's Tariq?"

"He's out the back, helping Oliver put everything away."

I'd not heard anyone mention Oliver before. He must be new. Not paying it much thought, I took the proffered cloth and spray from Harry – who no doubt looked forward to getting home soon – and started to wipe down the tables and chairs. Will started to upend the chairs onto the tables.

We'd finished all but the table where Josh and Erin sat when Tariq appeared. Unlike Erin and Will, Tariq didn't have Down syndrome. Apparently, he had been deprived of oxygen at birth, but his learning disabilities hadn't been spotted for several years. On the surface his disability was invisible, only becoming apparent with his often-literal understanding or when he struggled with money. But he faced life with a laid-back approach, terrible jokes and a wonderful laugh.

"Maddie, I gotta new one for you. Why did the snowman go into the grocers?"

He waited until I dutifully responded, "I don't know, why did he go to the grocers?"

"To pick his nose."

Chuckling, I pointed towards the door. "Come on, we've got to go."

As I took Josh from Erin, a man stepped from the storeroom. His dark eyes locked with mine. I hesitated, feeling a strange pull towards him. But the moment didn't last, as our caravan had already started out the door, with Will in the lead.

"Bye, Oliver, bye, Harry," the trio shouted, echoed by Josh, while I pulled the door shut.

Again, my gaze met the stranger's through the glass. I glanced away, embarrassed. With Josh bouncing against my hip, we hurried to the car park, along a pavement that glittered beneath the lamp light. The frosty air cooled my flushed cheeks and nipped my nose. Above us the wind rushed through bare branches and bowed the tips of the leylandii trees. Josh's teeth began to chatter, so I pulled his hood up and hugged him closer.

Tariq jumped into the front, leaving Will standing outside while I clipped Josh into his car seat, assisted by Erin, who'd settled in the rear seat beside him. When I started the engine, cold air blasted into the car. I twisted the dial and rubbed my hands together.

"Maddie, I've got another joke," Tariq said.

"Okay, but then you can tell me all about this Oliver. Is he a new helper? Or was he at the café just for tonight?"

Tariq shrugged. In the rear-view mirror, Will and Erin reflected his blank expression.

Bemused, I said, "Don't any of you ask the helpers about their lives?"

Since Josh's father had left during my pregnancy, I hadn't even thought about a new relationship, yet the few seconds I'd spent with Oliver had affected me in a way I couldn't comprehend. I longed to see him again. My three potential informants sat in baffled silence, which meant I'd have to find out about this Oliver some other way.

Exasperated, I shook my head. "Okay, Tariq, fire away with your joke."

Will tapped Tariq on the shoulder. "Tell her the one about the boobies."

Chapter 4

THE NEXT MORNING, I AWOKE wondering why I'd been so keen to find out more about Oliver. He might be good-looking, but I didn't have time for a relationship. Not when I had Josh, Dad, Will and work. Within days, Oliver had slipped from my mind and I became engrossed in work and family stuff again.

One work project that interested me involved supporting a community group to set up a youth club on an estate that had issues with young people hanging around the precinct at night. I'd found out about it from Dana Orwell, a councillor in another ward. She said the group needed help, but she couldn't provide it as there was an unwritten rule that you couldn't step on another councillor's toes in their patch. Later Emma had told me that the councillor for the Dealsham area wasn't interested in young people. His funding and support went elsewhere. But it was part of my remit, so I could assist them. Plus, it meant I could find out more about the area.

In addition to the main town of Holdenwell, the council I worked for encompassed several other small market towns and villages. In the villages and some areas of town the bus services were sporadic, something which hadn't improved from when I'd been a teenager. My childhood home had been in a part of Holdenwell where the bus services stopped at six o'clock midweek. They still did. When I'd finally managed to find a waitressing job at a local café at the weekends – earning riches after the little pocket money I'd previously been given – I was still stymied by the lack of transport in the evenings. Saying that, not all my friends had been so lucky. Jobs had been scarce for the under-sixteens, and even more so now with the restrictions on working hours.

We'd hung out at the rec, which annoyed parents with young children. When forced to move on, we loitered at the crossroads in the centre of the estate, sitting on the telephone junction box until a fed-up resident smeared it with grease. I had less free time than most of our gang, as I had to babysit Will while Dad worked, but sometimes I dragged Will along. My friends loved my funny little brother, who'd laughed and cuddled them without constraint.

Now I wanted to help other young people, especially ones on the poorer estates: latchkey children, those with parents unable to ferry them around, or ones who simply could not afford the cost of after-school activities. My ideals had been why I'd taken the job at a charity, but I'd been forced to move onto a job in sales when I needed more money. Now my role fulfilled both my objectives: giving me scope to help people and to earn a decent salary.

Worried about being late to the youth club meeting, I'd arrived fifteen minutes early and spent the time reading the minutes from previous meetings while keeping an eye on the digital clock on the dashboard. At five minutes to the hour, I stuffed the papers into my bag and stepped from the car, smoothing down the woollen dress I'd bought on a shopping trip the previous weekend. Fingers crossed, it looked suitable. I wasn't sure how neighbourhood managers were expected to dress for meetings involving youth workers and local residents.

Across the road was a junior school, while beside the small car park stood a precinct with four shops – a convenience store, a fish and chip shop, a second-hand furniture place, with whitewashed windows on the last one, along with a 'for let' board – next door to an ugly community centre. The smell of chips hung in the air and I wondered whether I should treat Josh and myself when I finished our meeting, but I decided against it. By the time I reached Chelsea's house, the chips would have gone cold. And Josh would have eaten. Also, I had leftover stew at home, which would go to waste if I didn't finish it tonight. It wouldn't fit in the fridge's ice box.

Nerves mounting, I pulled open the heavy glass door and stepped inside the community centre. A noticeboard hung on the wall to my left, filled with posters about keep-fit and weight-loss classes. Through a further set of double doors lay a hall, but beside it a door labelled 'Meeting Room' had been propped open, where four people sat around a table, chatting. They looked up as I entered and one of them stood to shake my hand.

"Madeleine! How lovely. I'm Kavita. Everyone, this is Madeleine from the council's neighbourhood team."

She introduced me to each of the group – two other women and a man who were residents looking to volunteer at the youth club – and explained that they were expecting a few more but they'd had three apologies too.

Then she glanced at the clock, gasped, "Oh no! Excuse me!" and shot out of the door.

While I pulled my notepad and pen from my bag, one of the women leaned forward, smiling. Crimson lipstick smeared her front teeth.

"Do you work in David's team?"

"If you mean David Garnett, then yes."

"I can imagine he's a nice boss."

I frowned. "I wouldn't know. He's not my boss."

I stopped myself from adding, 'Or anyone's, for that matter.' Nor did I point out my seniority to him. Thank goodness I didn't have to line-manage him, especially when he barely spoke to me or – if he had no choice – he was curt in tone. Oddly for a grown man, I was sure he'd hissed "Cow" or something like that when I'd passed his desk the other day, but I may have misheard. According to other team members, he believed I'd swiped his much-deserved promotion. From what they said, I had a feeling he'd never forgive me.

"He's not sent you here to do the minutes, then? David told me he'd found us a secretary to come tonight."

Why would David be working for this group? This wasn't his area.

"That's nice. How do you know David?"

"He attends another group I'm on. The Radfield Residents' Association. A right proper Mr Fixit. Reckons there's nothing he can't do." She took off her glasses and wiped them with the tip of her shawl. "So, you're not his secretary?"

A grey-haired man pointed his pen in my direction. "You could do the minutes. You've got a pen and paper."

I couldn't believe it when the other two women nodded. But I hid my annoyance. "We've all got paper and pens. Why don't one of you do the minutes? I'm here to offer help with fundraising sources or other…" I nearly said 'matters', leaving myself open to anything, but I swiftly amended it to, "non-secretarial matters."

The man scowled. "I'm the treasurer."

Thankfully, the front door clanged and Kavita rushed in. "I'd forgotten that I'd changed the venue and hadn't told everyone, but I've found them now."

She ushered a woman and a man into the room who seemed to know the others from the way they greeted each other. Kavita looked expectantly towards the door. Moments later a younger man hefted a box into the room, which he placed on the table.

"Thanks for bringing that for me."

The man ran a finger across his fringe, rippling it away from his eyes and grinned. "What have you got in there? Lead bars?"

He turned, catching my gaze, and a jolt of recognition passed between us. Smiling, he sauntered over, while I tried to look nonchalant, praying my cheeks didn't look like the fireballs they felt.

"Hello again." Oliver pulled out the vacant chair beside me and sat down. "You're Will's sister."

He spoke well. Leah would have called him posh. Either way, he was out of my league.

I nodded but I couldn't summon a response. His coat sleeve brushed against my arm. It felt damp from the chill outside. I shivered, but not from the cold. Why did he arouse this reaction in me? It felt rude not to look at him, so I flickered a smile. Then I wrote the date on my pad and the name of the group, because it gave me something to do.

Kavita called the meeting to order but was interrupted by the man across from me. "We need a minute-taker. I've asked her…" He stabbed his pen in my direction. "But she wouldn't do it."

"Madeleine's not here to take minutes." Kavita shook her head as if he'd said the daftest thing in the world. I loved her for it.

Oliver cleared his throat. "I'll take them this time, Bob. Someone else can take them the next. Until you get a secretary."

Kavita threw Oliver a look of gratitude. Bob looked pleased, as did the woman who'd originally nominated me. And I felt churlish in my earlier refusal to help.

Oliver scribbled something down and slid the sheet along to me. He didn't wear a ring, but that didn't mean he wasn't taken. *They spent twenty mins fighting about the minutes at the last meeting.* He took the paper back and wrote another line. *Be careful they don't try to co-opt you.* I chuckled and wrote on my pad. *They did. I told Bob to take them instead.* Grinning, Oliver wrote: *Minutes of the last meeting agreed without amendment. Good for you. I bet that didn't go down too well.* He underlined the final two sentences and added a smiley face.

We settled down. I forced myself to concentrate on what was being said and to ignore Oliver's presence, even though I could smell his aftershave and his arm kept touching mine because our chairs were penned between the table legs.

When Kavita brought the meeting to a close, Oliver turned to me. "I have to shoot off to another meeting. But I'll see you on Wednesday, won't I? Harry's asked me to help out at Samson's from now on."

As he went to leave the room, Kavita called him over and they chatted for a moment until he pointed to the clock. After calling "Goodbye!" to everyone, he hurried away. I hadn't realised that I'd been watching him, but I came to with a start and began to stuff my papers into my bag.

"I think we're all smitten with Oliver." I hadn't spotted Kavita standing beside me. "Well, us ladies, anyhow. Although there's little—" She paused and shook her head. "Forget I said that."

Her words knocked me off-kilter. But they made perfect sense. Oliver was one of those men women fell for: caring, intelligent and good-looking. With a combination like that, no wonder I'd been attracted to him – something no doubt she'd been about to confess. I had no chance.

She slid gracefully into the chair he'd vacated, her ringed fingers resting on the table. "So, do you think you'll be able to help us with funding?"

"I've already got a few ideas. I'll speak to my colleagues about support for your procedures too."

"Oliver can deal with those," she said. "He works for a youth organisation and knows all about safeguarding. But he'll be very interested in your fundraising abilities. They're always strapped for cash."

The thought of having a one-to-one meeting with Oliver made me tingle. But I told myself not to be daft. He wouldn't go for an average-looking woman, who lived on the Court Place estate, with a ready-made family and friends who would mock his posh accent. Most likely he already had someone special. If he came for help for funding – or anything else to do with work – I'd happily oblige. But I'd do what I promised myself earlier and forget any notion of romance. Josh didn't need the upheaval … and neither did I.

Chapter 5

WILL ANSWERED THE DOOR. "You've come to see Alan?"

I frowned. "I've come to see Dad *and* you."

"Where's Josh?"

"Chelsea's looking after him. I've got an evening meeting but thought I'd pop by for a moment and check on you both."

"Alan's in there." He pointed through to the lounge and disappeared off to his bedroom.

In the lounge, Dad slumped into the back of the settee, his hands clasped over his stomach, head back, dozing through a film which showed a steamy bedroom scene. I nudged his knee.

"What on earth are you watching?"

One eye blinked open, then the other. When his gaze fell upon the TV, he picked up the remote control and switched it over. "I have no idea. I was watching a rerun of some show or other and this must have come on."

A letter lay on the coffee table. Not one from the hospital or a utility bill. I twisted it around to read it.

"I'll have to come round your house and read your letters," Dad said.

"Chance'd be a fine thing. You've not been inside my place yet."

"Those steps are a killer."

My heart sank as I scanned the lines. Yet another 'thanks, but no thanks'. No one wanted to recruit a sixty-three-year-old man, let alone one who'd had to take time off work to fight cancer. He'd been free of the disease for a year, but his old company had since relocated too far for Dad to travel. In a few more years he'd be drawing his pension but, until then, he had to keep sending out those CVs and sleeping off the rejections. Maybe something would come up. Even part-time work in a shop would give him something to do.

Not wanting to dwell on it, I changed the subject. "How come Will's calling you Alan?"

"It's my name."

When I pulled a face, he sighed. "It's his latest thing. At least he's gone off boobies."

Will strolled into the lounge wearing a huge parka. The hood hung over his eyes and shadowed his nose. His tongue poked between his teeth as he zipped it up.

"I'm going to the shops."

"Let me give you a lift. I'm going past them to my meeting."

His eyes narrowed. No doubt he was wondering if he'd be forced to work to my timescale, especially if Erin happened to be at work.

"You'll have to walk back, so you can spend as long as you like there. But give me five minutes."

A nod settled it. Not one for patience, Will kept his parka on as he hovered by the door while I chatted to Dad. After the allotted time, I gave Dad a peck on the cheek and ushered Will outside. He plumped himself down in the passenger seat and clipped his seatbelt. In silence we drove down the road, but at the junction I took a moment to look at him. While his lack of conversation might stem from being unable to talk and chew his thumbnail, he seemed uptight. Lines pinched the skin between his eyebrows and his face was paler than usual.

"Is Erin working this evening?"

"I'm going to ask her out."

I hadn't expected him to say that. "What, as in out-out or just the usual friends going out?"

"I've saved up money to go for a meal."

"Wow, that's posh. No man has ever taken me for a meal."

Until I spoke, I hadn't realised it was true. Before I met Josh's father, I'd hung around in a gang with Leah and Rachel and others – male and female – and we'd all gone out together, even with our respective dates. It was fun going to restaurants with a bunch of people, although not so great for the waiting staff serving a group of ten or more. Josh's father had often pulled in at a fast-food outlet drive-thru or we'd ordered a plate of chips at the pub or a takeaway Chinese, but we'd never been to an actual restaurant for a one-to-one date.

"Well, I'm taking Erin," Will said.

I didn't want to leave him alone if Erin rebuffed him because she didn't see him as anything more than a friend. After I'd parked outside the convenience store where Erin worked, I checked the dashboard clock to make sure I wasn't going to make myself late for the meeting. I had ten minutes to play with. Maximum. Next to Erin's workplace stood a pizza parlour. I had a feeling Will would make a detour there after speaking with her. I hadn't noticed any food smells at Dad's house.

"I could do with a bottle of water." I reached for my handbag.

Will frowned but didn't instruct me not to go near him in the shop. He left me to lock the car and I followed at a pace slower than his, first picking up a bottle of water from the chiller cabinet before going in search of him. I found him in the next aisle, standing over Erin, who knelt while stacking tins of carrots onto the shelf.

"Will, I'm far too busy to talk to you. Anyhow." She tossed her hair from her face. "I'm at work, and you know I'm not allowed to chat to friends."

Will's shoulders slumped. "What time do you finish?"

"Ten o'clock. My dad's picking me up. You can call me tomorrow."

Will hurried away down the aisle, his shoes scuffing the floor. After giving Erin a brief wave, I dumped my bottle of water back in the chiller cabinet and rushed off in pursuit. I caught up with Will by the door.

"You okay?"

He nodded. "Erin's not allowed to speak to me at work."

"That's a shame. You can speak to her tomorrow, though. Let me know how you get on." I hesitated – it would put me under pressure – but I couldn't not ask. "Do you need a lift back?"

"No. I want to walk." His gaze strayed to the pizza parlour and I chuckled.

"Take a few slices back for Dad. He'll be hungry." I left him open-mouthed and scratching his head, clearly wondering how I knew where he would be going.

♦

At first I'd made good progress but, when I entered Chartley, the traffic slowed to a crawl and then a stop. No amount of gripping the steering wheel while calling, "Oh come on!" made it move faster, but I finally reached the community centre with a few

49

minutes to spare before the meeting started. It meant I didn't have time to feel nervous. Not that I needed to be worried; I wouldn't be playing a leading role. That would be the job of the local councillor and the police team. My remit was to watch, learn, and come away with ideas about what we could do to help residents and the police to resolve the issues.

The room crackled with tension. Feelings were running high after a toddler had been injured by a hit-and-run driver a few weeks before. The toddler had got out through an open gate and made his way to the road, where he'd been clipped by a vehicle travelling at 25 mph. The driver hadn't spotted the child, who had dashed out from behind a tree. The driver had then sped off in fright. He'd handed himself in to the police an hour later, leaving an angry community split on what should be done. The council's issue was the lack of available funding for an expensive road safety scheme, particularly when speed hadn't been a factor in this accident. But many residents wanted a pedestrian crossing at any cost, others favoured a reduction in road speed, while other unworkable ideas had also sallied back and forth.

The panel milled at the front, ready to take their seats, so I went over to introduce myself to the local councillor, Mark Carradine. Emma had explained that he had joined the council after winning a by-election the previous year. According to her, he was a new councillor with a passion for local projects. He was prone to being wayward, but he'd be a fabulous asset if his enthusiasm could be steered in the right direction. Drumming his fingers on the plastic-backed chair, he frowned as he gazed at the throng of people that continued to file through the door.

"Why don't you sit with me up here?" he said.

"Thank you, but I only joined the team a month ago. I'd be better off watching proceedings this time."

The police sergeant overheard and pointed to a vacant chair tucked at the end of the top table. "I got a heads-up you were coming so I saved that one for you."

I looked at Mark Carradine, who shrugged and nodded to the crowd settling into their seats. "I need you to save me from that lot."

As an expectant hush fell over the room, I whispered to Mark Carradine (it felt a bit informal calling him Mark and too formal calling him Mr or Councillor Carradine), "Who's coming from the highways team?"

He gave me a confused look. "Highways? I was told that you'd be able to deal with any questions."

Me? Not only had I been at the council for just a month, but I wasn't in Highways. I went to refute him, but the scrape of a chair diverted our attention. The police sergeant stood to address the audience, giving the background to the toddler being hurt but omitting to mention the open back gate. Rubbing his hands together, he turned to introduce the top table, starting on the opposite side with the Neighbourhood Action Group chairman, the head of the Community Speedwatch group, to his other side the chairman of the town council – who'd organised this meeting – and finally, Mark Carradine and me. He slapped his hands together as he called our names. "Both from Holdenwell Council."

The air filled with boos. Dumbstruck, I looked around the room. Why were they angry with us? We hadn't left the gate open or pressed the accelerator on the car that sped off after hitting the toddler.

Mark Carradine got to his feet. He raised then lowered his outstretched arms until the crowd hushed.

"Gentlemen," he said, although over half the people present were women. "I'm on your side."

Bewildered, I turned to him, but his focus was on the crowd.

"I'm your representative for the Berryway division, which means I'm here for you, not them."

Them? He meant me! In one sentence he'd made me the pariah and him the saviour. But he and his councillor colleagues *were* the council. They made the rules, while I was paid to follow them.

The meeting moved on. My heart thudded with every question from the audience. The police sergeant – Glenn, I learned – seemed to enjoy leading all the residents down a path of fury, enticing them to hate each representative in turn, while the various chairmen – one of them a woman – vied to be seen as the spokesperson for the people and 'on their side' against all others. As each representative staunchly defended their position, my nerves began to mount. They needed a scapegoat. And I knew it would be me.

"No one could be here from Highways, unfortunately." Mark Carradine spoke to a toad-eyed man who liked to raise his fist each time he made a point. "But Madeleine here could take your question."

Mark Carradine passed me the molten baton. I hesitated. The man had asked about funding a pedestrian crossing. I had no idea of the answer. Councillor sodding Carradine would know but, obviously, there would be no money for that, or else he would have snatched the question and moulded it into a present to be gifted back to the audience.

The room hushed and a hundred eyes burned into me. I cleared my throat. Emma's mantra to manage expectations ran through my mind, but I'd be slayed if I tried too hard.

"Unfortunately, I cannot advise what funding is available for a pedestrian crossing. My colleagues from Highways and Councillor Carradine will need to have discussions about that. As your representative, he will be able to report back to you and the town council."

As I spoke, Mark Carradine's eyes narrowed and he pursed his lips. I ignored him.

"So, you can't tell us now?" Glenn, the police sergeant, raised his eyebrows in a show of disbelief.

"This will be up to my Highways colleagues and your councillor, Mark Carradine." Inside I shook but my voice rang clear. I braced myself for more booing. After all, I'd rebuffed their question – and no one had even thought to invite Highways – but Glenn stepped in, holding up his hands. Perhaps he'd seen enough blood for one night.

"When is the next meeting?" He swivelled around to the town council chairman, who advised that it was just a fortnight away. Everyone turned to Mark Carradine. The police sergeant said, "To make it clear, will you have a response for the residents within a fortnight, Mark?"

Mark Carradine clenched his teeth and a muscle bulged along his jaw. I looked at his grim expression. Would I still have a job tomorrow?

Facing the audience, he beamed. "Of course!" He held his palms up. "We're all in this together. I'll make sure I get the answers for you and, if those answers are not in all our interests, I'll make sure we hold them to account."

Them?

The council, he meant.

But the council *was* him and all his fellow councillors…

This politician obviously wasn't going to let that fact stand in the way of a good story. At any moment I expected him to break out into 'Friends, Countrymen, Berryway residents'. Instead I allowed my resentment to fester beyond indignation. When Glenn called the meeting to a close, it took all my willpower not to vent my fury.

Mark Carradine slumped back into his chair. "Thank goodness that's over."

His cheeks were blotched; grey smudged his eyes. I glanced at my watch. Ten to nine. I needed to pick up Josh. But I couldn't let his earlier comments pass unchecked. Giving no consideration to my newbie status, he'd offered me to the audience as their whipping girl.

I pointed a trembling finger at him. "*You* councillors *are* the council. *You* make the rules. My job is to do what *you've* agreed."

I picked up my bag and swung it onto my shoulder, not bothering to say goodbye to anyone. But when I strode out of the building into the chill wind, I wondered if I'd just made a huge mistake.

Chapter 6

EMMA PURSED HER LIPS and gazed across the foyer, where a grey-suited, silver-haired group of men stood. One of them turned and, spotting her, nodded. She lifted her hand, giving him a glimmer of a smile.

"Peter Cavendish," she said, as if his name should mean something to me. "Portfolio Holder for Legal and Finance. Also, Mark Carradine's uncle. You might be wise buttering them both up."

Spotting my expression, she added, "I know Mark was out of order the other night, but you need friends in high places, especially in your role."

"If friends hang you out to dry, how much worse would an enemy be?"

Her gaze tracked back to the huddle by the doors. "They can close down our service. Not all the councillors agree that a neighbourhood team is needed, especially when youth clubs, older people's groups, libraries and so on are facing budget cuts. We're only here while we're useful." Sighing heavily, she checked her watch. "Where is he? Look, wait here for another five minutes. If he hasn't arrived by then, come to the meeting. If we don't get started, I'll never make it to the next."

Heels clacking on the marble tiled floor, she rushed off towards the meeting room, leaving me to look for a man I'd never met before. At least I didn't have to ask for a description. He'd be wearing a police uniform. As I trained my gaze on the sliding doors, a familiar person appeared. It took me a moment to associate his face with the smart white shirt, tie and dark trousers he wore. He'd even swapped his favoured trainers for well-polished black shoes. Grinning, he loped over.

"Tariq! What are you doing here?"

"I have a job interview. For the café."

"You kept that quiet."

He chuckled and tapped his nose. "I'm good with secrets."

I had a feeling there was a little more to that statement than keeping schtum about his interview. Did he know something about Will that I didn't? But I let it slide. Out of the corner of my eye I spotted a policeman leaning against the reception desk. How had I missed seeing him arrive?

Tariq grinned. "I've got a good one for you."

"Sorry, Tariq, but I have to go."

"What did the policeman say to his belly button?"

I shrugged. "You're an innie and I wanted an outie?"

He frowned. "That's silly! He said, 'You're under a vest.'"

"Very funny." Chuckling, I hooked my bag over my shoulder. "Good luck with your job interview. You'll need to go to the reception desk over there."

When I introduced myself to the policeman, I found Tariq hovering by my side. The policeman gave me a friendly handshake – he seemed much nicer than the sergeant, Glenn, who I'd met the other night. Then he turned and beamed in delight.

"Tariq! Long time no see. What have you been up to?"

He grasped Tariq's proffered hand and patted his shoulder in an oddly personal gesture.

'Oh, he's not with us,' I went to say, but thankfully I didn't. I wasn't being mean to Tariq, but I didn't want the policeman to think he was greeting a colleague rather than my friend.

"I'm going to a job interview at the café." Tariq held up his letter as proof.

At that moment a woman came up to us. "Are you Tariq? I'm Elaine. I've come to take you to your interview."

The policeman smiled. "Good luck, Tariq. Not that you'll need it." He turned to Elaine. "Believe me, if he gets the job, he'll be your best asset. He was great with the customers at Mike's Bap."

I led the way to the meeting room. The first set of double doors clanged behind us. "That was lovely of you."

"Not really. He's a nice bloke, although every time he sees me, he tells the same joke."

"About your belly button?" I grinned.

Chuckling, he patted his stomach. "It's famous. So are you, by all accounts."

"Me? How?"

"The other night when you got to meet Chartley's illustrious sarge, Glenn…"

I felt myself redden. "More like infamous. What did you hear?"

"It's a long story. All I know is that Glenn heard you telling your councillor off. He's not keen on Mark Carradine, so he's now become a fan of yours."

I shook my head. "I need a PhD in customer relations to navigate all the politics in this job."

♦

Will opened the door to me and Josh. He gave a deep sigh, his slumped shoulders and jutting lip telling me more about his feelings than any words could. He didn't hold his hands out to Josh, although that didn't prevent Josh from wriggling from my arms to grasp his leg.

Gazing adoringly at his uncle, he said, "Watch *Sinsons*?"

Will shook his head. "Nah. I'm not in the mood."

He shuffled off to his bedroom, Josh trotting behind him. I closed the front door and paused in the darkened hallway. Should I find out why Will seemed unhappy, or give him a bit of peace? I decided to leave it for now. If I took the wrong approach, I risked antagonising him. Perhaps Josh would cheer him up and then he might be more willing to speak.

Unusually for a Saturday afternoon, I couldn't hear football commentary. In the lounge I was met by a blank TV screen and my father sleeping, his hands resting on his stomach, a full cup of tea on the coffee table. I touched the cup. Cold. The milk had congealed on the top, which meant he must have fallen asleep hours ago. Frowning, I sat down on the neighbouring armchair. Was he depressed, or was something else wrong? He'd had the all-clear at the hospital, yet once again I'd found him asleep during the day. I couldn't remember him ever missing the football on TV by choice. My gaze strayed to the photographs on the mantelpiece – there were school photographs of Will and me on either side, while the centre one showed Dad and Will, decked in woolly hats, scarfs and thick coats, their noses nipped red as they stood beside the touchline one winter's day.

My childhood had followed a routine. While my friends went out shopping with their mums, or to the cinema, my childhood memories were of a Saturday afternoon spent on the settee watching *Match of the Day*. Or, more accurately, Dad watching it while I read a book, coloured by numbers or fought off Will, who didn't believe in sitting quietly.

Sundays had been the day for spring-cleaning. After six days creating mess, the house needed it, although we couldn't have done an intensive clean or we'd have found Will's stash of peas down the settee. My favourite Sunday mornings were when Dad dragged us to the rec, on the pretext that Will and I needed fresh air and a go on the swings, although these outings often coincided with the local team playing at home. Perhaps he'd learned the art of marketing. Sell it with swings rather than football.

When I reached my teens, my world had changed: I had discovered shops and the joys of hanging around doing nothing with friends – magical after spending time cloistered in our small family. Dad probably missed me, especially after Will got a TV for Christmas and holed himself up in his room for the next decade. But I'd been too wrapped up in my new social life to think too hard about Dad, who wasn't able to leave my little brother on his own.

Dad let out a gentle snore. I *would* wake him. He'd be disappointed to find I'd been and gone without saying hello.

I got to my feet and tapped his knee. "Fancy a cuppa?"

It took him a moment to register me. "Please. I must have just dozed off."

Just? His cold cup of tea gave him away.

"Do you want me to put the football on?"

"I turned it off. I had a headache. Can you fetch the paracetamol too?"

That didn't seem to add up. Dad plus a headache plus paracetamol had never equalled minus football. But I didn't say a word. I went through to the small kitchen to pour him a glass of water and pull out the medicine box from the top cupboard. After switching on the kettle, I took them through to Dad then went back to finish making the tea.

Will came into the kitchen and pulled off the lid to the biscuit tin. "Josh wants one."

He looked a bit better, but carried an air of dejection.

"You look sad, Will. Are you okay?"

He shrugged and snapped a ginger nut in half, popping it into his mouth. Then he pointed to show he couldn't speak, making a big deal of chewing the biscuit until, finally, he swallowed it with a grimace. Still not answering, he moved to the sink, where he grabbed a glass from the draining board and slotted it beneath the tap, which he turned on full blast. Water splashed the tiles, the worktop, the floor and Will.

"Oops," he said and shook his sodden arm. But instead of wiping the sides, he glugged the water that had made it into the glass. He plainly didn't want to talk. Something about his reticence made me think of Erin. He'd gone to ask her for a date the other day, but I hadn't talked to him about it since.

"Have you seen Erin since we went to the supermarket?"

He kept his empty glass horizontal to his lips – no doubt an attempt to conceal himself from my gaze. His lip quivered. Poor Will. I put my arm around his shoulders.

"Did she just want to be friends?"

He put his glass on the worktop and turned to look out of the window. A blanket of grey cloud hung low.

"You're a nice man, Will. You'll find someone."

"But I like *her*." He snatched a handful of biscuits from the tin. "Josh is waiting for these."

"Will?" I called.

He hesitated by the door. "Yes?"

"I like someone too." I knew I was on dodgy ground. There was a high chance Will would come straight out and tell Oliver. But telling him this might mean Will didn't feel alone in his one-sided affection…

He stood open-mouthed. "Scott?"

Trust him to bring up Josh's father, even though we hadn't bumped into each other for over a year. "Nooo! Someone you know."

Josh called for him from the bedroom. Without another word, Will shot off to share his booty. Behind me, the kettle clicked off. I picked up Dad's mug and popped a teabag into it. I didn't like to see Will unhappy, but I couldn't make Erin like him. Outside two pigeons huddled beside each other on the fence, while a third hovered several feet away, alone. Maybe Erin already had someone but she hadn't told Will? Or maybe she simply wanted to be friends. I'd been in that situation before – but usually the one yearning for a change in status, rather than doing the turning down.

I'd have a chat with Rachel and Leah when they came around later. They'd postponed our usual Friday night sit-in to tonight as Leah had arranged a date with a man she'd met at work. Maybe Rachel would come up with a plan to help Will. I could rely on her to come up with good ideas.

Chapter 7

RACHEL ARRIVED AN HOUR EARLIER than usual so she could see Josh before he went to bed. When Leah arrived, she found us with cars lined up on pretend roads around the lounge, while Josh gave directions to the garage beside the TV, insisting we adhered to his version of the Highway Code. Leah stood by the lounge door, balancing herself against the wall as she toed off her stilettoes and kicked them to one side. Rachel's eyes narrowed to slits when Leah shrugged off her coat to reveal a spangled black top and dark jeans.

"Date went well last night, then?"

"Not really. He had to leave early, so I hung on at the Nag's Head. Good job I did because I ended up chatting with this guy, Paul."

"So, you've dropped us for this Paul?"

Leah had the grace to blush, while I chuckled. Not for her a staid night of babysitting. Refusing to join us on the floor, she plumped down into the armchair where she surveyed traffic operations while sipping her Prosecco. I hoped she'd leave it behind. I hadn't tried Prosecco until she'd introduced me to it a few weeks before. Now I preferred it to my usual cheap wine.

When I announced it was Josh's bedtime both Leah and Rachel overruled me, so he got to stay up an extra half hour. But soon he was rubbing his eyes. After a murmured protest and an insistence on kissing both women on each cheek, he snuggled into me as I carried him upstairs. When I returned, Rachel had cleared away the mess and lined his cars up beside the garage.

"Have you seen your neighbour since he caught us nosing at

him being arrested?" Rachel said. She gave Leah a pointed glare.

"He looked at me a bit strangely, but that's all," I said. "I think it was a one-off. He's usually quiet."

Absorbed in her phone, Leah had ignored our discussion. She got to her feet.

"Turn the light off and I'll show you him."

For a moment I thought she might be talking about my neighbour, but the expression on her face told me otherwise.

She waited until I'd switched off the lounge light, then stepped through the back door onto the small balcony, where I kept the clothes horse, to point out a car parked below, its headlights dimmed. A cloud of exhaust fumes belched into the night. I could make out a man's face, partly lit by his mobile phone, but darkness shrouded the rest.

"You sent him round the back?" Rachel said. "The front not good enough for you?"

"No offence, but back or front is all the same round here."

Leah had a point. Each block looked similar, with its large seventies-style windows, exterior walkways out front and squat balconies at the rear on every other floor. Two blocks were just four floors high – one of them mine – while the rest had five floors.

"I said to meet me there, 'cause if it doesn't go well, then he won't know where either of you live." Leah called over her shoulder as she headed into the hallway to fetch her coat and shoes. "I'm not saying he might be a problem, only that I met him last night."

I stood by the lounge doorway. "Good point about not sending him here."

"You're getting in a car with a bloke you've just met?" Rachel said.

Leah called from the hallway. "Mike, the landlord at the Nag's, knows him."

Rachel accepted her response with a nod. The Nag's Head was one of their watering holes on their usual Saturday nights out, so she knew Mike.

Leah angled her feet into her stilettos and her arms into her coat. Her Prosecco stood on the table. I offered it to her and she grinned.

"Don't pretend I wouldn't have to wrestle it from you. Keep it."

She gave us a little wave and slammed the door. I hoped Josh wouldn't come down to investigate.

Rachel picked up the bottle and held it out to me, grinning. She filled both our glasses and shook out the dregs and we curled into the settee opposite each other. I decided to tell her about Will's feelings for Erin. She frowned when I reached the point about Will being upset.

"It's difficult, because he's the one who's moved the goalposts. To her, he's a friend."

"I know, but I don't like to see him unhappy."

"Poor Will." Rachel sighed. She'd known him ever since she'd dated a lad on my childhood estate and started hanging out with our gang. She knew Erin too, and could be relied upon to give a balanced viewpoint.

"Maybe another love interest is needed?"

But how? It had taken Will twenty-six years to form his first true attachment. While he was a loving, kind man, having Down syndrome in a town the size of Holdenwell meant he didn't have a huge amount of choice of potential romantic liaisons. Perhaps if I arrived earlier at the café, I could chat for longer with Will and his friends. See what other activities they could do. Yes, Oliver would be there, but I didn't care about that. Will's happiness was more important.

♦

With my mobile phone planted to my ear, I gazed through the rain-splattered windscreen, praying Will would answer my call. I'd offered to take him to the café and bring him back as the weather was so bad. Outside the wind shuddered through the skeletal branches of trees, but these would soon burst into life when the tight buds unfurled into lime-green leaves. I sighed. My holiday was just a fortnight away. I'd booked four days off, giving myself a fabulous ten days, including the Easter bank holiday weekend. Although I'd saved up to take Josh on a few day trips – including a blow-the-budget outing to Legoland – it wouldn't be so much fun if the weather didn't improve.

Will hurried up the path, holding his jacket above his head. Thank goodness he'd spotted us waiting. When he yanked the handle, I leaned across the seat to pull at the catch. He ducked inside, sprinkling me with droplets of rain, while giving me a look that suggested the few seconds he'd had to wait had caused him to get wet.

"Uncle Will, look at my car," Josh called from the back seat. Through glasses beaded with rain, Will assessed the red Mini with its go-faster stripes.

"We went to the charity shop and bought a few more cars for his garage," I said.

"Nice car." Will gave Josh a thumbs-up and settled into his seat.

I drove off, feeling a little guilty for not saying hello to Dad. But I could pop in briefly when I dropped Will back. I'd managed to leave work an hour earlier than usual so, once I'd dropped Will at Samson's Café, I had time to get home and eat with Josh before going back out again. That's after I'd put on a bit of lippie and retouched my mascara, since Oliver might be there. I was under no illusions about a relationship, but I wanted him to see me at my best.

The sky darkened and passing headlights cut into the gloom. I turned the windscreen wipers to full so they slapped back and forth, but they couldn't keep up with the downpour. Ahead the traffic lights turned red, reflecting on the river of tarmac. We came to a halt at the front of the queue. A squall shook the car and raindrops scudded across the junction, reminding me of a starling murmuration. Will and I used to love watching them dipping and soaring above our house, but Dad had hated them. He'd rush outside and call us to help him tear the washing from the line.

"Do you remember…" Something about Will's expression stopped me from asking him about the starlings. Instead, I asked, "Are you okay?"

The lights turned green and I pulled away. "Will?"

"Eh?" Wrinkling his nose, he lifted his head to gaze at me over the rim of his glasses.

"Are you worried about seeing Erin tonight?"

He frowned and crossed his arms. "No!"

I stole a glance at him. Will wasn't usually one for lying and, when he did try, he was unable to keep it up under pressure. The edges of his mouth arced downwards but his hands were still folded across his chest. If he was nervous, he'd be chewing his nails.

"What's upset you then?"

Will jabbed his finger towards the window. "This! We were meant to be doing Pooh sticks. But the stupid rain means we'll be stuck inside. I won the cup last year too."

I'd forgotten he'd been crowned the champion last year. Unlike the gentle Pooh sticks of my childhood, Samson's championship involved hard-fought stages and silver cups both for the stick owners and for the person who'd picked the overall winner in a sweepstake.

We'd reached the row of shops and Samson's Café. Outside a car sat, its hazard lights flashing, on double yellow lines, so I pulled up behind it. Inside the brightly lit café people moved around. Was Oliver in there, hastily rearranging the schedule so they had something interesting to do tonight? The abandoned Pooh sticks also meant that Will would have to spend more time with Erin; they were on the same table. Neither Tariq and Erin had needed a lift there, but I'd be taking them all home. I hoped tonight went well, or it would be a strained journey later.

♦

The rain had ceased by the time I stepped from the car to pay for a ticket. Usually it took no more than five or ten minutes to fetch Will, but once or twice it had taken half an hour and I couldn't afford a parking fine. This car park was often busy in the evening, with people going to the pubs and restaurants, so it was one of the few in the area where parking had to be paid for after six o'clock. I'd seen the warden out checking tickets a few times too, so didn't dare risk it.

After popping the ticket on the dashboard, I unclipped Josh from his seat. I'd dressed him in a red mackintosh and his yellow wellies but, in my haste to leave after hanging on to watch a local news item mentioning the council, I'd forgotten my umbrella. Holding Josh at arm's length as he splashed through the shallow puddles on the pavement, I clasped my coat collar tight to my neck. It may have stopped raining, but drips fell from the tree branches with every blast of wind. One scored a direct hit in my eye beneath the sign for Samson's Café and I wrestled the door open with my eye screwed shut, while Josh insisted on stomping in the puddle by the doorstep.

Erin ran over to admire Josh's coat, leaving me to dab my eye with the heel of my hand.

"You're crying." Eyes wide, she assessed me. "What's the matter?"

Heads turned in my direction and Will scurried over, while Tariq lumbered behind.

"It's just—"

"Has someone hurt you?" Erin peeled my hand away.

"No, I'm fine, honest. It's—"

"Your eye is black." Will's gaze met mine.

"Seriously, it's—"

"Is everything okay?" Oliver headed over.

So much for trying to look good. "I'm fine. A raindrop fell in my eye, that's all."

Taking no notice of my protestations, Erin ushered me over to the table and levered me onto the chair. She patted my shoulder. "Do you need a drink?"

I shook my head. "That's very kind of you, though."

Behind her, a grinning Oliver sauntered away. Will sat down opposite me, next to a woman I hadn't met before, while Erin pulled up another seat – I must have taken hers – and Tariq took the chair beside me. I held my arms out to Josh but he clambered onto Erin's lap. Now it was her turn to be inspected. Josh studied her lips.

"Is that juice?"

"It's my lipstick."

Will watched as she pressed her puckered lips against her hand and showed Josh the purple kiss-shaped imprint. Beside him, the new woman twiddled a strand of her dark hair. Her gaze tracked Will's movements.

Tariq nudged me. "Why do cows lie down when it rains?" He didn't wait for me to respond, but said with a flourish, "To keep each other dry."

I'd heard this one before and knew the punchline should be 'udder' rather than 'other', but I didn't correct him. When Will burst into laughter and clapped his hands, the new woman glowed with happiness. She hadn't once glanced at Tariq, so it was nothing to do with the joke. Erin seemed to have noticed this interloper's attention, but Will remained oblivious, his attention focused on Erin's mouth.

I turned to the woman. "I'm Maddie. And you are?"

"Christabel."

"That's a lovely name," I said.

For the first time since I'd arrived, Will turned to look at Christabel. A frown creased Erin's forehead and she tapped Will's arm.

"Do you like my bracelet?" A chain hung from Erin's wrist,

weighted down by a collection of little charms. I could make out a heart and a silver bell.

Oliver appeared beside her. "Very nice."

She twisted her wrist so the charms jangled together. With Will's attention returned to the rightful owner – or so she believed – she graced him with a smile.

Oliver grinned. "A ménage à trois in the making, do you think?" He turned to go, then hesitated. "I've got a meeting at the council next Tuesday. Could you spare twenty minutes before then for a coffee?"

A thrill ran through me, which only slightly abated when he added, "I've a few queries about the Dealsham youth group that you may be able to help with."

Chapter 8

ON THE WAY HOME FROM SAMSON'S CAFÉ, Tariq had told me that he'd got the job and started on Monday, but when I went into the café on Tuesday it felt odd to see him standing behind the counter. After an early start dealing with a fretful Josh, who didn't want to go to Chelsea's house before nursery, I'd left home, forgetting to pick up my lunch box. Instead, I decided to treat myself to a jacket potato ahead of the meeting with Oliver.

The clock showed five past twelve, so most people wouldn't have come down to lunch yet, but I'd expected to find the place buzzing with informal meetings, especially when finding a room at short notice was impossible. But the café was quiet, with just a small group huddled at a corner table.

Behind the counter, Elaine stood beside Tariq, pointing to various items while he listened intently and nodded. I'd seen her many times before, but I hadn't known her name until she'd introduced herself to Tariq in the reception area before his job interview. I hung back, letting her finish what she needed to say, but she glanced up. Spotting me, she nudged Tariq. Other than a slight widening of his eyes, no one would have guessed we knew each other.

"How can I help you?" he stuttered, wiping his hands down the front of his apron.

"Hello, Tariq. How are you doing?"

"Hello." He glanced around to Elaine, as if to check whether he could fraternise, then he turned back. "I started yesterday."

A phone shrilled from the little office behind the counter and

Elaine told Tariq to serve me while she took the call.

"I was thinking of getting a jacket potato with cheese. Can you do that?"

He gave me an uncertain nod and crossed over to the potato oven, where he picked up a pair of prongs and eased a jacket potato out. His tongue stuck between his teeth, he carried the potato back to the counter and placed it in a carton. After sawing the potato in half, he dug into the butter with his knife and used his finger to slide it from the blade. Elaine stood in the office behind with her back to us, the phone tucked between her ear and her shoulder, writing something on a pad. I didn't want to attract her attention, in case it got Tariq into trouble, so I waved at him, but he didn't look up as he took the spoon from the container and scooped grated cheese onto my potato. I wilted inside when he used his finger to press the cheese into the potato.

"Tariq!" I hissed.

Six prods – three on each potato half – and he folded the lid closed, smeared his hands down the front of his apron and handed me the carton with a look of satisfaction.

"Erm. I think that's three pounds, but hold on and I'll ask."

Finally, I'd got his attention. Putting my finger to my mouth, I signalled for him to follow me to the end of the counter. When I got there, I turned to find him standing where I'd left him. When I flapped my hand to call him over, he frowned but did so.

"You should be wearing gloves," I said.

He slapped his hand over his mouth. "Oh no! I forgot."

"Don't worry. Elaine shouldn't have left you when you're new. You mustn't stick your fingers in the food either." He'd worked at Mike's Bap, so he should know that. But perhaps he'd forgotten in the excitement of serving me. "You should use a fork or spoon."

His face fell. "I get confused. I haven't done food before. Only cleaning and washing-up."

Now I felt bad. Will struggled to remember things when he was given too many instructions at once. It would be the same for Tariq, especially with the job being so new.

"Can you ask Elaine to write you a list? You need to tell her if you're not sure, so she can help you."

Elaine came out of the office, looking surprised to see us at the other end of the counter.

"We were just working out how much I owe," I said.

She lifted the carton lid. "Jacket potato with cheese. That's three pounds."

Tariq beamed as I gave him a thumbs-up. He'd added it perfectly. I handed over a five-pound note, waiting while Elaine showed Tariq which buttons to press on the till. He counted out two pounds and went to pass it to me, but paused, hand hovering in mid-air, his attention taken by the restaurant doors whirring open behind me.

I swung around to find Oliver sauntering over, looking amazing in jeans teamed with a white shirt and a smart jacket. My heart sank. I'd wanted to eat before he arrived. It was bad enough having a formal work meeting with Oliver – especially when I would spend much of the time worrying about how many times my gaze met his – let alone having to eat and talk to him at the same time. I'd leave my jacket potato until after the meeting then heat it up in the office kitchen.

"Hello, Oliver. What are you doing here?" Tariq said.

"I've a meeting with Madeleine."

Tariq looked around, as if expecting to see someone else with Oliver.

"I'll be over there." I pointed towards the other side of the room. "See you later, Tariq."

"You've got food," Oliver said. "Good. I could do with something hot."

Change of plan. I'd have to eat in front of him.

I picked a table in the corner – not for intimacy, but to be further away from the draught that swept in each time the doors opened. The chairs, while modern in look, were hard plastic and not made for comfort, especially for shorter people like myself where they bit into the back of my legs, cutting off my circulation. I'd spent previous meetings in here stretching my feet, trying to ward off pins and needles, so I perched on the lip of the seat to pull the bits I needed from my bag. All the tables accommodated four people, so if I put my notebook in front of my food Oliver would have to sit diagonally from me, giving us a bit more distance. Unless he decided to sit beside me, which would be odd. I stuck my bottle of water in front of that chair, just in case.

Once I'd set out the table, I opened the lid to assess my food. I'd known Tariq long enough to be able to deal with a few finger-prod marks. Thank goodness he'd done it to me, not someone else. Chuckling, I unwrapped my plastic knife and fork from the napkin. From the counter, Tariq looked across as he pulled on a pair of blue gloves, rewarding me with a brief rendition of jazz hands. Then, under Elaine's watchful gaze, he crossed over to the oven. It wouldn't be long before he had gained enough confidence to be able to tell potato jokes while serving our food.

When Oliver came over a few minutes later, he chose the seat

I'd planned. While he tucked into his jacket potato, he made small talk about the previous week at Samson's Café. It was only when he was halfway through his meal that he put his knife and fork down and faced me, his expression serious.

"I wanted to speak to you about your colleague, David Garnett. But I'd appreciate it if you didn't tell anyone about this yet. It's linked to the youth club, but I think there's more to it than that."

"That sounds mysterious," I joked.

"I don't like to see decent people being treated badly." He paused. "You've got enough to deal with as it is."

He'd said 'you'. What was going on? I had few dealings with David. While he might be in my team, he kept out of my way. Perhaps Oliver was about to tell me that David wasn't happy that I'd got 'his' job.

"I think David is out to cause trouble for you." He shifted around in his chair, fixing his dark eyes on mine. Shocked, I met his eyes. I opened my mouth to say 'Why?' but found I couldn't speak.

"Kavita told me that David had been offering your services to one of the youth committee members as a secretary, hence the confusion at the meeting. Someone overheard her and told me that David had boasted about setting you up at a residents' meeting." He shrugged. "I don't know much about that one, but they told me he'd manoeuvred things to make you look stupid in front of a councillor."

"I took it a stage further, though. I had a go at the councillor – Mark Carradine – that night."

Oliver pursed his lips, reminding me of Emma's expression when she'd told me how important it was to keep Mark Carradine on side. I needed this job. There was no one but me to pay for our rent, the nursery fees, food and my much-needed car. Even though my old boss had been unable to believe I would last at the council, saying that I'd find it too restrictive and that I'd be begging to go back to my position in sales within six weeks, I didn't want to prove him right.

"I've come across David many times. He's a back-slapping man's man. Not only will he hate having a female boss, but he'll also hate the fact that a woman has taken the role he wanted. Right now, he's using his network to his advantage, but it won't be long before you have your own. You're making good inroads as it is. I'm amazed at how much you do."

I knew he didn't just mean work. He'd seen me at the café with Will, Josh and the others.

For the past few minutes, Oliver had been twisting his pen round and round but now he laid it down on the table. The café doors brushed open and a group strode past, laughing. He waited until they were out of earshot.

"Look, all I can say is, take care with David. His self-importance will be his downfall, but keep your wits about you in the meantime."

Chapter 9

DAVID WASN'T AT HIS DESK when I went back. Not that I had expected to see him. His 'work' consisted of leaning back in his seat, his legs splayed in front of him, while he chatted to a contact on the phone, or bashing the keyboard with his index fingers. I had no idea what he did the rest of the time. Everyone else in the team seemed to do more work than their salary covered, while David spent his time telling people how hard he worked. It paid off in the community because people didn't know the reality – that someone else had produced his results.

I'd seen this behaviour before in previous workplaces, and it had irked me. But David had taken it further than a simple boast. I debated whether to seek Emma's advice – the jacket slung over the back of her chair told me she was around somewhere – but decided against it.

As I pulled my mobile from my bag, it started to ring. Dad. I'd asked him not to call me at work unless it was urgent, so I hurried away from my desk towards the back of the office for some privacy.

"What's up? Are you okay?"

"I am, but Will isn't."

"Is he ill?"

"His bank account has been emptied. He says he hasn't touched it. He's come home from work in a right state. The bank won't speak to me but he doesn't understand what they're telling him."

I bit my lip. I had a report to write, which I'd promised to send to Emma before her morning meeting. I could write it this evening, but that would spell the end of my quiet night watching TV with Josh and the start of one spent cooking a rushed meal before settling back down to work.

"What did the police say?"

Dad sighed. "They took his details and said they'd be in touch. Three hundred pounds is probably nothing to them."

"*Three hundred pounds!*" I gasped. I had no idea Will had managed to save that much money, but then it hit me. It wouldn't all be savings. It would be the money he needed to take him through to his next pay day. "And it's gone from his account? Are you sure?" I checked my watch. One o'clock. If I rushed, I could be back in time to finish the report. "I'll pick you up and then we'll get Will."

I pulled my pen lid off with my teeth and jotted a note to Emma to say I'd had to shoot out and would be gone a couple of hours.

"You could just take him."

I rolled my eyes. Each day it was becoming more difficult to shift Dad from the settee. But I didn't have time to worry about it today. "You know more about it than me. I'll be over to pick you both up in twenty minutes."

♦

I'd forgotten Tuesday was market day in Holdenwell shopping centre. The sign listing the car parks said that all were full or almost full. I told Dad he'd have to take Will into the bank while I waited in a nearby side street. If a traffic warden appeared, I'd be able to move on. From the rear-view mirror I could see Will gazing through the window, his bottom lip quivering. He swiped the back of his hand across his face.

"How did you find out?" I asked him.

He shrugged, so Dad responded.

"He tried using his card in the canteen but it wouldn't work. His boss took him to a cashpoint as he was so worried, but it said he had no money. It had all gone."

"But how did his money get taken?"

"We have no idea, but he needs it back soon. He doesn't get paid or get his disability allowance for another fortnight."

I sighed. Our family had never been wealthy. When Mum died, Dad changed his job from postman to gardener. That meant he could take Will with him during the school holidays, although the council's summer club had been a godsend. But the work had been sporadic in winter and he'd relied on ad-hoc jobs in shops or working from home counting out screws and other fittings into little bags for a local pre-packed furniture supplier. When Will went to college, Dad got a full-time job that he enjoyed working in the offices of a seed company, but after his cancer diagnosis things had gone downhill and his chemotherapy had left him too weak to work. The little savings he had wouldn't stretch to bailing Will out. I hoped the bank would be sympathetic to Will's predicament.

In the street behind the bank, the half dozen parking bays were full. I pulled up on a stretch of double yellow lines, making sure I didn't block the road, and put my hazard lights on.

"If a space becomes available, I'll come in," I said.

Dad grimaced and struggled from his seat. Clearly, he would have liked me to go with them, but I couldn't risk a parking ticket. Will slammed his door, making the car judder, and shuffled off behind Dad, even more loath to face the people at the bank. When they turned the corner, I picked up my phone and started scrolling through my emails while glancing up every now and again to check if a space had become available.

A familiar-looking man was coming towards me. I squinted. David! What was he doing here? Did he have the day off? I sank lower into my seat and reached down to find my sunglasses. A poor disguise, but better than being spotted. He paused by the car ahead of mine and placed two bags on the ground – one labelled M&S and the other a pinkish colour through which packs of meat bulged and a bag of spuds poked from the top – to rifle through his pockets. Car keys found, he hefted the bags into the boot and got into the car. Soon his reversing light brightened and I put my indicators on. When he pulled away, I took his space, waiting until he disappeared down the road before I got out to buy a ticket.

The bank was busy, with three queues: for the cashpoints, the cashiers and the helpdesk. I chose the latter as I couldn't see Dad or Will anywhere. Half a dozen people stood in front of me and I resorted to my trusty phone – this time my Facebook feed – to stave off a boring wait. It meant I almost missed Will rushing past me, Dad in pursuit. Heads turned as Will yanked open the door and fled, almost crashing into an elderly woman.

After muttering an apology, Dad rushed off, leaving me to push through the queue and sprint after them, calling, "Dad! Will!" Neither heard me.

Even though Dad was not as fit as he'd once been, Will's health issues meant he couldn't outrun him for long and I caught up with them by the bakery. Will's arms flailed as he fought to keep Dad at bay but, corralled between us and the wall, he sank into Dad's chest, sobbing.

"Why did he do that? He was my friend."

"Not everyone is nice, Will." Dad's voice trembled.

Catching my puzzled expression, Dad mouthed 'I'll tell you later'. The smell of baking wafted past, warm against the chill breeze that buffeted my back. My lunchtime sandwich lay heavy in my stomach. I felt sick. Did Will's tears mean he wouldn't get his money back? Surely, if someone had stolen cash from his bank account, it couldn't be his fault?

We stood in silence, comforting Will. When his sobs calmed, Dad pointed towards the café window. "Do you want a hot chocolate?"

Will knuckled his fists to dry his eyes. He sniffed, hard. After a moment he allowed Dad to lead him into the café, where the comforting smell of pastries embraced us. While Dad and Will ordered cake, I opted for a cup of tea. The server invited us to take a seat while she prepared our order, so we settled for a table away from the door. Dad needed the warmth, but I needed the shadows. I'd spied David out and about and I didn't want the same to happen to me.

"Aren't they reimbursing Will?" I asked when we were all seated.

Dad fired me a look, so I gave Will's hand a squeeze. "It'll work out, I'm sure."

Not knowing what else to say, I gazed around, cricking my neck to look at a framed black-and-white photograph hanging above us. It showed a laden horse and cart outside a grocer's store.

"That's the building over there, isn't it?" I jerked my head towards the mobile phone shop across the street. Neither of them responded, their attention taken by the woman walking towards us, biting her lip as she held a tray. She slid it onto the table and handed out the drinks and cakes.

While I sipped my tea, Dad and Will munched their cakes, each looking lost in their thoughts. Their silence frustrated me. When would they get around to telling me what had happened? Will dabbed the last of the crumbs from his plate and popped his finger in his mouth. He grinned, his equilibrium restored. While Dad ate his cake, Will moved on to his hot chocolate. I'd never get back to work at this rate.

When Will announced that he needed to use the toilet, I waited until he was out of earshot and asked Dad about the bank.

He shook his head. "It's worse than I thought."

"How?"

"We'll have to get the police involved."

Whatever had happened to Will sounded serious, but we didn't have time for a full-length discussion. "Just give me the basics."

Dad brushed his hands together, dropping crumbs on his plate. "Will made friends with a visitor of a patient at the cottage hospital. During their chats Will mentioned he struggled to get out at lunchtime, so the man said that if Will gave him his bank card, he could get a few things from the shop for him."

I frowned. There was a small canteen at the cottage hospital where Will worked, so he could get food and drink. Then I remembered Will talking about how the canteen had 'gone all healthy' and stopped selling chips. It made more sense now, except for one thing. "But how did he take three hundred pounds without having Will's PIN number?"

Dad swiped his sleeve across his face. "That's the worst of it. He did! After Will handed over his PIN number, this man withdrew fifty pounds the first day and gave Will a tenner or so change. But then he came back a few days later and took two hundred and fifty pounds. The limit from the cashpoint. It's odd that he gave Will his card back, but he probably thought there'd be more for the taking. Will says the person this man was visiting has left hospital but, hopefully, the police can find out who it is."

"I hope they bloody well find him before I do." I'd spewed the words in anger, but they were just that. I couldn't do much other than ring the police.

Dad tapped my hand to warn me that Will was on his way back. Will slumped onto the seat and picked up his cup, disappointed to find he'd drunk all his hot chocolate. Instead, he slurped the dregs and licked his lips.

A bank stood next to the mobile phone shop. It gave me an idea, but presented a quandary. If I gave Will some of the money I'd saved for my Easter break, it meant Josh and I wouldn't be able to do all the things I'd arranged. While I could take Josh to the park instead of spending money on a pricey day out, I didn't really want to give up our special day at Legoland, especially when I'd planned it to compensate for the sacrifices we'd both had to make with my new job. But Will couldn't live on air and Dad had little to give him. Finally, I made up my mind.

Dad pushed his plate away. "Let's go. I'm not that hungry."

I scraped my chair back and stood up. "Wait one moment. I just need to get something."

I slung my handbag over my shoulder and headed outside. At the cashpoint I hesitated – was I being too stingy? – but I ignored my inner angel and pressed the button for sixty pounds. I pocketed a tenner. The rest was for Will. It wasn't enough, but it would help him to get by until the end of the month – he had a bus pass and could take packed lunches to work – while also meaning that Josh and I could still have our big day out.

Back in the café I grabbed Will's hand and folded it over the notes. He opened his hand in confusion and the money fell to the table.

"Where's that from?" Dad asked.

"I'm doing okay now, so I can afford it. It's not much, but he needs to get by until they sort him out."

"That's if they ever do," Dad muttered. "I'm not happy about you doing this, though."

"Well, no doubt you'll have to sub him too."

Beaming, Will fanned out the money. "Look, Alan, I'm rich!"

"Well, he's back to normal calling me Alan," Dad said in a voice that reminded me of Eeyore.

I gazed at Will, loving the simplicity in his happiness. "Sorry it's not quite the riches you lost." When he gave me a blank look, I sighed. "Right, let's get you both home. I need to get back to work."

Chapter 10

RACHEL'S HOUSE STANK OF RANCID SOCKS, or how I would expect them to smell. I never let mine – or Josh's – get to that stage. In my childhood, Dad had done the washing using an old twin-tub, even when he could have bought a second-hand front-loading washing machine from the local electrical shop. Dad was finally forced to by a new machine when the twin-tub mangled his trousers and shaved chunks of wool from his favourite jumper. I'd never forget his look of dismay when he held up his mutilated jumper, as Will and I dissolved into fits of giggles. Dad told us to stop laughing but then he'd put it on and paraded about looking like Worzel Gummidge, while we begged to have a turn wearing it too. Strange how smells could lead to a journey of long-forgotten memories, although I had no idea what the reek in Rachel's kitchen could be or why it had made me think of Dad's washing machine.

Josh pinched his nose and flapped his hand in front of his face. "It stinks."

Blue paint smudged his cheek from his latest creation at nursery. I'd never have guessed the painting was a horse, had he not told me. The painting, crinkled from an afternoon spent drying on the radiator, had been abandoned on the back seat of the car, along with his nursery bag. There was little point ferrying either over to Rachel's. We'd collect them while walking home.

"Rabbit," Rachel told us. "Kieran's decided it's his new thing. He had it at his friend's the other night and loved it."

I wrinkled my nose. "I hope the taste is worth it. Want to try a bit, Josh?" I teased, knowing what the answer would be. He shook his head and raced off to the lounge, in the hope of finding Kieran. Rachel's partner could always be relied upon to throw Josh around, either pretending to be a fairground ride or a wrestler. I didn't mind. Most people wanted their child calmed down before bed, but the games – combined with the stroll back to our block – made for a tired little boy who welcomed an evening snack, a bit of TV, then bath and bed.

Soon I heard an adult voice making zooming noises, matched by Josh's high-pitched squeals.

"We won't stay long. You'll be wanting to eat."

Rachel absentmindedly scratched the nicotine patch on her arm. "Tea? You're needing your bed, by the look of you."

"Please." I rubbed my eyes and yawned. "I was up until one this morning writing a report. It had to be in this morning."

For the next few minutes, I relayed the previous day's events, with Will losing his money to the fraudster and how I'd made it back to the office with only an hour to go before I had to leave to collect Josh from the nursery. David hadn't arrived back; he'd apparently been – I made air quotes – 'out at a meeting'. But I hadn't said a word. After all, I'd spent the afternoon with my family.

"I'm gutted for Will."

"What sort of person would do that?" Rachel handed me a mug of tea.

"He's easy pickings. I hope the police find the bloke. But there's probably little chance of Will getting his money back. I'm going to ask Oliver to give a talk about looking after money at Samson's Café, though."

"Oliver?" she said. "I thought Harry ran it."

"He still does. Either of them could do it."

I hadn't said anything to make her curious, but I felt my face flush. No matter how often I told myself that Oliver would have a girlfriend, that he wouldn't want to be with a single parent and certainly not one living on Court Place, I found myself getting embarrassed if anyone mentioned him. I didn't want anyone finding out about my schoolgirl-style crush. Oliver might not be a pop star, but I had as much chance with him as I would have done with one of the members of Take That.

"While you're asking him about the talk, you could invite him to my party."

"Party?" Then what she'd just said hit me. How had she guessed? I looked her straight in the eye, hoping my cheeks wouldn't illuminate the room. "Oliver's not my type."

"Gay, is he?" She chuckled. "Oops, wrong friend. Saying that, you could both do with mixing things up a bit. There's her, the man collector, and you, the man barrier. Anyhow, do you reckon Chelsea will look after Josh? It's the Saturday before the Easter weekend."

"I can ask."

"Feel free to bring a bloke. Josh doesn't count. Unless you can't find a sitter and want to pop in, then you can bring him. It won't get messy until gone ten." She tucked her hands into a pair of oven gloves and opened the oven door. Hot air, laden with the stench of hot hare – or, more accurately, rabbit – blasted out. After giving the concoction a stir, she put the lid back on. "It needs fifteen minutes more, I reckon."

While she wiped the steam from her glasses, I sipped my tea. "We'll be gone by then."

"No hurry. Believe me, I'm not desperate to eat it."

Who could blame her? I'd had a sandwich at lunchtime and tonight's dinner would be beans on toast, maybe with an egg if Josh wanted one. Not exciting, but it was preferable to hers.

"I forgot to tell you, my brother's got an admirer."

"Has he now?"

Rachel's eyes lit up. "Not Erin, I take it. Although, give it time and I reckon she'll be on his tail too."

♦

David sat opposite me in the team meeting, his eyes glinting behind his black-rimmed glasses as Emma told us that the library service needed to make cutbacks, and the easiest way to make the saving was in staff costs. Not that it got sold to us as such. Our Portfolio Holder had been quoted in the press release as saying this was a golden opportunity for communities to get involved in running their libraries. At least it meant there wouldn't be library closures. Yet. Emma explained that some local protests were being planned, but our team's job would be to go out – on behalf of the library team – to drum up community support and to find people willing to give up a few hours to help at their local library.

I prickled with discomfort. Josh and I often popped into Holdenwell library for him to choose a few books. While I wasn't on first-name terms with the staff, they always said hello. Now I'd joined the council and the library was yards away, it was even easier to pop by. Just last week one of the staff had spotted my identity badge and asked if I was enjoying my new job. Now I felt like a traitor. My job would be to encourage people to take hers.

David shifted forward in his seat. "Who's leading this project from our team? I'm happy to do so."

Emma rifled through a set of papers and handed them to the person next to her to pass around the table.

"You'll be working with a few of the groups. We need volunteers to take on the new roles. But, as expected, Madeleine will be the team lead."

"So once again experience doesn't count here."

Uncomfortable glances passed between the team members as David shifted back in his seat and folded his arms. Emma ignored his outburst and continued to talk about the planned strategy while he glowered at me. I was more surprised about being elected to lead the project than his behaviour. Although I shouldn't have been. Emma dealt with general council strategy – in other words, she would be involved in decisions relating to the proposed fate of the libraries. David worked with community groups, acting as their allies. My role straddled the two, linking service areas with the relevant people in the communities, including working with local councillors. I'd never thought about it in this way before, but I would be seen as a double agent, ostensibly wanting to help the community but also seen as a council lackey, while the people with jobs at risk in the other service areas – including libraries and youth services – would see me as council staff, there to do the leadership's bidding. Were any of them wrong?

Soon after I'd joined the team, I'd wondered why they'd recruited an outsider for a job that would be better suited to someone who understood the council and local community. Now I wondered if I'd been chosen because it was better that I *didn't* know them. It would be horrible to upset people you knew. Saying that, David's expression told me he didn't have a problem with it. I would have gladly handed this poisoned chalice to him and he'd have snatched it from me, gulped down the contents and would no doubt survive, whereas I doubted I'd reach the other side of this unscathed.

Why hadn't Emma forewarned me? Usually, she went out of her way to do so. When the others filed out after the meeting ended, I waited to speak with her. I didn't meet David's eye as he got up, but I felt him pause behind me.

His breath patted my ear as he hissed, "Brown tongue."

I jerked around in shock. What a strange thing for a grown man to say. He reached the door, where he stood out of Emma's sight, smirking.

"Do you have a moment?" I asked Emma.

She glanced at the clock, even though she'd checked the time to bring the meeting to a halt. "I'm seeing Derek in ten minutes, so walk with me."

David's shadow slid away. By the time Emma had stuffed her laptop into her bag and swung it onto her shoulder, he'd disappeared.

"Let's take the stairs." She led me towards the stairwell and pushed the double doors open. "Sorry I didn't speak to you about this. I got your note about having to shoot out but I had a four o'clock meeting on the other side of Chartley, so I couldn't get back."

I flushed. My note had said I'd be a couple of hours; I hadn't anticipated needing three hours to take Dad and Will to the bank. Emma hadn't been able to speak to me yesterday because she'd booked the day off to attend a funeral.

"We need to get started on this urgently before Derek changes his mind. He wants to close the two village libraries and leave the three main ones in the town centres, but he won't consider replacing the village ones with a mobile library."

She fell silent. Soon I understood why. Two people chatted at the foot of the stairs, one clutching papers, the other a stern-faced woman in a red dress with a large pearl necklace strung around her neck. The women glanced at Emma and nodded.

Emma pushed through a set of double doors and headed down a corridor. "Councillor Margery Arscott. Another one who doesn't like people being late no matter what the reason," she hissed. "Anyhow, Isobel, the head of libraries, wants the volunteer solution. It's not perfect but it's better than the other option, which would cut staff *and* lose two libraries in places with poor bus routes. The councillors in those areas wouldn't be happy either. Isobel's going to ask for voluntary redundancies. Hopefully," – Emma held up her crossed fingers – "it will be enough."

"Why does Derek want to close the two village libraries?"

Shrugging, she said, "Who knows? It could be that there will be less fall-out from the villages. Fewer people to complain. Or perhaps because one of the libraries is in Didlingbury, which has a councillor from the other side."

She must have read my confused expression. "The political opposition."

We'd reached the reception area, where she came to a halt. "There are some documents in a folder marked 'Libraries'. IT has set it up so you and a select few others have access to them. Spend a bit of time reading through them, as you'll be meeting with the library team tomorrow to start taking it forward."

She strode off towards Derek's office. It was almost one o'clock, so I decided to go via the café and see how Tariq was getting on. Perhaps I'd treat myself to lunch. I'd been too tired to eat more than a couple of mouthfuls of beans on toast last night, with the unforeseen consequences that I'd eaten my sandwiches within minutes of arriving in the office this morning.

I'd reached the front of the queue and Tariq was cutting me a slice of cake when the lovely councillor I'd met soon after I'd joined the council came over. She touched my arm.

"Madeleine, isn't it? How's it going with the youth club? Has it started yet?"

I couldn't recollect her name, but thankfully her identity badge faced outwards. Dana Orwell. But as I went to speak, Tariq butted in.

"It's not Madeleine. It's Maddie! Everyone keeps getting her name wrong." He frowned at me. "And you sound strange too."

Dana's laugh tinkled in the air. Not unkindly, she said, "Tariq, you are funny."

I stood there, shamefaced. He'd noticed my work voice – which was not unlike the telephone voice my friends' mothers had been mocked for using.

"You can call me whichever you feel most comfortable with," I told him.

Had I just spoken to Tariq in a voice that would make the Queen proud? I cringed. If Rachel and Leah were here, they would be rolling on the floor almost wetting themselves, but Tariq stood open-mouthed, holding a knife in mid-air.

I turned to Dana Orwell and cleared my throat before moderating my work voice. "Tariq's known me for years. I haven't always spoken like this."

She laid a hand on my shoulder. "You sound fine to me."

Tariq shook his head. I'd try to explain to him at Samson's Café next week, but I doubted he'd understand. Why would he? What was so wrong with my name and how I spoke that I had to pretend to be someone else? But then I remembered Derek and his comments about my social-housing estate and I knew exactly why. While Dana was lovely and would accept me for who I was, I'd met people like Derek before. If I spoke the way I used to, he'd ignore anything I said. Because, to him, 'my kind' were – how had he put it? Oh yes. Scum.

Chapter 11

I'D EMAILED OLIVER AND HARRY to tell them what had happened to Will and asked them to chat to the people at Samson's Café to ensure the same didn't happen to anyone else. I'd asked them to be discreet, so Will didn't get upset. When I arrived a bit later than usual to pick up Will the following week, I found clearing up in progress.

Josh wriggled out of my arms. We couldn't be long; I needed to get him to bed. He had grey smudges beneath his eyes and his ears burned red, a sure sign of tiredness. He popped his thumb into his mouth and curled his free arm around my leg, anchoring me to the spot. A grinning Erin rushed over, dragging Will behind her, while Christabel watched from a distance.

Erin bent to give Josh a kiss. Then, in a voice breathless with excitement, she said, "Poor Will. Those terrible people stole his money." She pulled Will tight to her chest. He didn't push himself free.

As Oliver turned around, leaving Tariq to finish upending the chairs onto the tables, Erin released Will.

"We didn't mention names or give the same scenario." Oliver looked from me to Will. "But Will wanted to tell everyone what had happened to him, and to warn them too."

"He was very brave." Erin patted Will's shoulder. "Now we know to take care with people pretending to be our friends."

"Maddie pretends to be Madeleine at work." Tariq butted in. "Don't you?"

"Josh, watch out!"

I shifted him out of the way to let two lads past. They cast 'goodnights' back into the room and stepped outside, leaving the door ajar. As cold air rushed in, I pushed it shut then turned back, to find Tariq waiting for me to respond. Beside him, Oliver raised his hand to his mouth to stifle a seeming cough but his crinkling eyes gave him away.

Then it hit me: I'd told Josh to 'watch aht' rather than 'watch owt'. No wonder Oliver had laughed. The old me was never far from the surface.

I had to answer Tariq. He wouldn't let it drop until I did. "I do. But it *is* my name."

"And you talk differently."

Oliver grinned. "Tariq, you should have joined the police."

It made sense that Tariq would notice. He'd known me for years as Maddie, but Oliver's reaction told me he'd seen through my work persona. Did that mean that other people laughed at me behind my back? I wanted to speak well, to rediscover the 't's and aitches Dad had moaned at me for dropping in my youth. Surely that wasn't a bad thing?

"Am I that obvious?"

"Not really. I'd noticed the name change but I hadn't thought much about it until Tariq mentioned it. On the few occasions I've met you at work, you sound fine." His twinkling eyes met mine. "There's nothing wrong with the way you speak, full stop."

His voice hinted at his life: living in a detached house, with holidays abroad and parents who'd taught him to enunciate every syllable without affectation. Maybe I should concentrate on pronouncing all the letters in my words, rather than trying to sound posh.

"Right, are we ready to go?" I thought I'd spoken in my usual voice, but Tariq shook his head.

"You're doing it again."

Laughing, I dropped into my best Estuary English. "Flaming 'eck. Ain't a woman allowed to speak proper round 'ere?" Holding open the door, I ushered them out. "Come on. Let's get you lot 'ome. Is that all right nah, Tariq?"

♦

As I zipped my laptop and popped it and a pile of papers into my bag, my gaze fell upon David's empty chair. He hadn't spoken to me since Emma's announcement the previous week. In fact, I'd hardly seen him. On the few occasions he'd been in the office, I'd been at meetings and colleagues would tell me – without being asked – that David had popped by but had left five minutes ago. Anyone would think he'd checked my calendar and planned his itinerary around my diary.

Now I had a whole ten work-free days in front of me, and little to do but to spend time with Josh, see my family, and go to Rachel's party. As I hefted my bag onto my shoulder, I had a feeling David would make the most of my absence. How? I had no idea. But I was sure I'd find out.

Emma caught me by the doors. "Did you get the meeting booked with the Chartley library group? And what about the residents' meeting Derek wanted you to organise?"

"They're both happening the week I return. The Didlingbury one is in progress too."

"Great!" Her smile transformed into a frown. "That reminds

me. I'll put a meeting in your diary for first thing Tuesday when you get back. I need to bring you up to speed about something, but I won't bother you with it now. Have a lovely week off."

Leaving me with that ominous offering, she waltzed away. I thought about going after her and finding out more, but I didn't want to be late collecting Josh from nursery. Why had she said that? Now I'd spend the week fretting that something terrible would happen on my return to work.

As I hurried down the stairs, my mobile phone buzzed in my pocket. Rachel. She got straight to the point.

"Have you invited someone for tomorrow night?"

"No. And I don't need you to do that for me either."

Rachel and Leah had been winding me up for the past few days, telling me about a handsome man they'd found for me, threatening to pair me up with him at the party. I had an idea it might be one of Leah's new boyfriend's mates. She'd managed to last three whole weeks with this guy and had stunned Rachel and me by announcing that he was 'the one'.

There was little point in me asking anyone. Seeing Oliver for five minutes at Samson's Café on Wednesday had reinforced how rushed my life felt. My trio of men – Josh, Dad and Will – were more than enough for me to deal with. Much as I loved them, they absorbed most of my hours outside work, leaving no room to fit another man into the mix, especially with all the recent palaver around Will and the police. The person who had stolen from him had been found and the police told us he would be charged, but that led to further worries: would Will have to go to court? How would he cope?

"Are you taking your dad shopping tomorrow?" Rachel had

moved on.

"At ten."

"I've got everything but baguettes. Can you pick up about six for me? I can't be arsed to fight the Saturday crowds."

I'd reached reception, which seemed unusually busy for a late Friday afternoon, and had to cover my other ear to hear Rachel above the hubbub.

"Okay. Is there anything else you need?"

"For you to bring a man. Josh and Will don't count."

I sighed. "I'll bring the baguettes."

♦

The next morning, I stood in the bakery section putting half a dozen baguettes into the trolley in which Josh sat. When he insisted on holding one across his thighs, I decided to go for a seventh. His one wouldn't be making it out intact. I'd bent down to pick up a loaf of bread from the bottom shelf when I heard a familiar voice.

"Hello. Are you Will's brother?"

Knees cracking, I stood up to find Christabel holding the trolley handle, while Josh chewed the end of the baguette. I didn't correct her.

"Sorry I didn't say hello on Wednesday night. Josh was tired. How are you?"

She tipped her head shyly to one side. "We're getting food for tonight. My grandad's coming to see us all. Is Will here?"

I'd abandoned Dad and Will in the tinned food aisle, where they were arguing over the merits of tinned and frozen sweetcorn, but they should have moved on by now.

"He's probably by the baked beans. If not there, it'll be the soups." I knew Dad and Will's shopping habits. After giving us a wave, she shot off. Chuckling, I turned to Josh. "She likes Will. A lot."

"I like Will. He's funny." Josh ripped a chunk of baguette off with his teeth. Was it shoplifting if he started on the baguette before we got to the till? I hoped not. Deciding to leave him gnawing in peace, I pushed the trolley over to the eggs.

Josh pointed. Soggy bread oozed between his teeth. "Look! Sanson."

A man came towards us. Oliver! How strange. We came shopping here around the same time each Saturday, but I hadn't bumped into him or Christabel before. Having said that, they'd both joined the café just a month or so ago, so we may have stood in a queue together without realising. Although I would have seen Christabel. Having a brother with Down syndrome meant I was more likely to notice others with it.

I wouldn't have spotted Oliver, though. No matter how good-looking he was, I'd never found myself eyeing up men in the queue. Usually because I had to stand guard to stop Josh snatching sweets or to intervene when Will and Dad bickered over who'd put the pack of doughnuts/peanuts/tub of ice cream into the trolley.

Smiling, Oliver ruffled Josh's hair. "Your dinner is taller than you are."

He wore his usual jeans and jacket, but he'd swapped his shirt for a grey fleece. A faint trace of stubble shadowed his face, but it suited him, especially against his tousled hair, which shone beneath the harsh strip lights. He'd slung a shopping basket over his arm, filled with an assortment of fruit and vegetables and a carton of almond milk. In comparison, I had committed 'carbicide'.

"I'm going to a friend's party," I said by way of explanation for the baguettes and crisps.

"You were nominated for the bread run?"

His dark eyes met mine and I flushed. The words 'Would you like to come?' tingled on my lips – I tried mouthing the 'W' – but they wouldn't spill. Why would a man like him want to come out with me? And to Court Place too. He probably lived in Radley Heights or the Planefield area. He hesitated – could he sense that I wanted to say something? – then gestured up the aisle.

"I don't suppose you've bumped into Christabel?"

"She went off in search of Will."

He grinned. "My sister has a thing for your brother."

And I have a thing for you. I blushed at my unbidden thought. "Your sister? I didn't realise."

"We agreed not to say anything. Harry asked me to help out because of my youth group experience and mentioned about Christabel coming along too. She hadn't wanted to go on her own before – she's quite shy – so it worked well. But I didn't want her to become the teacher's kid, if you see what I mean. Different to the others."

"I understand. I won't say anything."

We fell into silence. I searched for something to say. Anything other than inviting him to the party, which part of me urged my more restrained self to do. He glanced down the aisle.

"I've got to go." Smiling, he turned to Josh and held out his fist. "Fist bump?"

Josh frowned, but obliged by 'bumping' Oliver with a fistful of squished bread.

"See you both soon, I hope."

"Probably in the next aisle," I joked.

As he strolled away, I longed to call out, to invite him to come with me tonight. But I simply couldn't. My courage wouldn't stretch to making a fool of myself. Instead, I picked up a carton of eggs while I rewound the conversation, trying to work out if he'd betrayed an inkling of anything but friendship. My memory told me not.

By the time I found Dad and Will, Christabel and Oliver had disappeared. I spent the rest of the shopping trip scanning every aisle in the hope of seeing them, but I didn't. For once Josh – with his half baguette – left me in peace while I stood at the checkout, ignoring Dad and Will as they argued about money and the potential shopping bill. Instead, my gaze combed each of the till queues and out through the huge windows into the car park until, despondent, I gave up. Oliver and his lovely sister were long gone.

Chapter 12

A CRUMPLED CAN FLEW OVER THE BALCONY, landing on the grass verge. I didn't need to see more than the puff of smoke and fingers clutching the railing to know who had thrown it. Who else but the Flying Scotsman?

"Oi!" I shouted. "Watch where you throw stuff."

"Oh, bugger off," he slurred back in a bored voice.

Strange that I had the courage to shout at the local imbecile, who'd even tattooed 'die' across three of his fingers, but I didn't have the nerve to ask Oliver to come to a party with me. The usual cigarette ends littered the area outside Rachel's kitchen window. Not hers, but flicked away by the moron above. Thank goodness I hadn't invited Oliver. It would be the last I'd see of him.

Strains of a familiar pop song reached me. Before pressing Rachel's doorbell, I smoothed down my skirt. I'd dropped off the bread and a bottle of Prosecco earlier, taken Josh to Chelsea's for the night, and now I just had myself to look after. Hopefully, I wouldn't spend the evening fending off whichever bloke Rachel and Leah had chosen for me. I hadn't dressed to impress. Underneath my jacket, I wore a baggy roll-neck top. My skirt, while above the knee, lay above tights the thickness of leggings, while I'd bottomed off my look with boots.

The door juddered open and music and laughter blasted out, as if someone had turned up the dial. Rachel grinned. "Finally! I thought you'd got lost."

She'd put on a black dress patterned with huge cerise flowers and pink stiletto heels. She looked amazing, making me appear dowdy in comparison. I didn't care. It was her party and she wanted to shine. She'd even decked the top rim of her glasses with stick-on stars, which must be annoying each time she looked up. When I bent to kiss her cheek I smelled a scent I didn't recognise.

"New perfume?"

She shrugged. "One of those little giveaway bottles."

"You should get it. It smells great."

"Yeah. When I've got a spare seventy quid to throw away."

She ushered me through a hallway filled with unfamiliar faces and into the kitchen, where she reached up to a cupboard. "I tucked your Prosecco in here so it wouldn't get nicked. Leah's is in the next one. Everyone else has brought cheap plonk. They know me too well."

She poured a glass for me. I took a sip and grinned. "Warm Prosecco. Yum."

"If I'd put it in the fridge, you'd have none."

Clutching our drinks, we turned sideways to squeeze through the crowded hallway. As we moved along, Rachel gave me brief introductions to her friends, most from the pub:

"David, meet Maddie."

"Have you met Mika before?"

Strange – I'd known Rachel for years, but this was another world of people from her other, fun-loving life. But I couldn't be jealous. She'd do anything to be stuck at home in the evening with her child.

The steady thump of music rose as we entered the lounge, along with the babble of voices interspersed with laughter, but it didn't reach an annoying level. Rachel wouldn't have her music too loud, not wanting to upset the neighbours. It's a shame the Flying

Scotsman wasn't so thoughtful. I envied him being outside on the walkway, though. I felt suffocated by all the bodies pressing against me, hemming me in their warmth.

Rachel pushed through groups of people, aiming for the corner where Leah had jammed herself. As she reached it, the gap between us closed, pinning me between two blokes and I couldn't get past them. When I grasped Leah's arm to help me, she frowned until she realised whose hand it was. Grinning, she dragged me through to her huddle of friends.

"Elbow 'em next time." Her breath tickled my ear. She nodded towards the men's crotches. "For us shorties, they're a perfect height."

She tapped the arm of the balding guy standing next to her. He turned to me. He had even teeth and a generous smile.

"Maddie, meet Paul."

Other than a glimpse of his face in the car when he'd come to pick up Leah a few weeks ago, I'd not met Paul in the flesh. He had kind eyes. Instinctively, I knew Leah had chosen well with him.

I held out my hand. "Pleased to meet you."

He looked from my hand to my face. What on earth had made me do that? Politely, he gave it a firm, but not painful, shake. Leah nudged him.

"She thinks she's at work."

I laughed. "You can call me Madeleine, then."

The joke went over his head, but Leah grinned. She tapped her neighbour's shoulder, ignoring the fact he seemed to be in an intense discussion with someone else.

"Mad-e-leine, meet Sean."

I didn't want to meet Sean. Or, at least, not the type of meeting Leah had obviously planned, going by the determined look on her face. A few years ago, I'd had a thing about Sean Bean in *Sharpe* when Dad had watched the reruns. I'd loved his deep Sheffield accent, his unruly blond hair and gorgeous eyes. But while he was similar in colouring, this Sean was more beanstalk. He towered over me: my eyes were level with his chest.

He held out his hand. I couldn't refuse as I'd shaken Paul's hand, even though it was a daft thing to do at a party. Strangely, he held it rather than reciprocating my attempted handshake.

Not releasing his grip, he said, "So we finally get to meet."

I answered as a statement rather than a question, even though I had no idea what he meant. "We do."

Leah slapped his hand away. "Get over teasing her."

I took a sip of my drink to hide my uncertainty. I hated being lined up with potential dates – for good reason. For a start, I had no idea whether men liked me or were just being polite – although usually towards the end of the night I found out. Either they went in for a clumsy, drunken kiss or they made their excuses and I spotted them walking out of the club with someone else thirty minutes later (this had happened). And, as I'd told myself countless times, I had no room for another man in my life.

Someone banged into me, spilling my Prosecco. I dabbed my hand to my mouth. To make matters worse, the person then moved into my space, their warm backside rubbing against mine. I scowled, desperate to move away from them, but that meant getting closer to Sean.

"Can't waste a drop?" Sean raised his can to me.

"I don't blame her," Leah said. "The price of this stuff. So,

Maddie, are you gonna send Sean to sleep by telling him about your job?"

I chuckled. Leah knew I didn't have much else to talk to a potential suitor about. Chatting about my son would probably put him off. Who wanted to date a single mother when there were less complicated relationships to be found elsewhere?

"Or we could talk about Josh, my son. He's lovely."

If Sean had any interest in me, that would see him off. Leah rolled her eyes at me. 'What are you doing?' her look said.

But Sean's eyes widened in interest. "My sister's got a kid. She's lovely. How old is yours?"

"He's two. Nearly three."

"I bet you're looking forward to the end of the terrible twos. My sister couldn't wait. But her one – she's amazing, mind – has just moved into the 'trocious threes."

"I can't believe it gets worse." I grinned. "Josh can be a nightmare at times. I'd only been at my job a few days when he found the fake penis cupboard and brought out what he thought was a lollipop."

"Fake penises?" He laughed. "Please tell me more."

After a while, Sean and I decamped to the quieter kitchen with Leah and Paul and a couple of others. I found Sean and I had a lot to talk about. He loved reading and walking and had travelled widely, even taking a gap year. Something no one from my childhood had done. Rachel popped over every now and again, her hostess skills stretched between her various cliques of friends. It was a lovely evening but, by midnight, I longed for my bed. Leah had disappeared, leaving me with Paul and Sean, who'd spent the past ten minutes laughing at my muffled yawns and calling me a lightweight. But I rarely saw this time of night unless Josh was ill. After polite goodnights – Sean didn't try anything more than a "It's been a lovely night. Have a great weekend with your little man" – I went to use the toilet. When I returned, the group I'd been with had left the kitchen, replaced by an unfamiliar bunch. I went to take my phone from where I'd left it on the side, but it wasn't there.

I went off in search of Rachel and found her in the lounge. Her glassy eyes met mine.

"I can't find my phone."

"Where did you lose it?"

Even in my inebriated state, I could tell that was a daft question.

"After I took my jacket off, I put it on the side in the kitchen next to me in case Chelsea needed to call about Josh."

Leah staggered over. "You've lost your phone? That's bad."

She followed me back to the kitchen, which had sprouted a pile of rubbish since I'd left. Used cans, bottles and glasses crammed the sides, and crisps and bits of pizza crust littered the floor. While I went back to double-check the area beside the fridge where I'd last seen my phone, Leah pushed through a group of people to scan the crowded worktop and the area around the sink. Even though every surface was filled, it would be easy to spot my phone: there would need to be a gap between the bottles and cans, and there wasn't one. I even lifted the kettle from its base unit and checked inside cupboard doors and the fridge. I know it sounds odd, but I couldn't think where else it could be.

I turned to Leah in the hope she'd found it.

"Not here." She toppled backwards, knocking a can to the floor and treading on a man's toe. Grabbing his shoulder to steady herself, she said, "Oops. Sorry."

She stumbled back towards the lounge, where many of the partygoers still congregated.

"Everyone!" She cupped her hands around her mouth and, slurring, bellowed, "Listen! Maddie's lost her phone. Anyone seen it?"

Most people shook their heads, while a few turned around to check their immediate vicinity. Unlike mine, Rachel's flat was on one level, but she'd kept her bedroom door shut, leaving her kitchen, lounge and bathroom open. Just three rooms to check. I'd last seen my phone in the kitchen, where I'd spent most of the evening. I'd left it once to go into the lounge for fifteen minutes or so to chat with Rachel. But I was sure I hadn't picked up my phone – and, even if I had, I could only have left it on the table, which looked just like the kitchen worktops, with an assortment of cans, bottles and glasses ranging from half-full to empty. I'd lost it before I went to the toilet, so I didn't bother looking there.

"I'll call it." Leah tottered out to the quieter hallway. I followed her. When the ring tone started at her end, I hurried through to the kitchen to see if I could hear my phone. Nothing. Arriving back in the hallway, I found Leah speaking to someone.

"You've got her phone?"

I could hear a tinny voice through the speaker. Whatever they'd said had annoyed Leah, as she raised her voice.

"Why not? You need to give it back."

A flushed Rachel wobbled over and leaned against the wall beside us. Although not so drunk as Leah, her voice had a blurred edge. "What's up?"

"He's flipping hung up on me. Can you believe it? This John guy has nicked Maddie's phone and he won't give it back."

Rachel frowned. "But there wasn't anyone called John at the party."

Leah tapped her phone to call him again. "See for yourself. He's got her phone."

Rachel held the phone to her ear. I leaned close, able to make out a man's voice.

"Rachel," she said. She frowned. "No, you look here." She jabbed the air as if the man stood in front of her. "This is *my* phone and *you're* the one who's got my mate's phone, so you need to bring it back here now."

The man must have cut her off. Rachel shook her head and passed the phone back to Leah. "The cheek of it! He just had a go at me for bothering him at this time of night and – can you believe it? – he reckons *I've* stolen someone's phone."

"Well, you did say it was yours when it's mine," Leah said.

In our drink-fuddled state – I'd had four Proseccos, which made me feel blurry rather than blotto – it seemed a reasonable statement.

We stood in silence. What should we do next? Paul came back in without Sean, who must have left. Looking puzzled, he asked Leah what was going on, but she hissed that she needed time to think.

I did too. I couldn't go home without my phone in case Chelsea tried to call me. I couldn't even text Chelsea to let her know it had gone missing, as neither Leah or Rachel had her number.

Leah's phone pinged. While she read the message, her phone pinged again.

"I don't get it," she muttered.

Then the phone pinged for a third time. She clamped her hand to her mouth. "You're kidding me!"

She held out the phone so Rachel and I could read the messages.

What's going on? Why are you being rude to John?

Has someone got your phone?

You do know this is Mandie from work?

"Oh no!" she wailed. "I'm such a div. I called Mandie instead of Maddie. John must be her husband or something."

"No wonder he accused me of pinching your phone," Rachel said.

"I can't believe I did that." Leah didn't look up, typing a frantic response. "I hope she's not too mad."

"Well, she's definitely not Maddie either." Rachel sniggered. She reached into the back pocket of her jeans and pulled out her phone, frowning. "Wait a minute – this isn't mine."

The phone had a sparkly gold case. I snatched it from her. We'd bought the casings and screen covers at the repair shop after she'd smashed the screen on her phone for the second time. She'd chosen a blue backing.

"That's because it's mine!" I checked the screen. Thankfully, I didn't have any messages or missed calls from Chelsea.

"You let me call Mandie at midnight when you flaming well had the phone all along?" Leah glared at her. "How drunk are you?"

"Pots and kettles," Rachel fired back.

"I'm not the one who nicked Maddie's phone."

Leaving them to bicker, I unhooked my jacket from beneath the other coats draped over the hooks and put it on. Then I tapped my coat pocket, satisfied to hear the jingle of keys.

"Goodnight."

I slipped out of the front door, dismayed to find it had started raining. At least it meant a mild night. As I stood beneath the porch to pull up my collar and to wrap my jacket tightly around me, the door opened and Rachel popped her head out. I couldn't help greeting her with a walrus yawn.

"I don't s'pose you saw my phone when you were looking for yours?" she asked.

"Sorry. You'd best get Leah to phone it. Just make sure her boss isn't called Raquel or something."

Chapter 13

MY TEN DAYS OFF WORK had been busier, yet lazier, than I'd imagined. Josh had allowed me a few lie-ins by bringing his book, cars or dinosaurs into bed with me. My chest became a mountain range to roar or vroom along – slightly less annoying than him using my nose as a launch pad. When we'd got up – no later than nine o'clock – we spent our days at the park, at the local children's activity centre, or around my dad's or Rachel's. Josh and I had a wonderful time at Legoland and we also managed to take Will – Dad didn't feel up to it – for a day trip to London on his Wednesday off. Will and I been paid by then, so we could afford it. In fact, I'd been so busy, I hadn't thought about work or checked my work emails.

While I enjoyed work, it was wonderful spending time with Josh, so it was with mixed feelings that I placed my bag on my desk on the Tuesday morning and gazed around the office. In an hour, I had a meeting booked with Emma, when I'd find out the reason for her worrying comment just before I went on leave. Before then, no doubt, I had an inbox full of emails to sift through. I opened my laptop and went to grab a coffee while it started up.

When the meeting reminder flashed onto my screen, I couldn't believe the hour had passed so quickly. Emma hadn't come into the office yet – most likely because she'd decided to work in the café before our discussion. With meeting rooms at a premium, anywhere with a few chairs and a table was considered a prime meeting spot.

I found her, as expected, typing on her laptop. Tariq wasn't at the counter, so I went over to her and slipped into the chair opposite. She appeared lost in thought, and it took her a while to register me or my muttered, "Good morning."

After a few moments she looked up and snapped her laptop shut. She opened her notebook and flicked through until she found the page she wanted. It was titled 'Madeleine', below which rows of scribbled notes ran down the page, in various colours of ink. She must have added to the list each time she remembered something.

I brought out my pad and a pen, readying myself to jot down notes.

"Good break?"

"Lovely."

She pursed her lips. "Back to work with a bang, then."

That sounded ominous. I clasped my hands together on the table.

"Right." She took a deep breath. "The last time I spoke to you, this was just a rumour, but Didlingbury library is proving to be a problem. They're refusing to consider moving to volunteers – they want to keep their library staff."

"That's lovely, although I can see the issue."

"It's ironic that all the libraries are going to have volunteers so we can save Didlingbury and Potterham, then this happens."

"What will happen if they don't accept?"

"We'll go back to plan A. Close the two small libraries to save the three town ones. But, even if we do that, it'll be a hybrid option for the three bigger ones – Derek likes the idea of volunteers."

"Can Didlingbury find a way to raise funds towards the salaries?" I asked.

"That's one for you to investigate. Didlingbury's councillor,

Agnes Drew, is on the opposition. She's got her community at heart but doesn't realise the tightrope we're treading right now. Or, if she does, she's stirring things up. Derek won't be happy. Arrange a meeting with her and the chairman of the parish council. But *do not*, and I mean this…" She pointed her pen at me. "Do not let her know that the library closure is Derek's preferred option."

She ticked off the first item on the sheet in front of her. "Right, now on to Derek's residents' meeting. I've lined us up to talk it through with him at 1pm, so it would be good if we could briefly go through your plans. He might want to bolt on some issues he's been having."

I readied my pen, preparing myself for coming away with a mound of work.

◆

I'd booked the small church hall at the top of Meadow Manor for the residents' meeting, which was going better than expected. The small gathering of irate residents seemed to respect Derek. When the meeting started, a genteel lady assured him that more people had wanted to come but they couldn't make a mid-afternoon meeting. Derek looked accusingly at me over the top of his glasses. Why had I chosen a time no one could make? But I hadn't. The group's leader, Mrs Whatever-her-name-was-in-the-powder-blue-top, had told me quite specifically on the phone that three o'clock would be the most suitable time. If I expected her to confess this, though, I was mistaken. Phone conversations could not be proven.

I'd been both excited and apprehensive to meet residents who lived near me. When I say 'near', we all lived in the Hadfield Green area of Holdenwell, so there was a chance we could bump into each other at the convenience store. But, although they lived less than half a mile from the Court Place estate, we could not have been further apart in wealth and expectation.

The residents raised low-level issues with high expectations of what could be achieved. Slowly, they took us through a list as long as Emma's had been. As I had done with her, Derek promised to do all he could to resolve their issues. There were far worse potholes on the main roads near my estate and Dad's estates, but these residents deemed the ones on Meadow Manor more urgent even though, in my view, they were more like grazes than craters. Speeding was also an issue, they said. How? Even a Grand Prix car couldn't get up to any speed between the humps that lined the winding road. But Derek said he – meaning me – would speak to the speed reduction team about it. And the parking issues they faced! I hid my stunned expression at that point. Most of these people had driveways, whereas those living in the roads near Dad's estate had problems with people who worked at the college and the small business park nearby, but these residents all nodded, bemoaning the fact that outsiders chose to park in their road. I could understand their anger if their driveways were being blocked or the parking issues meant emergency vehicles couldn't get through, but this didn't appear to be the case.

Emma had told me that managing expectations was important in all dealings, because the council's money belt had tightened beyond the final notch, but Derek didn't seem to care about this.

"Madeleine will ask the parking team to assess the issues." Derek pointed towards my pad, as if I needed to be told what to write.

Mrs Whatever-her-name-was-in-the-powder-blue-top cleared her throat. "A residents' parking scheme would be the preferred solution, but don't give something like that to the people in the social-housing estate. They never get involved, so why should they benefit?"

This opinion didn't gain a consensus. While most nodded, two people commented that it wouldn't harm to include them, or else everyone would park at the bottom of the road. I gazed from face to face, unable to believe that no one had condemned her remarks.

"It's near the shops," Mrs Whatever-her-name-was-in-the-powder-blue-top said. "So, an eminently suitable place for shoppers to park."

No doubt she meant herself. Meadow Manor started at the bottom of the hill near the shops. A clump of council houses and flats sat there but as the road wound its way up the hill the houses thinned, so those in the centre had the largest gardens and longest drives. From that point it was all downhill again, both in geography and status. As the road sloped downwards, the plots diminished in size, ending with a stretch of Victorian terraced houses. People who lived here were the only ones – apart from those in the social housing at the other end of the road – who had a justified complaint about parking, as none had a driveway and commuters or shoppers parked outside their houses.

"Our final point is the one that concerns us most. Those wretched Court Place teenagers are using Meadow Manor as a shortcut to the college and shops." Mrs Whatever-her-name-was-in-the-powder-blue-top spat the words 'Court Place' as if they contained germs. She straightened her back and pursed her biro-line lips as she surveyed us.

Stuck-up cow. My face burned and I shook with fury. But I had no choice but to sit mute, firing imaginary barbs of hatred at her. After spending every penny on my Easter break with Josh, I couldn't afford the luxury of free speech. My job here was to be Derek's lackey.

Another person spoke up. "It's a shame we can't make it a private road like Charlton Heights. They barricaded their road during the floods to stop cars using it as a cut-through."

I remembered the photograph in the paper. When everyone else had been trying to help the shops and homes damaged in the floods, those unneighbourly residents had manned a homemade barrier to stop cars driving along their road to skirt the terrible flooding. Instead, cars had been forced through sewage-laden water, creating a wake that rolled into the neighbouring properties.

Derek sighed, returning to the point about the teenagers. "But walking isn't a crime, so I can't see what we can do about that."

Finally, he'd said something to counter her! Was that because he knew I lived there? I doubted he'd remembered our previous conversation, as he didn't glance in my direction. Most likely, he still assumed I'd been joking.

"They don't just walk. The other day, one of them kicked a can into my drive."

"And I found one of them hanging around by my house," said another lady.

A man, who'd stayed quiet until this point, spoke up. "Most of them are fine." He ignored his neighbour's harrumph of disbelief and continued, "But the one I'm worried about is not a teenager, but a balding older man who often walks along swigging from a bottle of Scotch." The woman next to him tutted. I turned to gaze

117

at Derek's thread-veined cheeks and bulbous nose, realising that he had something in common with the Flying Scotsman. Although Derek's nose was worse, like purple broccoli.

"He's taken to shouting at my wife each time he sees her, after she told him to pick up his litter. She's scared of him. He showed her his fist the other day."

The man held his fist towards his face to demonstrate what had happened. "Written on it was 'death' or 'dead' or something. I phoned the police, but they say he hasn't actually threatened her. But what else do you call that?"

I couldn't imagine the Flying Scotsman walking anywhere, but there was a betting shop in the precinct in Lower Street which led from Meadow Manor, so perhaps that gave him a reason to venture from Court Place and his usual drinking haunts.

"Madeleine will speak to our housing department for you."

A fat lot of good that would do. How many times had Rachel or her neighbours called them about his flying cans, bottles, cigarette butts, abuse and the TV? But I dutifully jotted down Derek's instruction.

"Well, it's been nice meeting you all again." Derek splayed his hands on the table to push himself to his feet. "It's a shame, but I have to be somewhere else now."

I followed him out. When he reached his car – we'd arrived separately – he signalled me over. "Don't waste too much time on this. We haven't got the money for much more than 'slow' markings on the road or for the parking team to come out and suggest some cheap measures. But make sure we're seen to be doing as much as we can. The elections are coming up in May."

The man who'd told us about the Flying Scotsman came out of

the building, raising his hand in acknowledgement. He patted his pocket and pulled out a set of keys. He'd driven here, even though the church hall was at the end of his road. But then I told myself off for being judgemental. Perhaps he was going somewhere else before going home, or he had a physical issue which meant he couldn't walk far.

Derek inhaled, air whistling between his teeth. "I do feel for him, though. While we can't do much about those Court Place kids going along Meadow Manor – why do you think I bought in Charlton Heights? – we need to do something. His wife had a stroke last year. Get hold of the housing department. We can't have thugs like that awful man destroying people's lives."

For once, he'd said something I agreed with.

♦

I put the phone down. Well, I never! I hadn't expected that to be so easy. Needing to talk to someone about the surprising turn of events, I spun around in my chair to find David had returned. He slumped back in his chair, legs apart, chatting on the phone. When he met my eye he sneered, scrunching his nose like a child. No way would I tell him. Then I came to my senses. I wouldn't tell *anyone* at work about my life at Court Place. Instead, I buttoned my thoughts until later when I could speak to Rachel. She'd be as stunned as I was.

Before leaving for the day, I checked tomorrow's calendar. I had another youth club meeting, this one scheduled for two o'clock. Would Oliver be there? I hoped so, although I'd see him that evening when I went to pick up Will. David's laugh boomed across the office. Being nosey, I clicked his calendar to see what he was up to. According to his diary, he was also attending the youth club meeting. But why? That wasn't his area.

When he put the phone down, I turned to him. "I see you're attending the Dealsham youth meeting."

He glanced up, a flush touching his cheeks. I'd hit a nerve. "How come?"

His eyes narrowed. "What do you mean by 'how come'?"

"It's not in your area. It doesn't need both of us to attend."

"Don't go, then."

"That's ridiculous. Are you telling me that I shouldn't do my job because you want to do it?"

He grasped both chair arms and leaned forward, his face puce, his eyes bright with fury. "I've been asked to go because I have far more experience than you. They need someone with a solid background to help get this off the ground."

He might have a point about experience, but he had no idea that I'd already managed to get agreement on a funding stream from a local organisation. It wouldn't be formally announced for a few days, but the grants supervisor had called yesterday to let me know the good news. I'd phoned Kavita immediately afterwards, but I'd asked her to keep it under wraps until we had a letter confirming it.

"Did Kavita ask you?" Strange that she hadn't mentioned inviting David to come along when we'd spoken.

"Kavita isn't the whole group," he said.

"No, she's just the person leading the committee."

He snatched his mug from his desk and snarled, "You women are all the same," before stomping off in the direction of the kitchen.

Other people had been watching us from their desks. While a few gave me supportive smiles, others ducked behind their screens when they caught my eye. Neither David or I had won admirers during that episode. Next time I had an issue with him, I'd make sure to air it in private.

Chapter 14

RACHEL PULLED A FACE. "Yeah. They might say they'll sort him, but they won't bother. It's all talk. What are they going to do? Stop him from walking down a road? I've called them a dozen times about him throwing stuff and they've done sod all about it."

"Seriously, I mentioned Derek Hamilton OBE and the housing woman's attitude changed. It was like…" I searched for the words to say that just the mention of Derek's name had been like Excalibur slicing through reels of red tape. "Unbelievable."

"Did you really use the OBE bit on her?"

"Of course not. But I did tell her he was our Portfolio Holder, in case she needed reminding."

Rachel shrugged. "I dunno what a Portfolio Holder is, but this Derek sounds like a tosspot. He's the one that thinks we're scum, isn't he?"

"He's a VIP at the council but he'll forever be a VIT to us."

For a moment she frowned, but then she caught on and grinned. "I know loads of tosspots but he's my first very important one." She put her mug to her lips and took a sip. "Well, time will tell if the Flying Scotsman is dealt with."

Josh ambled into the lounge from the kitchen, where he'd been helping Kieran with the washing-up. A tide of wet hemmed his sleeves. As I rolled them back, he opened his mouth to reveal a blue tongue.

"Kieran gave me a sweetie."

Kieran came through, giving me an apologetic look. He slumped into the settee, followed by Josh, who bounded onto his lap, giggling at the 'ooof' Kieran made. When Kieran pointed the remote at the TV and switched it on, Josh shouted – thanks to the sugar hit he'd just been given – "Yeah! *Sinsons*!"

"*The Simpsons*," I corrected him. "You don't have to watch, Kieran. Will's got him into it."

Kieran shrugged and settled back, smiling as he was given a rundown of the characters according to Josh. I didn't know where Josh got half of it from, especially when he mimicked the action of an axe.

"Chop, chop, chop! Aargghhh!"

Rachel looked fondly at them, and I felt a pang of sadness for her. How wonderful it would be for Rachel and Kieran to have a child of their own. A skin-deep veneer masked her longing but her eyes were a window to her soul. She and Kieran would make wonderful parents to a lucky child. They might not be rich in money, but they were in love. If I had a wand, I'd wish their dreams into reality.

Rachel's fingernails chinked against the side of her mug. "Have you seen Sean since the party?"

I frowned. What an odd thing to say. It had been almost a fortnight and she hadn't mentioned his name before. "Why?"

"Leah and I bumped into him down the pub at the weekend and he raved on and on about you. He asked Leah for your number, but she said she'd check with you first."

"Raving mad, more like." I nodded towards Josh. "He's a bit young for this 'bringing a man home' lark."

She shrugged. "Or he could be the perfect age to accept it."

I took a swig of tea, wincing as it scalded my mouth. Blinking away tears of pain, I said, "I don't want Sean to have my number."

She had a point about Josh being young enough to adjust but, if I was going to bring anyone into Josh's life, I wanted it to be worth the effort. That would be Oliver.

◆

Oliver had taken the seat across from me at the meeting, chatting to Kavita. I said hello to them both, but was too shy to go over to chat. As I glanced around the table, I frowned in disbelief when I spotted David sneaking in. While he'd said he would come today, I'd half hoped that, following our disagreement, he'd stay away and let me get on with my job. He took a seat beside the woman who'd insisted I must be his secretary at my first meeting.

When Kavita called for everyone's attention, the woman next to David looked pointedly at me.

"Who's going to be our secretary today?"

Kavita sighed. "We've sorted this. Ben is going to take the minutes." Next to me, Ben waggled his pen at the woman. Kavita continued, "Right, minutes of the last meeting. Are we all in agreement?"

The meeting set off at a good pace: Oliver confirmed the insurance was in place, the safeguarding forms had been completed, while Ben paused in taking the minutes to tell everyone he'd recruited enough volunteers to run the club.

We'd reached item number five. Funding. Kavita's finger hovered over the page and she smiled at me. "We might have some news on that front soon, I hear, but it's under wraps at the moment."

David extracted a sheet from the sheaf in front of him on the table with a flourish and cleared his throat. "Well, I have some news for you all."

Kavita turned to him, her mouth open, her brow furrowed, looking as confused as I felt. What was going on? The room fell silent as he unfolded the paper.

"I picked this up at lunchtime from Serena at Horizons for Holdenwell."

Serena? I'd been working with her to get the grant. But how did he have the funding agreement? It was impossible for us to have duplicated the work. Only one application could have been considered by the panel, and they'd approved mine.

"I'm pleased to award the Dealsham youth committee the sum of five thousand pounds towards the initial set-up costs, equipment as set out below, and hall hire for one year."

Gasps ran around the room and the woman next to David patted his arm. "You are brilliant. I said we needed you here."

Kavita threaded her necklace through her fingers and glanced uncomfortably from me to him, while I was rooted to my seat, in shock. It took all my willpower not to demand that he hand the letter over, but he kept a tight grip on it. For good reason: it would be addressed to me. After yesterday's confrontation in the office, I didn't want to make a scene here. Emma would be livid if I exposed the civil war brewing in her team.

Beside me Ben scrawled 'David has secured £5,000 funding'. My achievement would forever be David's. It had been memorialised in the minutes, to be remembered by anyone who bothered to read them.

"So, we're all set." Kavita's voice quivered. I noticed she no longer looked at either David or me. She probably didn't know who

125

to believe. "We've got everything in place now. The next meeting will look at final preparations and marketing."

We had other items to go through before the meeting ended. I sat in silence, sickened by the David love-in taking place. When I'd got written approval of the funding, I would have let Kavita tell everyone by email. I didn't need praise. But David basked in the attention, seeming to forget that he hadn't done anything but read out an email meant for someone else. Me.

For some reason, the participants got hung up on item seven – the purchase of equipment – which I thought had been decided. I checked my watch. I had to leave or I'd be late for my next meeting. My work here was done, anyhow. By David.

Muttering apologies, I pushed my seat back and headed out of the room, my back stiff. As I passed David, he beamed triumphantly and winked at me.

♦

I'd trembled with fury throughout my next meeting. When I got back to the office, I opened my laptop to find Serena had emailed me a copy of the grant letter. 'The awards won't formally be announced until this Friday,' her email read. 'David popped by earlier and asked for a copy to give to you, as he said you needed it for a meeting. As I explained to you yesterday, please keep it in confidence until the embargo date.'

Did she think I'd sent David to ask for a copy of the letter, so I could announce it earlier? The tone of her email seemed to suggest it.

I bashed out a reply, my fingers trembling with anger,

explaining that I hadn't been aware that David had even known I'd applied for funding, let alone been awarded it. I added that I'd been dumbfounded when he'd informed everyone at the meeting about our funding success, then deleted that line. The award could still be retracted if we broke the conditions of the agreement. David had risked the youth club for plaudits.

But someone must have told him. Had Kavita been indiscreet after our previous phone conversation? But she'd looked just as surprised at his revelation. Then I realised: he didn't have to know that we'd got the funding, just that we'd applied. His friend, the silly woman who kept going on about me being a secretary, had no doubt told him about that and he'd decided to take a detour to Serena's office to find out whether we'd been successful.

After revising my email to Serena to a shortened, but polite, version, I forwarded a copy to Kavita, warning her that she should ask the committee to keep the funding under their hats until Friday. I then forwarded the email chain to Emma, with a request to talk to her.

Then I simmered for the rest of the day, and into the evening. Outwardly, I went through the motions: laughing, joking and singing along to the songs on Josh's CD. It wasn't his fault that I'd had a bad afternoon. But I couldn't shake my agitation, even when we strolled across the car park on our way to Samson's Café that evening and Josh pointed excitedly at the bushes and trees. He'd spent the day at nursery in their little 'forest woodland' – more of a copse – learning about nature. Usually, I would have loved to examine the blossom with him, but why did he have to choose the one night when I felt out of sorts with the world and couldn't see much beauty in even the daintiest bud?

Even in my sales job, I hadn't met anyone who'd behaved like David. My role at the council seemed to attract polar opposites. There were so many wonderful people who wanted to help their communities, either as councillors, residents or staff. But there were also those who used their roles for their own agendas – like Mrs Whatever-her-name-was-in-the-powder-blue-top (I later found out she was called Daphne), Derek and David. Sadly, the upset I felt thanks to those three Ds had outweighed the kindness of ten times more good people. It shouldn't be that way.

"Look!" Josh yanked my arm to draw me closer to a bush covered in buds with small white petals and tiny stamens. Dusk was drawing in, and the petals seemed to glow in the murky light. The delicacy of the flowers was lost on Josh, who grabbed at a stem.

"Josh!" I prised open his fingers and sighed at the smear of orange on his hand. "You have to be gentle. You've hurt the poor petal."

For a moment he examined the pollen stain, and I guessed what his next move would be. When he stuck his tongue out to lick his palm clean, I grabbed his hand and swiped away the pollen.

"Come on. Let's get Will."

I held out my arms to pick him up, but he shook his head, so we dawdled to the café. Our progress was reminiscent of that of a dog on a street full of lamp posts, as Josh stopped at every bush and knelt to examine each dandelion and other assorted weeds.

In the end, I did what I shouldn't – for other people it might be a carrot and a stick, but for Josh it was the promise of cake – and his eyes lit up. We trotted the final hundred yards and headed, breathless, into the warmth and bustle of Samson's Café, which buzzed with chatter and the bang of chairs being upended on tables. Erin rushed over, dragging Will and Christabel with her. The two ladies had hooked their arms through Will's. While Erin bent to give Josh a one-armed cuddle, Christabel gave me a shy grin. Will's beam was enhanced by a brownish curl at the edges of his mouth. The cat who'd got the girls, the hot chocolate, and the cream.

The word 'cake' reached me and Josh's pleading eyes met mine.

"I don't suppose there's a slice left over?" I asked Erin.

She glanced from Will to Christabel, clearly assessing the potential harm that could be done if they were left alone for a few minutes. But then her kind nature took over and she extricated her arm from Will's and gave Josh's shoulder a squeeze.

"You want cake? Come with me."

Oliver appeared from the back room, where he paused to listen to Erin. Nodding, he stepped to one side to allow her to take Josh through.

He came over, Tariq trailing behind. "Maddie!" He hesitated. "If I can call you that."

The man of my dreams stood in front of me, but I couldn't shake my despondency. Oliver had been at the meeting earlier. Had he fallen for David's story? But I didn't have the energy to debate the whys and wherefores of the whole episode or to voice my indignation.

"I'm so sorry about earlier. I did wonder how David had managed to get that funding. I thought … well, I assumed you'd asked him to do it, until Kavita sent out an email asking us to keep it quiet until Friday. Then I guessed." He shrugged. "David's not to be trusted. But you knew that."

I was unable to speak. A big fat ball of hurt at David's treachery, and thankfulness for Oliver's kindness, leapt into my throat and I couldn't swallow it back. *Don't cry, don't cry,* I thought desperately. That would be terrible. I forced a smile. At the back of the room, Josh came out squeezing a slab of chocolate cake in each fist, like hand weights. Crumbs littered the floor and he crouched to pick them up, almost dropping the cakes he held.

Erin's voice rang out, reprimanding him. "Dirty! I'll get you more if you finish that."

'Don't get more,' I wanted to call. But I didn't need to worry. Josh had more than enough to handle there.

Oliver lowered his voice to a caress. "Don't let David get to you. I'll help."

"I don't mean to be rude, but how?"

He chuckled. "We'll have to put our heads together. But, for now, I'll find the wet wipes."

Josh pushed a fistful of cake into his mouth, some squishing into his face, most of it landing on the floor. I had only myself to blame for the state of him.

"I'll get the dustpan and brush," I said.

As Oliver disappeared, Tariq came over. "Maddie, you look sad tonight. I've got a joke to make you better."

"Have you? I'd love that."

"What do you give a sick baby bird?"

I shrugged. "I don't know. What do you give it?"

"Tweetment."

I couldn't help laughing. "Oh Tariq. Where on earth do you find all these?"

He gave me a serious look. "I've got a book at home."

My eyes welled with tears. I would cry, but for all the right reasons. Strange that before coming here I'd felt sad, but just a few minutes with this lot had made me feel so much better. Oliver returned, dustpan and brush in hand. He handed me a packet of wet wipes.

"I think we should swap roles. You wipe the choccy monster and I'll sweep."

Chapter 15

I'D MANAGE TO SNATCH TWENTY MINUTES with Emma before leaving the office to pick up Josh. We'd tucked ourselves into a corner in the empty café, where I'd told her the whole story: about the altercation I'd had with David in the office, then how he'd gone into the funding organisation's office and taken the letter meant for me.

Emma had remained silent, but her anger showed in her cheeks – which had transformed into flaming orbs – and the compressed sliver of her lips. When I reached the part where he'd claimed the credit for obtaining funding, she burst out, "He did *what?*"

She scribbled David's name on her pad, underlining it twice. "Look, I can't say much, but I can assure you this will be taken very seriously indeed. It's unlikely that the funding would be withdrawn because of this, but he knew he could be putting it at risk. And taking credit for other people's work is not on – especially the way he did it."

But I wanted more. Although Oliver had promised to support me at the youth club meetings in future, it was easier if he didn't have to do so. Who knew how many grenades David had stored up for me?

"Can you tell him not to attend the youth club meetings?"

"I'll do more than that. It's Kavita who runs it, isn't it?"

I nodded.

"She's excellent. Although she must be wondering what on earth is going on." Emma jotted Kavita's name below David's. "And Serena was the person in funding who gave him the paperwork?" She ran her hands through her hair and sighed. "Things might get a bit bumpy in the office, but that was going to happen anyhow."

I frowned. That sounded cryptic. "I don't understand."

She swept a stray hair from where it lay on the table, letting it drop onto the carpet. "Look, this is all I'll say and I do *not* want it repeated. I inherited David when I took over this team. There are things going on behind the scenes which don't need to concern you, but *this*…" She jabbed her notes about the meeting. "Ratchets it up to a whole other level." Her chair scraped the floor as she got to her feet. "You need to pick up your son. You're working from home tomorrow morning, aren't you?" When I nodded, she continued, "See you next week then."

She strode off towards the stairs to her finance meeting with the service director. I didn't envy her. Soon I'd be outside, enjoying the warm April sun, which the weather forecasters promised would shine all weekend. Stifling a yawn, I slung my laptop bag over my shoulder and headed in the opposite direction. I hadn't slept well last night, so I hoped Josh wasn't in too lively a mood. Tea in front of the TV followed by a bath and bed was the most I could manage tonight.

♦

Josh had been brilliant all morning, playing quietly with his garage in the lounge while I finished a report on my laptop. At one o'clock, I snapped the laptop lid shut and went through to the kitchen to make us a sandwich. Josh followed me out, his interest perking up when I opened the fridge door.

"Ham or cheese in your sandwich?"

"Jam," he said.

"Only if you eat your apple." I'd last spotted it discarded on the carpet, whole but for a gnawed strip where the flesh had browned.

His bottom lip quivered and he frowned, but I put my hands on my hips and stood calm. I'd finished work and didn't need to worry about bribing him to behave.

"Cheese." When I gave him the look, he added, "Please."

After lunch, we strolled to the park. I'd tucked his coat in my bag but, as I shaded my eyes to check for rain clouds, just a few cotton-wool clouds hung in the milky blue sky. Still in his nature phase, Josh stooped every now and again to examine a leaf, blossom petal or weed. I kept at his pace, finding joy in his curiosity – or to save the life of a ladybird when I spotted his pincer fingers moving towards it.

The park lay several roads away, behind what had been a council estate but, thanks to its prime location, wide roads and crescent-shaped greens, most of the houses had been sold and extended, so it bore little resemblance to what I remembered from my childhood. My old school friend's house stood on the corner, one of the first to be upgraded, the lighter tone of brick evident in the side extension. Its white mock-Georgian door and lattice-paned windows once had an air of superiority, but now it seemed dowdy in comparison to its neighbours with their oak doors and block-paved driveways.

I didn't know a single person on this estate now, unlike my dad's, where many of the older residents still lived, not having bought their homes and sold up to better themselves on private estates. There, the only changes seemed to be in the gardens. Gone was the old chain-linked fencing that spanned concrete posts; front gardens were now surrounded by privet hedges or wooden fencing. Many had taken the council up on its offer a few decades ago to build driveways for a small price, although the estate still suffered from overcrowded roads, since most families had more than one car. But that was a small price to pay for living in a friendly neighbourhood.

When I thought about Court Place, I could see why people shied from it and its inhabitants. The ugly concrete blocks had a forbidding air. Outsiders didn't see the young couples and families who lived there quietly, striving to do their best, but had to contend with its visible occupants like the Flying Scotsman, who slurred obscenities in a thick south London accent, even though I'd been told he'd moved here from Chartley, just six miles up the road.

But wherever we lived, we could all share the park with its wonderful play area, which neighboured the tennis courts, and a multi-use games area, beside which teens hung out in the youth shelter watching their more athletic friends. Further away lay the football pitches and tucked in the corner alongside the woods, which bordered a little stream, was the bowling club.

Today, Josh and I seemed to have the rec to ourselves. I let him race the final hundred yards to the swings, while I sauntered behind, only picking up speed when he reached the closed gate to the fenced play area and shouted for me to open it. He had an insatiable appetite for the swings. Although we chatted while I pushed him, it wasn't a stimulating conversation and I found my mind wandering, until squeals of joy broke into my thoughts. This was different to his usual shriek when the swing reached its peak; this one had purpose.

"Look!" He pointed into the distance to a person skipping towards us, her dark ringlets bouncing. It looked like Christabel, but she'd changed her hairstyle to the one now favoured by Erin.

She gripped the metal bar of the playground gate. "Is Will around?"

"He's at work, I'm afraid."

Josh fought to extract himself from the baby swing, so I hefted him out. He raced over. The lock clanked as he rattled the gate.

"Come to play?"

She shook her head and pointed to a distant figure at the corner of the field. For the briefest moment my heart leapt, until I realised it wasn't Oliver but a woman with a dog.

"I'm walking Robbie dog with my aunt. She lives in Meadow Manor."

I grinned. "Not the hotbed of crime, speeding and potholes?"

She frowned.

"Don't worry," I said. "I went to a meeting the other day where they talked about it."

I'd still lost her. But then she smiled.

"Oliver goes to lots of meetings too. He likes you and I like Will. Do you think he'll like my new hairstyle?"

Stunned by her revelation, I stuttered, "I-It's lovely. Really pretty."

Oliver likes me!

But I didn't have time to dwell on it. Josh reached through the gap between the gate and the fence post to tug at her sleeve. "Come on the swing?"

She looked doubtfully across to her aunt, who had moved closer to us while launching balls to her unflagging dog, but then she shrugged and unclipped the latch. She flopped onto the swing next to Josh's toddler swing, curling her hands around the chain, while I fed his legs through the bars. Once in, he threw his legs back and forth before I'd even pushed him.

With Christabel here, I could fact-check her earlier comment. While Oliver 'liking' me might be an auspicious revelation, she could have simply meant that Oliver and I were friends. But she'd used it in the same context as her and Will, and she definitely had a thing for him.

"You said Oliver liked me?"

"Yes." She turned her wide brown eyes to mine. "What time does Will finish work? I'm going home at six."

"Where do you live?" Why had I asked her that? It wasn't as if I would stalk Oliver. But if her aunt lived in Meadow Manor – most likely in the posh houses in the centre, if Oliver's accent was anything to go by – it would be interesting to know if she and Oliver lived in a nice road too. Not too posh, I hoped.

"Cantwell Place."

I frowned. Wasn't that where the sheltered accommodation and the older people's bungalows had once been sited, until a purpose-built unit had been constructed on the other side of town? I hadn't been that way for ages so, for all I knew, they could have knocked them down and developed the land into a housing estate.

"I've got my own flat now. It's nice. I've told Will to come and live there but he won't."

Now it made sense. They must have converted the old buildings into supported-living housing. I decided not to probe further about Oliver.

Christabel's aunt strode towards us, her dog on the lead. She'd tucked her trousers into green wellies, even though the ground had been hardened by a week of sun. When she neared the playground, Christabel stuck her feet out to slow down, scuffing the tips of her shoes, and slipped from the swing.

She signalled to Josh. "Come and say hello to Robbie dog."

Once I'd extricated him from the swing, we followed her over. Christabel's aunt greeted us warmly while the dog bounded up and down, evading Christabel's attempts to clasp her arms around him. Eventually, she won and seized the dog in a tight embrace before smothering him with kisses. When she came up for air, she invited Josh to pat Robbie dog's head.

"Is that okay?" I asked.

"He loves children." Like Oliver, Christabel's aunt spoke well. She gave me a welcoming smile. "By the way, I'm Laura."

"Madel— Maddie," I corrected myself and held out my hand, which she shook, although I had a feeling that I'd been overly formal.

"I think I've heard you mentioned previously."

"Oliver likes her," Christabel said. "And I like Will."

She'd said it again. Oliver likes me!

I hoped my face didn't show my true feelings, but I couldn't hide the tremor of excitement in my voice as I told her, "Will's my brother."

Laura's eyes met mine and she chuckled. "Your brother sounds quite a catch." Then she checked her watch. "We have to get back. Lovely to meet you."

Christabel gave us a little wave and hurried off after her aunt. For a moment Josh and I watched them walk away, the dog's tail whipping their legs. Then we turned back to the swings. I'd promised Josh an afternoon at the park and I wouldn't short-change him. While I pushed him on the swing under the warm spring sun, I could dream about Oliver. Strange how simply being told that Oliver liked me had allowed me to release my feelings.

I liked him too. A lot.

Chapter 16

ON OUR WAY BACK FROM THE PARK, we passed Rachel's flat. Puzzled, I took in the cans, bottles and other objects littering the verge – was that really a toilet brush? Josh tugged my hand, pointing towards her flat. I went to tell him that we'd see Rachel later, but her front door opened and she called us over. The skin beneath her eyes was bruised grey beneath the frames of her glasses, her hair untamed by a brush. She stifled a yawn.

"I hope you don't mind, but I won't come round yours later. We had a bit of a to-do last night."

Josh squirmed between her legs and the door frame in a bid to get inside. I grabbed hold of the back of his collar but he leaned forward, as if ready to plummet from a ski-jump.

"Josh, not today." I turned back to Rachel. "Are you okay?"

"I'm not ill, just knackered." She stepped aside. "Come in, though. You'll want to hear this."

I picked Josh up and dropped him inside her door. Like a wound clockwork mouse, he raced into the lounge, turning full circle. Then he raised his palms in confusion.

"Kieran'll be home in thirty minutes," Rachel said. "I'll put the TV on for you."

Once she'd provided Josh with the home comforts – juice, a biscuit and TV – we went through to the kitchen where she switched on the kettle and pulled two mugs from the cupboard.

"Well, your Derek certainly got some action going here."

"My Derek?" Then I remembered she meant our Portfolio Holder at the council, and my subsequent phone conversation with the housing team. "They spoke to the Flying Scotsman?"

"They did that all right." She drew a carton of milk from the fridge and sniffed the contents. "A day out of date, but it's fine."

"It's sorted, then?"

"You're kidding me! Didn't you see the war zone outside?"

"I saw some cans and other bits."

She ushered me to her front door and pointed past the debris to a black Vauxhall parked in a bay. I shielded my eyes from the sun, which had dipped low. Stunned, I surveyed the spider's-web crack that radiated out from a dent in the centre of the windscreen. It was incredible that the screen hadn't shattered. The tyres had deflated, becoming folded rugs for the metal rims.

"Did he have a go at the housing officers?"

She gave a thin-lipped smile. "He was as good as gold with them. I saw him shake their hands goodbye. I wouldn't have known who they were, had it not been for later."

I frowned. "Later?"

"He thinks Janice next door grassed him up. But he didn't say a word until he got home at midnight, tanked up from the pub, and started on her."

A cloud obscured the sun, shading the scene, and I gasped at the now-visible dents in the passenger door and the word 'grass' gouged in the paintwork.

"What did he do to her?"

"When we heard the commotion, we went outside to find him hammering on her door. Kieran and Nige, her other neighbour, went to stop him but he barricaded himself in his flat and promised to calm down. Janice said she was fine and didn't want the police called. But within twenty minutes he was out by her car, smashing it up. Kieran and Nige chased him back to his place, where he started throwing stuff at people. Anything he could find."

She yawned and stretched, the hem of her T-shirt rising to show her pale stomach. "I was up all night looking after Janice. She was well upset."

"I'm so sorry. I had no idea this would happen."

"Don't be. It's not your fault."

"But I called them about him."

"Just like me, and just about everyone else here, and nothing's been done. I told the police about your Derek taking action against the Flying Scotsman and they said they'd speak to the housing team. Hopefully, this'll get him kicked out."

I pursed my lips. When I'd mentioned to Emma about the swift action taken after Derek had asked me to call the housing team, she'd said they were overstretched and could do little more than fight fires, rather than tackling issues before they blazed.

"Where is he now?"

If I'd realised what had happened, I wouldn't have brought Josh here. I couldn't put him at risk, even if it meant staying away from Rachel's for the time being. Thank goodness we lived in the Stuart House block. I'd often wished we didn't front the train line, but I preferred the clatter and screech of trains to the belching fury of the Flying Scotsman.

She shrugged. "As long as he's not here, I don't care where he is." Then she brightened. "Leah was asking what you're doing this weekend. Has she said anything to you?"

I narrowed my eyes. "No. Why?"

She lifted her mug to her lips and took a sip. "No idea. She just asked me…"

Behind us, the front door clicked open. She settled her mug on the worktop and went out to the hallway.

"Hi, darling. You look ready for bed too."

Kieran muttered something, but his words were cut off by Josh's squeal. "Kieran!"

He rushed through and launched himself at Kieran's leg, which he grasped while looking at him beseechingly. "Play zoom planes?"

"Kieran's too tired," I said.

But Kieran brushed me aside. "Nothing a bit of sleep won't sort. Come on then."

◆

I'd forgotten to interrogate Rachel further on Leah's plans. If I'd done so, I might not have boxed myself into a corner when Leah phoned to see if I could help her out the following evening by squaring the triangle and making a foursome. Her words, not mine.

I'd played my trump card – Josh – who could be relied upon at times like this. "I would go but I haven't got a babysitter."

But that's when Leah had chuckled down the phone and told me she'd sorted everything. I wasn't to worry about a single thing, just myself. Rachel would be around on the dot of six-thirty for her babysitting duties. Then she'd hung up.

The next evening, Rachel walked through my door and looked me up and down. "You look nice."

"Don't say a word," I growled. "I feel well and truly set up."

She gave my arm a squeeze. "Don't be. You'll have a lovely time."

A sense of gloom settled over me. I had a bad feeling about tonight. My lovely friends thought they were being helpful to me – the poor single mum who worked so hard and played so little. But, while a night out with Leah and her boyfriend would be fine, I didn't want a play date with Sean. He might be a lovely man but, by agreeing to go out with him tonight, it would make him think I was interested in him, and any attempt to show otherwise would be likely to cause offence and hurt.

I'd chosen to wear my black work trousers and a grey collarless top because they didn't reveal too much flesh. They made me look a bit mumsy, offset by the specks of glitter I removed from my cheek and trousers. (Thursday's artwork at nursery had involved creating cards with more glitter than the glue could catch. Consequently the car, house and every item of clothing I'd worn since sparkled pink, silver and blue.) My decision to team my clothes with a pair of heels had been made because 'Sean Beanstalk' was so tall, I felt like a child next to him.

I shrugged on my jacket. "Josh should be asleep, but if there's an issue you've got my number."

"I know, I know." Rachel ushered me outside. "Have a great evening."

She closed the door, leaving me to snatch a few gulps of air on the walkway to calm my nerves and my annoyance. Why hadn't I just said no? It's easy. N.O. spells no. But, when it came to my personal life, the page containing that word had been long ripped from my internal dictionary. Without the shield of poshness and my professional attire, I reverted to the unconfident girl of my childhood.

My heels clattered down the concrete steps, the noise echoing into the communal stairwell. On reaching the bottom, I spun back on myself, holding my nose as I hurried past the bin area, an unpleasant shortcut, but walking around the outside of the building wasn't much prettier or better-smelling. Then I crossed the sweeter-smelling grassed area – thanks to someone smoking weed nearby – which was enclosed by four of the estate's blocks.

I'd arranged to meet Leah at the pub, but as I started the short walk along the main road, my dread mounted. Not only would I have to go into the pub alone, but I'd also have to face Sean – who'd, rightfully, expect me to be looking forward to the evening. The thought made me feel sick. Less than fifty yards from the pub, I paused by a sign, on the pretext of shaking a stone from my shoe. To be honest, I didn't want to keep going. Would it be worse for Sean to be stood up at the beginning of the night or let down at the end?

A shiny crimson car slowed beside me. Leah's boyfriend, Paul, leaned out of the passenger window. "Get in. We'll give you a lift."

I angled my foot into my shoe. "It's only over the road."

Someone in the car pushed the rear door open, so I couldn't refuse. I ducked inside to find Leah wearing a sparkly black dress and glittery tights. Frowning, she eyed my attire.

"Did you think we were going to work?"

"It's smart casual."

"This is Saturday night. It's like a big deal."

At this rate, she'd be dragging me home to change into my old nightclubbing clobber that hung, unloved and forgotten, at the back of my wardrobe. A swift subject change was in order.

"Thank you for stopping to pick me up," I said, as Sean indicated to turn into the pub car park. "And hello, Paul."

Leah chuckled. "You'll be shaking their hands next."

Once we'd parked, Sean unfurled himself with some difficulty from the front seat. My eyes watered with sympathy when he banged his head, but mostly I looked on in disbelief. Why would someone of his height buy a low-slung sports model? My thoughts must have clearly showed on my face, as he turned to me.

"My car's in the garage. I borrowed my sister's."

"But your sister has a young child."

"Well remembered, but that's a different one." He gazed at me approvingly, no doubt thinking that I'd remembered this snippet from the party because our conversation had been memorable. However, my recollection stemmed from surprise that he hadn't been put off by the mention of Josh. "I've got four sisters. One has this car, one has a child, and the other two are twins off travelling the world."

I traipsed behind them into the busy pub, watching with amusement when Leah's head bobbed from side to side like a child crossing the road as she went over to the bar, greeting everyone. The tang of beer hung in the air and lay thick in the carpet. Sticky rings glistened on the mahogany tables and the chair fabric was mottled and stained. But the pub wasn't worse than most in the area, just in need of a refresh. Although, after placing my elbow on a wet patch on the bar, I decided it could also do with the occasional wipe.

While I rubbed my elbow dry, Leah stood at the bar, holding several notes. I didn't want to spend too much money, so I asked for a diet Coke but she laughed and ordered a bottle of Prosecco for us to share.

"It's your first time on the razzle for ages. The restaurant's not booked for another hour, so you might as well have a proper drink."

"I can't get too tipsy. I've got to get back for Josh."

She pulled a face as if about to argue, then shrugged. "Just be a super sipper then."

We had an enjoyable hour at the pub. At first, I found it draining to talk to Sean and Paul, knowing them so little, but I recalled feeling that way at Rachel's do and tried to relax. Again, I wondered why I could deal with almost any situation at work, but not on a personal level. But moving into work mode wouldn't save me here. Look how many eyebrows had raised when I'd tried to shake people's hands at the party. Sitting in the pub, listening to their banter, soon made me forget my worries, and the second half of the hour ticked around much quicker than the first. Before I knew it, Leah led us out to the car park.

"You're quiet." Sean pulled his car keys from his pocket. "Are you okay?"

I wrapped my jacket tighter against the biting wind. No doubt I'd be scraping frost off the car when I went out the next morning. "Just thinking."

I'd half expected him to say 'penny for them' or something similar, but he surprised me. "It's interesting how you seem at odds with this world. Not unhappy, just unsettled."

Puzzled, I said, "This world?"

He opened the rear car door and, as I slid into the seat, corrected himself. "I should have said environment."

Before I had time to respond, Leah bundled in beside me, her cheeks flushed by three glasses of Prosecco. She nudged me and looked across to Sean, who angled himself into the car seat.

"Having a good night?" When I nodded, she grinned and hissed loudly, "He's such a nice bloke."

Then someone ran a red light and she began a rant about moronic drivers, leaving me to spend the rest of the short car journey dwelling on what Sean had said. Had my shyness come across as stand-offishness? Or was it more than that? The way I spoke. But I couldn't change that. Not yet.

I thought back to how I may have come across. After a drink in the pub, I'd relaxed enough not to worry about what I said or how I said it. But I still had my limits. It would take another two or three glasses of Prosecco before I dropped my hard-won aitches. I wasn't trying to be a snob – or so I told myself – but I wanted to progress in the world and to make life better for Josh. Was that wrong? I had no idea. At present, my vocabulary reminded me of when I'd been a learner driver – having to think with every action – but one day enunciating every 't' and aitch would feel as instinctive to me as driving now did.

Sean found a parking space outside the Chinese restaurant. As he extricated himself from the car, I noticed that Sean Beanstalk had taken on another Bean persona. I bit my lip to hide a snigger. Mr Bean-stalk.

Leah elbowed me. "Don't laugh at him. Poor bloke."

"Your pity is better?" I grinned at her.

As Sean grasped the roof of his car and levered himself out, Leah failed to conceal a snigger behind her hand. He'd managed to free one leg and was twisting his foot to pull the other one out.

"I don't think he'll borrow his sister's car again."

"Strange how he can get in but not out," I said.

"It must be well uncomfortable for him, but he's got a heart of gold and wouldn't hear of letting us down after promising to drive.

His kindness has got him into some right scrapes. You'll have to ask him about the time he had to be rescued from a cat flap."

With that, she strode into the restaurant. I took off behind her, leaving the men to join us, once Sean had smoothed himself down.

We'd been allocated a circular table in the middle of the room, which felt like being in a goldfish bowl, as we became the focus of attention for bored customers waiting to pick up their takeaways. A table by the wall would have been better, but at least we had space so there would be no hand touching, although our knees were uncomfortably close, mostly down to Sean's lanky legs.

The gentle hubbub rose and dipped, as did the aroma of food, which was blown away by the chill evening air each time the door opened or closed. This happened often, as the restaurant seemed to have the world's busiest takeaway section. Where did everyone find the money? But in the days before Josh, I'd been able to indulge too.

We were served by an efficient waiter, who took our orders and brought out the starter minutes after bringing our drinks. Leah had ordered a second bottle of Prosecco, even though I would barely touch it. Paul opted for a pint of lager while Sean chose a small Coke. We'd gone for the option which offered us a soup starter, then pancakes, followed by a selection of dishes, with two choices each. It seemed a huge amount of food, but Leah held fast to the menu reading out our menu options so I couldn't see the price, laughing that, "She was in charge tonight".

I tried to push away anxious thoughts about how I would afford it, especially when we finished our soup and my favourite, duck pancakes, appeared. It took all my willpower to not steal an additional wrap, on the basis that I hadn't noticed it stuck to another

149

one, but I let honesty win and asked who hadn't had their second pancake yet.

"Me," Sean said. "But you can have it. If I could become anything right now, I'd ask to be a duck wrap. Look at the lust in your eyes."

I couldn't deny it. With that, he became my favourite person on the table and – by the look on her face – Leah's least favourite. She glanced across at Paul, who stuffed his second wrap into his mouth so his cheeks bulged.

Leah's expression of distaste transformed into a sickly smile and she patted Sean's hand. "Well, you've already worked out the way to her heart. Cupboard love."

I fired her an angry glance. *Don't use that four-letter word here!* But then I realised that I couldn't have it both ways. Accepting Sean's pancake might be a tiny notch upwards on his ladder of expectation – and I don't mean sex, just plain old dating – but I didn't want to lead him on.

"No, honestly. You have it," I said. "I'm saving myself for the main."

"I'll have it if you're not hungry," Leah said.

Sean shrugged. "Be my guest."

I had a feeling that neither he or I were happy with this outcome. As the waiter removed our plates, Leah told a story I'd heard before about a job she'd once had in a restaurant. I found myself half-listening and people-watching. I didn't recognise anyone here from work or the public meetings I'd attended.

A man at the neighbouring table placed his menu at the edge of his table but misjudged it and it clattered to the floor beside my feet. As I lifted it to hand back to him, I noticed the set menu we'd chosen. And the price. Seriously? Thirty pounds a head. That was before drinks were added on.

A quick tally told me the bill would be forty-five pounds each, most likely more. Although Leah had paid for the drinks in the pub, I hadn't banked on this. I'd spent the little I'd saved on the Easter break with Josh, and tonight would bust a hole in my bank balance. He needed new shoes more than I needed posh food. Why hadn't I told Leah that we couldn't go anywhere too expensive? The all-you-could-eat in town was half the price of this. As the waiter placed our dishes in front of us, the duck pancakes congealed in my stomach. We couldn't possibly eat all this food.

My companions tucked in, digging their serving spoons into mounds of rice and strips of meat. Candlelight reflected on my glass, the flame brightening the bubbles. Mesmerised, I watched them spinning to the surface like a soothing lava lamp until Sean broke in, giving me the line I'd expected to hear earlier.

"Penny for them."

Right now, I could do with more than a few quid for them. Then I shrugged to myself. Eating less wouldn't reduce the bill, so I might as well enjoy it. Smiling at him, I reached for my glass to take a sip while I waited for the others to finish serving themselves, but I clipped the edge with my fingers. As if in slow motion, the glass tumbled forward, evading my desperate grasp, before toppling onto the lemon chicken dish, soaking it – and the table – with Prosecco. The glass hadn't smashed, but that was all I could be thankful for. Moments earlier I'd been worrying about the cost of all this food, and now I'd just ruined it.

"Oh!" I lifted the empty glass from the dish, its side smeared with sauce. "What have I done? I'm so sorry."

Leah's lips were poised in an 'o' of surprise, her hands clasped to her cheeks, while a hush had fallen over the restaurant. All eyes focused on us. Or me, to be precise. If I'd felt as if we'd been sitting on view before, now I might as well have created my own circus ring, with me starring as the clown. My face burned brighter than the crimson lanterns above.

Sean grinned. "You're brilliant. How did you guess?"

Ignoring the waiting staff who scurried over to dab our table dry, he stretched over to take the Prosecco-ed chicken dish and heaped a pile on his plate.

He must have caught sight of my stunned expression, as he chuckled. "I just love coq au vin."

Chapter 17

WE LEFT THE RESTAURANT IN FITS OF LAUGHTER, just as we'd spent most of the evening since the coq au vin incident, or 'cocked-up van' as a very tipsy Leah insisted on calling it. Paul strung his arm around her, on the pretext of giving her a cuddle, but – from the way she dragged him from side to side – it was clear she'd be on the ground without him. When I'd asked about the bill, Leah waved me away, saying it had already been sorted, but my relief was shrouded by worry. Had Leah intended to pay, or was this a drunken gift she'd regret the next day? It was far too generous, especially after she'd bought the drinks in the pub. Paul spotted my concern and leaned over to whisper that Leah had planned this as a very late birthday gift to me after getting a bonus. But it still didn't feel right. I'd have to make it up to her somehow.

With help, Leah successfully negotiated the restaurant steps and we were making our way towards Sean's car when she stumbled out of the safety of Paul's arms, bumping into a man coming out of a convenience store.

"Whoa!" he laughed, holding his bottle of wine in the air.

Behind him stepped another man. Someone I recognised. Inside I wilted. Why had this happened to me? Now Oliver would think I was dating Sean. Much as I'd enjoyed our evening and found him amusing and interesting, I didn't want to be with him. And I certainly didn't want Oliver to be under any misunderstanding either.

While Paul apologised for Leah and readjusted his hold on her, I turned to Oliver. "What a surprise. I've just been eating next door with friends."

I hoped he'd catch the overt message – I'm still free – if that word could in any way be applied to my life.

As he stepped in front of the other man, his gorgeous smile lit up his face and his lovely dark eyes locked with mine. The familiar scent of his aftershave surrounded us.

"It's lovely to see you out on the town, Maddie. Let me introduce you. Maddie, this is Tom. Tom, meet Maddie." He turned to the other man, Tom. "We work together, and Maddie's brother also goes to Samson's with Christabel."

I shook Tom's hand, not feeling self-conscious or wrong in doing so, before turning to my friends. "Leah, Paul and Sean." I didn't point out the relationship between Leah and Paul – although it was obvious – in case anyone asked what my relationship was to Sean.

Tom tapped Oliver's shoulder. "We'd better get going."

Oliver shrugged. "He's like a sergeant major tonight. Marching me from one place to another."

After saying goodbye, they sauntered off in the opposite direction. I didn't want to watch them in case it gave my feelings away, but Leah paused.

"Nice couple," she slurred.

I frowned. What an odd thing to say.

"Couple?"

She tapped the side of her nose – missing the tip – and chuckled. "Years of practice has taught me." Giggling, she slapped her hand to her mouth. "Sorry, Paul, but you're the only one for me now. I—" She pointed to her chest, in case we didn't know who she meant. "I have one amazing gaydar."

"A what?" Sean had joined the conversation. I wished he hadn't.

Leah launched into an explanation. I didn't need to be told what Leah's gaydar was, other than something that had sucked all happiness from my soul. *Please don't let Oliver be gay.* But as my gaze tracked to where he and Tom strolled in the distance, my dreams shattered into fragments. They might not be holding hands, but their arms brushed together as they walked, just like any couple comfortable in their relationship.

Christabel had said that she liked Will and Oliver liked me. But she hadn't differentiated between Oliver's platonic 'like' and her fancying 'like'. Now, through no fault of hers but a misunderstanding on my part, I felt bruised and – I had to confess – heartbroken.

I turned to my companions, fixing them with the best smile I could manage. "Tonight's been such a great evening, but I'm exhausted. Do you mind if I go home?"

Sean's concerned gaze fell upon me and he ushered me into the car. "Of course, I understand. You'll want to get back for your son."

♦

I woke early the next day, feeling morose and stupid, so I took myself off to Dad's house where we could both sit in his gloomy lounge feeling sorry for ourselves. But when I arrived unannounced, I found Will huffing impatiently on the doorstep waiting for Dad, who was inside checking he'd turned off all the lights and shut the windows.

155

"We're going to the park," Will told me.

Surprise and relief flooded me. I'd got so used to arriving to find Dad asleep on the settee. So far this year, he hadn't left the house to go anywhere except the shops, the hospital or the bank, after Will's episode. I hoped this meant he'd turned the corner.

Josh frowned and his gaze moved from Will to the dark hallway beyond, where Dad was putting on his coat and gloves.

Knowing Josh was considering the loss of his beloved *The Simpsons*, I distracted him with, "You'll be able to go on the swings."

Dad appeared, raising his eyebrows when he saw us on the doorstep. "To what do we owe this pleasure? Twice in a weekend. That's a first."

"We've got a bit of free time."

While not exactly a lie, it wasn't the truth. I could find free time if I ignored the washing and ironing, I left the dust to grow extra layers and the carpet to become a montage of bits, fluff and glitter (the latter I still found stuck to my face and clothes every day).

"Lucky you." Dad tucked the door keys into his coat pocket. "We're rushed off our feet here. We've got just enough time to watch the memorial match and then we're back home to sort dinner."

Will and Josh plodded ahead, hand in hand. Josh's high-pitched voice swooped in the air so we caught the odd phrase, but Will's responses didn't reach us. Dad chuckled.

"Your lad likes to talk."

I laughed. Josh adored Will.

Dad bent to evade an overhanging bramble, but it snagged on the back of his collar. I pulled it free, pleased to see it hadn't caused any damage.

"Will's been a bit more talkative since they said he won't have to go to court."

"You never told me that."

He frowned. "I'm sure I did."

This was a typical conversation, although usually I was the one being accused of not saying anything. A caveated denial was the standard response. Just as Dad had done.

"So how come?"

He shrugged. "I was so relieved, I didn't ask too many questions. All I know is the man has admitted he's guilty."

"And Will's money?"

He shrugged. "We're hopeful of getting some of it back, if not all. But at least he won't fall for that one again."

We walked on in silence, both knowing there would be other incidents and learning curves for Will, as there would be for Josh and me.

"You're a bundle of joy today." Dad's words broke into my thoughts.

"Oh, you know." I shrugged. "Typical twenty-first-century issues. Girl likes boy but boy likes boy better."

I hadn't planned to tell Dad. It just came out. His expression told me that out of all the things I could have said, he hadn't expected that.

"I had a dog like that once." He checked his watch. "We need to walk faster. The game will be starting soon."

♦

Monday brought rain, meetings, and more gloom – in the form of David, whose expression could have soured milk. I tried to ignore him and get on with the preparation I needed to do, but his eyes burned into me, his hatred pulsing towards me in waves. It was a pleasure to pack up my laptop and head off to the bumpy waters of my first meeting with the Didlingbury library group. Hopefully, it would be easier than expected, just as my initial meeting with the Chartley group had been.

As I passed David's desk, I kept my head high, ignoring his muttered, "Snooty cow."

If only he knew. He'd have a field day if he followed me home.

When I reached my car, I jabbed the radio on, determined to drown my annoyance with a blast from the past. Or the 'guess the year' show which would be playing now. But the year seemed to be from the days of the ark, so I found another station.

My journey out of Holdenwell took me through roads lined by seventies-style houses with large windows, white cladding and flat-roofed porches, past the industrial estate and new housing developments that would soon swallow the surrounding fields. A bird dipped in the air, narrowly missing my car, before diving into a lime-green hedgerow. The late April sun had broken through the rain clouds of earlier, making the fresh colours glow. Its warmth burned through the windscreen. For a moment I basked in the heat, forgetting David and work, until I spotted the sign for Didlingbury. Its metal posts were flanked by tubs of tulips, their heads bobbing in the breeze.

The stark black-and-white sign brought Emma's warning to mind. I knew how Derek felt about the local councillor, Agnes Drew. Not only was she on the 'other side', but she was a forceful, capable woman who, while having the community's interests at heart, could unwittingly enable the closure of the library if we couldn't get her to agree to the proposals or to find another workable option.

I'd driven through Didlingbury twice, but always on the way to somewhere else. As I reversed into a tight parking space, outside a pub fronted by rickety benches that seemed to sway with each gust, I wondered why I'd never thought to bring Dad, Will and Josh here. They'd enjoy a day out to such a gorgeous place. The village green that stretched along the centre had a small recreation area at one end with wooden play equipment and a pond, where a woman stood with her toddler feeding the ducks. No Canada geese here, unlike the municipal park in the centre of Holdenwell. Opposite stood a church with a small graveyard that neighboured two mirror-image Victorian red-brick buildings, their windows arched with sandstone lintels. I guessed they must have once been the school and the large tarmacked frontage the playground. The sign that swung above the door showed that one of the buildings had since become a post office, while I knew about the library and the café sited in the other. This was where I would meet Councillor Drew, the chairman of the parish council, and two of the 'Save Didlingbury library' group members.

I took a deep breath to quell the nerves that threatened to surface and got out of my car, to be caught by a squall that whipped my badge and lanyard into my face. I stuffed my badge under my jacket and headed across the green, praying the meeting would go well and I wouldn't do anything to make a fraught situation worse.

Following the instructions, I found the group I was to meet in the café at the rear of the building. Councillor Drew smoothed down her tweed skirt, which she'd teamed with thick brown tights and boots, as she stood to present me to the trio of villagers.

"Call me Agnes." It was a command, not a request, but it was tempered with a welcoming smile.

She reached my height but looked better-fed, with a short blonde bob and plump rosy cheeks. Something about her reminded me of my childhood ideal of a down-to-earth farmer's wife, based on the old-fashioned books I'd read, where they forced huge slabs of cake and meat pies on visitors, along with fresh warm milk. I'd longed to be a farmer's daughter. That was until I'd moved on to books set at boarding schools, which won me over with midnight feasts, lashings of ginger beer and anchovies, although I had no idea what the latter involved. My favourite books revolved around food.

"We'll have a coffee and then you can meet our lovely library team and see why we don't want to lose them," Agnes said.

I didn't know which was worse. Being faced with a furious group or being won over with kindness while being introduced to the people whose jobs were at risk. The chairman of the parish council, Mary, passed me a mug of coffee but I wistfully declined her proffered plate of biscuits. I couldn't risk spitting crumbs while I spoke.

The small café was tucked behind the library. I wouldn't have known it was here but for the meeting instructions. Once this had been a classroom, but now it smelled of coffee and pastries. A man with grey hair and twinkling eyes told me he'd been schooled in this room – and caned here too. He pointed to the stone fireplace, above which hung a painting of Didlingbury church. The teacher's desk had been there, by the warmth of the fire. Now six tables filled the small classroom space, which looked out onto a paddock where horses grazed. I hadn't seen a horse so close in years, other than when I passed them while driving outside Holdenwell.

We spent the next half an hour talking about the history of their library, the reasoning behind the cuts (which Agnes knew, but swerved the conversation in another direction each time I mentioned the word), and the village's aspiration to make the library a social hub where lonely people could come and chat and where those looking for a job could get help with their CV. I thought of my dad at that point, alone at home and despondent as he opened each rejection letter. Holdenwell Library offered help with CVs and I was sure the staff would stop to chat to people, but its purpose lay in administration – the loaning of books – rather than friendship. The hard-working staff simply didn't have time for more.

I wanted the villagers to succeed, but I couldn't see how. If we didn't reduce costs – cut staff – Derek would close this library. I imagined him standing behind Agnes, rubbing his hands in glee. The loss of the library would not only hurt the community but, perhaps more importantly to him, reduce Agnes's chances of being re-elected.

Chairs scraped the parquet floor as we got to our feet. We made our way along the dark corridor, which still had coat hooks along one side, then Agnes pulled open a door which I'd passed unnoticed in my earlier haste. She ushered me into a space the size of the café. A trio of colourful beanbags lay scattered across a rug printed with a town scene and roads that children could drive their cars around. Josh would love it here. Three walls were filled with bookshelves, which ran from the door and ended beside a line of desks with three computers. They faced the windows that looked out over the village green. At the very end of the row a woman stood behind a desk stacked with leaning towers of books. She gave us an awkward smile and a shrug.

"I'm a bit behind. I hoped to have it cleared for your arrival, but it's been a busy morning."

We were the only people there. She must have read my thoughts, as she added, "We run a story-time session at nine-thirty on Mondays after the parents have dropped the older children at school. It finished twenty minutes ago but everyone stayed to take out books."

Agnes adopted a motherly air. "Karen does a wonderful job. She's a single mother and can't drive, and you know how few buses come through here. So it means we get her all to ourselves. And, believe me, she's an asset to this community."

Karen flushed. Embarrassed at her personal life being discussed or pleased with the compliment? She dropped her gaze to the pile of books on the desk and picked one up, pulling it to her chest. Armour in place, she looked up.

I'd expected her voice to wobble, but she sounded determined. "I have two teenage sons. I can't drive since I developed epilepsy a decade ago, but you don't want to hear about that."

She glanced at Agnes for approval who, I had a feeling, was the instigator behind this story.

"Although our hours were cut last year, we run activities for all age groups," Karen continued.

At that moment a stooped man walked in, clutching a carrier bag and a lead attached to an elderly Jack Russell with arthritic legs. He didn't seem surprised to see us standing there, giving us a nod before pulling three books from his bag and handing them over to Karen, who scanned them.

"This is Albert," she said. "He comes in every morning we're open, just to say hello." She turned to him. "This is the lady from the council." Obviously, he knew what she meant, as Karen didn't need to elaborate.

Albert touched his cap. "Morning." He tottered over to a chair by the bookshelves and slumped into the seat to pat his dog. There he stayed, watching from a distance, as the door buzzed open – someone had pressed the button – and a young woman came in backwards, pulling a buggy.

"I forgot Millie's book," she said and glanced at me. "Hello, everyone. What a surprise to see you all here."

"This one?" Karen picked a hardback from the side. The cover showed a red fire engine.

"That's it!" She bent down to the toddler in the buggy. "Oh look, there's Albert and Scottie. Shall we say hello?"

Not waiting for an answer, she stooped to drag one of the beanbags aside before settling the buggy next to Albert. Low murmurs reached us, as if they were deep in conversation, but I notice them casting surreptitious glances in our direction.

Soon the door opened again and two women appeared. I was once more introduced as the woman from the council. Neither asked what that meant. They knew.

"What would we do without Karen?" one said as Karen handed her some books.

Mary leaned over to me. "We have another lady who works here with Karen, but she's been offered a back-office position at the council. So we're looking at a solution that keeps Karen, with the help of volunteers."

I didn't care if they were leading me by the nose to help them keep their librarian. They'd made their point. I wanted to help this tiny community library that served a village with limited transport – and I wanted to help a single mum, who'd find it very difficult to get another job.

Internally I grimaced, wondering how on earth we'd fund that. But there had to be a way.

Within fifteen minutes, almost a dozen villagers, in addition to the original meeting attendees, had crammed into the library space. I checked my watch.

"I need to head off," I told Agnes. "But, before I do, can you tell me about the other rooms in this building and the one next door?"

She led me into the corridor, leaving the others to speculate on the impression made. She tried the door of the room opposite, but it had been locked. Through the narrow glass panel, I could make out a bare room with a beige carpet littered with boxes and papers.

"This used to be rented to a solicitor, but he moved out. I don't think he appreciated the sing-along sessions next door. It's a large office, double the size of the library and café. Then at the back of the building there's a kitchen and the toilets."

"What about the other building? The one with the post office?"

"Do you have time to see it? I've got an idea that might work, but we'd have to persuade Eric the postmaster to move."

"Go on. I need to leave by ten past."

We hurried across the tarmac to the twin building on the other side. The post office sign, which hung beneath a pole, creaked in the breeze.

"This was the girls' building in the days when the schools were segregated." She led me beneath a high stone archway into which the word 'Girls' had been chiselled. "The one with the library was the boys' school. This building is seldom used apart from the post office. We have a village hall by the playing fields."

Unlike its counterpart, this building didn't contain a colourful space filled with books or a warm café. Instead, the post office was a dank room with half-filled shelves littered with envelopes, cards and other stationery. Above us, cobwebs swathed beams that couldn't have seen a feather duster for decades.

A man hunched behind the glass counter. "Agnes." He sighed as if an already bad day had just been made worse. "To what do we owe this pleasure?"

"I've brought the lady from the council," she said.

Through dark-rimmed glasses he eyed me with interest.

Agnes folded her arms. "She's come to assess this building."

"Has she?" The man frowned. "And what do you mean by that?"

I blanched, not expecting things to take this turn, but Agnes shrugged. "They're looking at everything. As you know, Karen's job is at stake, and possibly the library. This building is owned by the council, so she needs to see it."

At that moment I knew what Agnes wanted. If he moved into the other building, perhaps this one could be sold or rented to make money to keep the library. But he'd need funds to help cover his costs. Also, the space on the other side was larger than this one. How could we make it work?

"I've got a lease," the man said.

"With a year left," Agnes said. "But don't worry. Nothing will happen … yet."

Leaving those ominous words hanging, she ushered me out, giving me no chance to say anything other than goodbye.

Once outside, well away from earshot, she said, "I can see his point. He can't afford to move. The post office won't cover his costs, which will be considerable. He'll need a strongroom, for a start."

"What if we can find a way around it? I mean, there isn't a shop in the village. And if the council can sell or lease this building, perhaps they'd look more kindly on contributing towards the move, especially if they can get a bit more rent too."

"Exactly my thoughts." Agnes held out her hand to shake mine. "Emma said good things about you, and I can see why. It'll be a pleasure working with you."

As I walked away, the rosy glow of dreams dissipated into reality. My two months at the council had shown that if all forty-seven councillors were placed on a scale from 1 to 10, with 1 meaning caring about their community and 10 meaning the party coming first, a few councillors would straggle from 1–3, with most located around the 4–7 mark, while Derek would score a 9. His primary aim was political ambition for his party and self, with the communities most likely to vote for him running a poor second. How could Derek be convinced to help Didlingbury when that would go against his own interests? The one plausible option could be if we were able to promote this as the goal he scored, with good publicity for him and his party.

I swallowed. But how would Agnes feel about that?

Chapter 18

WITH FIFTEEN MINUTES TO SPARE until my meeting with Kavita, I stopped to say hello to Tariq in the café and pick up a bottle of sparkling water. As I stood in the queue, I skimmed through the emails on my phone and checked my diary. Immediately after meeting with Kavita, I had a slot with Emma to discuss whether it would be feasible to move the post office and to let or sell the other building at Didlingbury. It had been two days since my meeting with Agnes Drew and her group, so I needed to get back to them with ideas.

Tariq beamed when I reached the front of the queue, but he kept his tone formal. "Hello. How can I help you?"

I went to make a joke about him being no different to me – we both adapted the way we spoke at work – when I realised he wouldn't see the funny side, especially not with his boss, Elaine, hovering nearby.

"I would like a bottle of sparkling water, if you don't mind."

He opened the chiller cabinet and put the bottle on the countertop. Then he ran his finger down the sheet in front of him until he found what he needed. "One pound twenty, please."

After I gave him the right change, he looked furtively around. One of the other workers had come in with tubs of fresh salad and Elaine had moved away to help rotate the stock.

"I've got a joke for you," he hissed.

When I nodded for him to continue, he glanced at the next person in line and leaned forward, cupping his hand around his mouth. His breath puffed my ear.

"What did one water bottle say to another?" He gave me a second to think before answering. "Water you doing later?"

"Nothing," I joked. "Samson's isn't on until next Wednesday."

He frowned. "Wat-er – *what are* – you doing later? Get it?"

I chuckled. "I got it the first time. Very good."

He graced me with a nod of the head before moving on to the next customer, who laughed. "Some people just ruin jokes, don't they?"

Tariq frowned. "Do they?"

The man stuttered, then settled on a shrug. I picked up the bottle of sparkling water and grinned at them both.

"Tariq, he meant me, not you. *I* ruined the joke."

"Oh!" But Tariq shook his head. "You got my joke. You said so." He turned to the man, his tone placid, and said, "You shouldn't be mean to Maddie."

One peek at the man's perplexed face told me I should leave that minute or else I would be doubled over, cackling.

After throwing me a look that said he'd done all he could, Tariq focused his attention back on the man. "How can I help you?"

With my mouth clamped tight, to fight back the giggles, and my shoulders shaking, I left the café. Passers-by shot curious glances at me. If they'd stopped and asked what was so amusing, I wouldn't have been able to speak for laughter. I'd known Tariq for years. While he had one of the best senses of humour around when it came to bad jokes or people falling over, it didn't stretch to sarcasm or dry wit. He wasn't alone in that regard. Sometimes I watched a comedian on TV and I couldn't work out why the audience had tears running down their faces, or someone would tell me a joke and I'd spend the next ten minutes trying to work it out. But the man in the café's face – that would be something I'd chuckle about for ages.

I reached reception, to find that Kavita hadn't arrived yet. A crowd milled outside, so I ambled over to the glass frontage. It was a wedding party, mostly people in their late teens or twenties, the men in shiny suits and the women in short dresses and heels, their bright colours enlivened by the midday sun. Around the periphery stood a few older people. Laughter and smoke drifted in the air.

"These people shouldn't be allowed to breed." A familiar voice broke into my thoughts.

"Eh?" I must have misheard him. I swung around to face the man, stunned to find Derek standing beside me.

Scowling, he gazed outside. "I said, these people shouldn't be allowed to breed."

Without thinking, I said, "These are *my* people."

They were. No matter how I sounded now, the young people dressed in the way I would have done at a wedding less than a decade ago. Back then I'd smoked too and I'd huddled with friends, having one last drag before being forced into the dusty registry office to watch our pregnant friend get hitched. Or that's how I'd seen it when I'd attended the wedding of a friend from school back then. No one in their right mind would settle down unless they had no choice. But I'd been proved wrong. My married friend didn't get pregnant until quite a few years later, while I'd ended up an unmarried single parent.

Derek chortled. "You are such a card, Madeleine. I never know when you're pulling my leg."

Believe me, it isn't a joke, I almost said. I longed to say worse, but I couldn't. It was no longer just about keeping up appearances

169

and paying my rent – although I couldn't deny that those things loomed in my thoughts – but Agnes Drew, Karen, the librarian, and the people of Didlingbury needed Derek on side more than I needed to tell him that he was a pompous oaf. Instead I gave him a terse smile and, spotting Kavita threading her way through the wedding party, rushed out to greet her.

I hadn't seen her in a sari before. Usually she favoured bright tops and dark trousers, but today she reflected the beautiful spring afternoon in yellow and cerise.

"You look amazing." I stepped back to admire her.

She pinched the material. "This old thing? It's not my usual fare but I'm off to see family later, and my aunt likes these colours."

We marched down the corridor to the small meeting room I'd managed to commandeer for half an hour. Already we'd eaten into ten minutes of our time. Deep in conversation, I didn't notice David coming towards us until he threw Kavita an excessively cheery, "Hello!" and paused, as if expecting her to stop and talk. She responded with a pleasant greeting but kept up the pace. I didn't look behind as we walked away.

Kavita had asked for a catch-up before the next youth group meeting but, during our short get-together, we said nothing that couldn't have been agreed by email or a phone call. I got the impression that she simply wanted to demonstrate that I was the main link between the council and their group after David's attempted coup the previous week.

When she mentioned Oliver's name, I glanced up, startled. *Oliver!* How could I have been so stupid as to think he'd like me? Thank goodness I hadn't told anyone. If Kavita had known, she might have tried to say something to make me feel better, which would have made it so much worse.

She turned to the next item on her agenda. "Oliver's sorted the insurance too, so we're all set."

"Just the publicity left to do for the opening."

"I was hoping you could get your press team to speak to the papers. My people can do the flyers. Are you up for a leaflet distribution session one evening?"

"I'm up for anything – if I can find a babysitter."

She raised her eyebrows. "I didn't know you had children."

"Just one. Josh. He's nearly three."

"Bring him. It's just a walkabout. I'm going to ask Oliver if the Samson's Café group could come along and help."

"In that case, I'll definitely come." She looked at me in surprise. Hurriedly, I added, "Not because of Oliver. I meant, if Josh can join us. Plus, my brother goes to that group. And Oliver's sister."

As my cheeks reached boiling point, she stifled a chuckle. With those hastily spoken words, I'd given away my feelings. Not that I had any chance, I wanted to say. But she'd know that too. Most likely everyone did, but me.

"That's what I thought," was all she said.

♦

Emma seemed enthused by the idea of moving the post office into the building with the library and café, so the other building could be leased or sold.

"But the space is too big for a post office, so they'll need a shop or something else there," I said.

She shrugged. "If the community is prepared to run it, you can find funding. Otherwise it's a business opportunity for someone. One that your postmaster should benefit from."

"And Derek?" I didn't need to say more. I wouldn't tell her what he'd said earlier either. That would be one for the weekend, when Leah and Rachel could rip him to shreds over a few glasses.

"Has anyone taught you to manage your manager?"

When I looked blank, she said, "As Portfolio Holder, Derek will want to look good to the whole of Holdenwell Borough, while Agnes needs her local community to know that *she* really did the work. I'll sow the seeds for Derek at the finance meeting on Friday. You can take the watering can next week." She chuckled. "Or rather, you can write a business plan setting out the options and potential costs versus income. You'll need to meet with property services first." She checked her list, reaching the final item. "By the way, how is the work with the Chartley library group going?"

"Fine. They're meeting again in a fortnight. I'm liaising with their lead, Richard Lewes."

Her face clouded and she opened her mouth as if to speak, but instead she slashed a blue line through the word 'Chartley!' on her pad.

"And is all well in the office?"

She meant David.

"As much as it can be."

A face peered through the glass panel on the door. The next meeting attendees had arrived five minutes early. I shut the lid on my laptop, assuming our discussion had ended.

Emma glanced behind. "They can wait. I don't suppose you've got a minute before your next meeting."

"I'm free all afternoon."

Her face lit up. "Great! That's just what I'd hoped to hear."

Minutes later, I left the room with a ton of work and the realisation that 'managing your manager' would be a useful skill to learn, in addition to never including 'I'm free' in a sentence.

Chapter 19

I REACHED THE NURSERY ON THE DOT OF FIVE-THIRTY, where I found Josh absorbed in a game of snap with one of the helpers. The pack featured animals rather than numbers. His eyes didn't stray from the cards, his grin widening each time another one appeared. I stood to one side, watching.

Josh laid down a card with a cow on it.

The helper laid a card... another cow.

"Snap!" Josh shouted, slapping his hand down. The table shuddered.

"What is this?" The man pointed to the letters and sounded them out. "C-O-W. Does that read dog?"

"Nooo, silly. Cow." Josh swept all the cards into a pile.

"I think you win," the man said. When Josh pouted, ready to demand another game, he lifted Josh's arm into the air. "I announce that Josh is the outright winner of the game. Make sure you put a gold star on your chart, because you are one."

Josh raced past me to collect his sticker, before allowing himself to be bundled into his mac and out of the door within minutes. As I passed the helper, I mouthed, "Thank you."

While Josh sang along to 'Old MacDonald had a Farm', I ran through the events of the day. From my fits of giggles with Tariq to my anger at Derek, the meetings with Kavita and Emma, and the pile of work I had to finish the next day before my evening meeting. Not one I needed to organise, thankfully, but a Neighbourhood Action Group meeting run by the police. With a jolt, I remembered my car tax. How on earth had I got almost two weeks into the month and forgotten to buy it? I had the money put aside but, with everything going on, I'd filed the letter and forgotten about it. The moment I got home, I'd go online and renew it.

The music had moved on to 'Wind the Bobbin Up'. Josh clapped along.

"Wind it back again," I joined in with the words, but I focused on the road, keeping a watchful eye for police cars while making sure I kept to the speed limit.

Finally, I slowed for the Court Park estate and, with a sigh of relief, turned the car towards the parking area for our block. As I edged along the road, lined with parked cars alongside Rachel's block, I frowned. Great! Not one but two police cars had double-parked, forcing me onto the muddy verge to get past. As I bumped the car up the kerb, I stole a look at the man sitting in one of the cars. Our eyes locked. Glenn, the police sergeant from the meeting with the Chartley residents. He spoke into his radio, while I eased the car back down the kerb, hoping he wouldn't think to check the status of my car tax.

Leaving everything in the car boot but my laptop, I piggy-backed Josh up the steps to our flat, pretending it was a game, but desperate to get inside. Once in the house, I turned on the laptop and slipped my debit card from my purse. Only when the screen told me that the car tax had been paid did I allow myself to breathe.

A message pinged on my phone. Rachel, I guessed when I saw it. She thought punctuation was a waste of energy, along with full words.

Theyre carting tfs off again

Glenn had come for the Flying Scotsman. Hopefully, whatever

he'd done this time would be the final straw for the housing department and we'd finally be rid of him. I wondered if it would be safe to go down to the car to fetch the bits I'd left behind, and decided it should be. We were far enough from Rachel's block and whatever was happening there.

I typed a quick response to her.

Just got back. I saw the police outside. You'll have to fill me in.

Josh gripped the rail as we went down the steps. He'd been excited to leave the flat, thinking we were going somewhere, but now slowed his pace when he realised it was a trip to the car and back. I opened the boot and pulled out the two bags, one with his nursery bits and the other with my work stuff. When I heard the rumble of an engine, I tucked Josh close to my legs. The car stopped beside us and I turned to find Glenn staring at me. He wound the window down and grinned, sarcasm and glee oozing from his voice.

"What are you doing here?"

I flushed. "I should ask the same of you. I thought you were based in Chartley." Then I panicked. What if the Flying Scotsman was in the car and thought I was a friend of Glenn's? In his view, that would make Josh and me his enemies.

Someone sat beside Glenn, his head cut from my view by the car roof, but I breathed a sigh of relief when I glanced at the rear seat. Empty. The Flying Scotsman must have been taken away in the other car. I wanted to find out what he'd done, but that would mean Glenn hanging about to tell me. Nervously, I glanced down the road, hoping the other car wouldn't drive past.

"I've moved to this neighbourhood team. It's a bit more exciting around these parts. Are you going to the NAG tomorrow?"

He must have seen my puzzled look, as he elaborated. "Neighbourhood Action Group."

Before I could answer, Josh tugged at my trousers. "Mummy."

I glanced down to find him staring at the police car, but when Glenn's gaze fell upon him, Josh burrowed his face into my leg.

"I didn't know you had a kid," Glenn said, in an oddly accusing tone.

"I've got ten more dotted around." Deflection with humour would be my best weapon here. My life was none of his business, and I wanted to keep it that way.

"Bring them all tomorrow night. That should double the meeting attendance."

He gave Josh a thumbs up and pulled away. Once the car moved out of sight, Josh said, "I got a peace car."

I reached for his hand. "Po-lice."

Rachel appeared around the corner, trailing a cloud of smoke. She'd failed in her bid to give up smoking again. I moved Josh and our bags across to the path, meeting her by the stairwell, where Josh squatted to examine a cluster of ants surrounding a half-eaten biscuit. I watched him while I chatted, fearing the odds of finding him eating an ant-infested biscuit were high.

She jerked her head in the direction Glenn had driven away. "Was that a social chat? Did they tell you what happened?"

"Nah – I mean, no. He was more interested in what I was doing here."

She tapped her head. "Duh! Going home."

Of course I hadn't told him that. I changed the subject to safer ground. "What was it about this time?"

"That bl—" She glanced at Josh. "Flaming man. He must've

lost a bet or something. Or maybe he got another letter from your council, but he was effing and jeffing in the walkway. People couldn't leave their flats in case he started on them." She ground her cigarette into the tarmac and kicked the stub down the drain.

I'd thought his last episode would justify evicting him, but I'd been wrong. Rather than giving Rachel more pointless platitudes such as 'this must be the last straw', I offered a cup of tea.

"Yeah, why not? Kieran's not home until late tonight."

Josh slipped his hand into hers and they walked together up the steps, while I followed with the bags.

When we reached the walkway, she said, "I meant to ask if you'd heard any more from that bloke you went out with."

"Sean? Why would I?"

When she raised her eyebrows, I added, "To be honest, I haven't given it a thought."

She accepted my truthful statement with a nod. Once inside, I switched on the kettle while Rachel sat on the floor with Josh and examined his police car. I brought the two mugs through on a tray, along with juice and a pot of yoghurt for Josh.

"Look at you – well posh. Next you'll be buying a teapot." She laughed as I placed the tray on the table.

"Dad's got one in the back of the cupboard somewhere. I might fetch it," I half-joked. Dad always said that tea tasted nicer from a pot, but he couldn't be bothered with the palaver for one person. Will didn't like tea.

Her comment about being posh reminded me of Derek's earlier remark. I didn't know whether I had the energy to face her indignation, but I ploughed on nonetheless. It would give us something else to talk about other than Sean or the Flying

Scotsman.

"You won't believe what Derek said today."

A roll of her eyes told me she'd believe anything he said. But when I relayed his words and how I thought I'd misheard him at first, she gasped.

"I know," I said. "I couldn't believe it either. But he actually repeated it." I put on Derek's pompous voice. "These people shouldn't be allowed to breed."

"Chance'd be a fine thing." Rachel's face fell and instinctively she touched her flat stomach. "No wonder we can't get IVF at the moment. Our address probably sends a red alarm flashing. 'Don't let them have a baby. They live in Court Place.'"

Her eyes glistened beneath her glasses. "I need the toilet."

I let her leave the room, blaming myself. Why hadn't I *thought* before telling her? She and Kieran would make amazing parents. Sod Derek and his disgusting attitude.

I'd always known that Court Place had a poor reputation, but I hadn't come across the likes of him in any of my previous jobs. Or had I simply not noticed? In the three months I'd been at the council, I'd come to realise it wasn't just him. In the meeting the other week, the woman in Meadow Manor had said she didn't want 'our sort' walking down their road, and even the police sergeant, Glenn, seemed bemused at the thought I might live here.

Rachel came back into the lounge, blowing her nose on a piece of tissue. "That's a sour face you're pulling."

"An impression of Derek."

Rachel glowered. "I wouldn't do too good an impersonation. Or I might thump you."

179

♦

I arrived ten minutes early for the Neighbourhood Action Group meeting at Holdenwell police station. Apparently, the location usually rotated between a trio of community centres, but the one chosen had suffered boiler issues a few days before, so this venue had been hurriedly announced. I'd assumed an evening residents' meeting held in a police station would put people off attending, so I was surprised to find all the visitor parking filled, with just one available space in the adjoining road. Maybe, like me, people were intrigued to see what the inside of a police station looked like.

Battered Venetian blinds hung along the rows of metal-framed windows on the stubby building. Paint flaked from the white fascia boards edging the flat-roofed porch, and weeds poked through the paving slabs. The dull concrete and unkempt appearance reminded me of the Court Park estate, minus the walkways and the balconies at the rear.

The reception area wasn't much more welcoming, even if the policeman behind the glass-fronted counter gave me a cheery, "Good evening." Plastic chairs lined two walls, behind which posters lectured on locks, keeping valuables hidden, and the difference between 101 and 999. I placed my bag on the floor beside the counter, wondering if the Flying Scotsman was somewhere in the depths of the station. Rachel hadn't reported his return.

"Can I help you?" the policeman said.

"I've come for the NAG."

Without making a joke – no doubt the acronym was too familiar to be funny – he asked for my details and handed me a pass. Then he pressed a button and the door beside me buzzed open.

"Second on the right, through the door."

A bland corridor with magnolia walls and blue carpet tiles – no different to those at the council – stretched out before me. I was disappointed to find I wouldn't be entering the hub of the station to see the police at work, but followed his directions into a typical meeting room, where all but one of the tables had been pushed against the wall. Rows of chairs lined the carpet, filled with an assortment of people: some sitting, arms crossed, while others turned in their seats, chatting to neighbours. Glenn and a policewoman sat at the top table, talking to a woman holding a Tesco carrier bag. Hoping he didn't spot me, I hurried over to the tea and coffee dispensers at the back of the room and poured myself a cup of weak tea.

I picked a spot behind a giant of a man whose muscular thighs rested on the adjacent seats. He stank of Deep Heat, at first comforting – in the sense it raised long-forgotten memories of Dad and his various pulled muscles – but it soon became cloying.

But while I wanted to learn about the issues faced by local residents, especially in areas where the work of the council and the police linked, I didn't want this meeting to mirror the one I'd attended in Chartley after the toddler had been hit by a car. There, in my unwanted position on the top table, I'd become the scapegoat for the residents' anger. Reasoning that the nauseous smell was a small price to pay to be hidden behind the man's broad frame, I sipped my tea, held my breath and waited for the meeting to start.

Glenn stood up and introduced himself and gave a brief rundown of the work recently undertaken by the police team. Residents joined in, with discussions centred around the speed

181

cameras being used in various locations. The jovial atmosphere contrasted with the previous meeting, and people snickered at Glenn's weak jokes. I listened with interest, knowing many of the roads and issues on a personal level. Finding it frustrating being unable to see anything, I shifted from behind my human barrier to the next seat. My view became the back of people's heads, which obscured the top table. Perfect! If I couldn't see Glenn, he couldn't see me, but I could see the audience.

A blonde woman put her hand up and Glenn invited her to speak. She stood up and cleared her throat. "I'm concerned about speeding on the bypass." She turned to the audience, her rings glinting beneath the harsh strip lights. "I was doing seventy down the bypass the other day and *still* cars were flying past me."

I wished I could see the expression on Glenn's face, but bemusement was clear in his voice. "You do know the speed limit is sixty there?"

Titters filled the room and a man two rows in front of me buried his head in his hands.

"That's my point," she said, missing his. "What are you going to do about it?"

"Well, I'm going to advise you strongly to keep to the speed limit for a start, because we have the speed van going out there soon. If you're doing seventy you'll be caught, along with all the others."

She clamped her mouth into a tight line. "So that's your answer?"

"What else do you propose?"

"A lower speed limit?"

Around me people sucked air between their teeth or shook their heads, while discontented mutterings came from near the front of the room.

Glenn continued to sound reasonable. "It's not an accident hotspot and, let's be honest, if you ignore a national speed limit sign telling you the limit is sixty, why would you obey one that said fifty? Now let's move on. We're still on speeding."

Hands shot up and Glenn picked another person, while the woman slumped into her chair, arms folded. Questions rolled on. Some I agreed with, others I thought pointless, but it certainly wasn't boring. I chuckled to myself. Two hours of speeding, burglary and anti-social behaviour had become compulsive listening, almost on a par with *EastEnders*.

"Right." Glenn sighed. "We've come to the exciting part. Any other business."

Another woman put up her hand and stood up. Her voice trembled. "The council has turned off the street-lights in my road. I can't see the entrance to my house. The other day I drove into the post on my driveway."

Had she really said that? Didn't her car have headlights? I sniggered, wondering how Glenn would respond.

"I think we've got someone from the council here." Glenn stretched so I could see the top of his head above the audience. "Where's Madeleine?" He stood up, craning his neck. "There you are. Do you want to take this one?"

Every single audience member twisted around to face me. Yet again Glenn had awarded me a seat on the top table, but this time without the buffer that a slab of wood – or melamine – would have offered. Deep Heat man's eyes bored into me.

What did I know about street-lighting? I knew there'd been a money-saving programme of street-light switch-offs in roads assessed not to need additional lighting, but that had been before I'd joined the council. Derek's sneering face swam into view. The original location for this meeting had been a community centre in his patch, which gave me an idea.

"Where do you live?" I asked her.

She frowned. "On the Barton Road."

That ran between Derek and another councillor's area. "I'm sure your councillor is Derek Hamilton. If you give me your details after the meeting, I'll ask him to get in contact with you."

He wouldn't like that. He'd probably try passing her back to me, so I'd tell him that she'd insisted on speaking to him.

The woman tried to continue but Glenn jumped in, clapping his hands together. "Well, I think we've directed that to the right person." He checked the time on the clock behind him. "I call this meeting to a close. Goodnight, everyone."

I threw my polystyrene cup of cold tea into the bin and walked over to the woman to write down her email address. Agitated, she tried to engage me in a longer conversation, pointing out that she was scared to pull on to her driveway in the dark. When I suggested installing lights on the posts, she flung her hands in the air and squealed in indignation. Nothing but the streetlights being turned back on would do. I stifled a yawn – not out of boredom but tiredness. Needing to get home for Josh, I kept it brief as I told her that Derek, as her councillor, would be her best option. If it wasn't him, I'd find the relevant person to respond to her. Then I hurried towards the door, where Glenn caught me.

"Sorry for catching you out there," he said.

"It seems to be a habit." I tempered my words with a smile.

He'd been right to ask me to respond to her issue. I did work for the council, after all. At least this time he hadn't tried to hang me out to dry.

"What were you doing at Court Place yesterday? Do you know people there?"

I frowned. What a strange thing to ask. But, recalling Derek's attitude, I found I couldn't deny my home any longer. If people only saw the likes of the Flying Scotsman there, no wonder they had such a bad impression of our estate.

"It's where I live."

"What? In single-mum city?" He looked stunned by my revelation.

Derek had once called it that. He'd followed it up by saying that people like me were 'scum'.

I glared at Glenn as I hissed, "Probably because I *am* a single mum." Then I shouldered past him into the corridor.

"Wait!" He hurried after me, catching up when I reached the closed door to the reception area. I pushed it. The door juddered against the frame.

Glenn stood behind me. "I'm sorry. I really am. I can't believe I said that. It's just…"

Again, I shoved the door, but it wouldn't budge. How did the stupid thing open?

I swung around to face him. "What? People on that estate are usually scum? Because that's the message I keep being told."

"No!" He stepped back in shock. "*No!* Not at all."

A woman walked out of the meeting room, throwing a curious glance in our direction. Glenn reached across to press a green button beside the door. It buzzed open.

"I'd be the last to think like that." He followed me through reception and into the chill evening. A welcome breeze cooled my face. "I was born there – lived in York House until I was eight. My cousin has a flat there and she's lovely. Although she's having a bit of hassle with one of the residents. You might know about him."

The light through the reception window bit into the night, but a few steps more and we'd be in darkness. I paused beneath trees that rustled in the breeze.

"The Flying Scotsman?"

Glenn nodded. "Janice is having a right time of it, but no one at the council is taking her seriously because she's from that estate."

Janice? Wasn't that the woman who lived by Rachel? The one the Flying Scotsman had blamed for 'grassing him up' when it had been me?

"Is that why you've transferred to this area?"

He shrugged. "One of many reasons. I'm hoping this latest incident will mean the courts aren't so lenient this time. We could go for an ASBO but it would be much better if the council moved him. I have no idea where, but those people don't deserve to live next to that."

Glenn's steady gaze met mine. If I tried again, would I be like Derek using my position to help my own kind? But that was flawed logic. The Flying Scotsman's behaviour affected so many people. That man at the meeting with the poorly wife who'd been threatened by him must be wondering why we hadn't done anything, even though I'd tried. Perhaps it wouldn't do any harm to take Derek's name in vain.

"I'll have another go with the housing people."

I could tell Derek I was pursuing his earlier request to help the man and his wife in Meadow Manor, while telling the housing department that Derek said they needed to sort the Flying Scotsman once and for all.

As I left Glenn and hurried across to my car, it occurred to me that life at the council had taught me one thing. Being duplicitous had its positives.

Chapter 20

THE FOLLOWING MORNING, after a constructive meeting with property services about the Didlingbury buildings, I called the housing department and asked to see someone in person. I didn't need to namedrop Derek because the moment I mentioned the Flying Scotsman – aka Melvin Scott, I learned – I was invited for an impromptu meeting with the relevant housing officer, who greeted me with a sigh and an explanation that they were doing all they could. And they were. When she dumped Melvin's bulky file on the table, I understood how much work he'd created. However, the legal process ground slowly and they had little choice but to follow it.

Apparently, she didn't particularly care about Derek, our Portfolio lead, demanding action either. She'd taken over the case recently and her previous excitement at the mention of Derek's name was due to her delight at finding more evidence against the Flying Scotsman, this time from outside the estate. While I felt better knowing how much was being done – and the sand *was* running out on his time at Court Place – I understood why other people would feel their issues were being ignored. They had no idea what was happening.

"Where will he go?" I asked the woman. "Once you sort this."

Her breath whistled between her teeth, taking with it her earlier enthusiasm. "Probably temporary accommodation. But that will be my colleagues' problem. And whoever has the joy of living near him."

Put him in Meadow Manor or Charlton Heights, I almost said.

That way they'd see how one bad egg could contaminate an estate. But I kept my sour words zipped.

"If you need more supporting documentation, let me know. There's a new police sergeant in the area—"

"Glenn." She chortled. "I spoke to him yesterday. He was keeping Mr Scott in the cells overnight to cool down and to give the residents a bit of peace."

Did she know I lived there too? I shrugged the thought away. Even if she did, this wasn't a self-serving act. The Flying Scotsman barely affected me, apart from when I needed to keep an eye out for airborne objects when walking to Rachel's door.

As I stood up to shake her hand, my tights snagged on a screw on the table leg, sending a gaping ladder down my shin. What a waste of money. No wonder I usually stuck to trousers. In disgust I ripped them off in the ladies and dumped them in the bin. When I walked back into the office, David glanced up from his keyboard. His gaze strayed to my bare legs and he sneered. Could he see the forest of hairs that my tights had barely covered? Stuff him if he could. I had just fifteen minutes to finish my emails before shutting down my laptop at one o'clock and leaving to collect Josh and then he would be out of my life for another weekend.

I spent an afternoon playing with Josh and watching TV while the washing machine churned in the background, creating Sunday's ironing pile.

My phone pinged a few hours later. Rachel.

All quiet on the western front

I typed back: *An exciting game of cars here.*

Bring them round for tea Im bored waiting for the gas man

Is he back yet?

189

She knew who I meant.

Janice says it wont be today

My bare knees had melded with the carpet fibres so when I eased myself upright, they resembled a pitted moonscape. As I brushed them down, embedded crumbs fell to the floor.

"Do you want to take your cars round to Rachel's?" I asked Josh, who had no difficulty in jumping to his feet. He grabbed a few favourite cars and dashed into the hallway, where I found him by the door.

"You need your shoes." I laughed. Gazing down at my crumpled clothes, I added, "And I need to get a pair of trousers on. I can't be seen out like this."

Even though we were just popping over to Rachel's I didn't want to spend the afternoon looking like I didn't know how to use an iron.

I thanked my lucky stars that I'd bothered to get changed when we reached the parking area outside Rachel's block and a police car pulled up. Glenn leaned out of the window. Even when smiling, he came across as smarmy.

"You following me?" he said.

I kept my tone dry. "I could ask the same thing."

He nodded towards the first floor and the Flying Scotsman's flat. "Just making our presence felt."

"So he's back?" I tightened my grip on Josh, who held his 'peace' car out. But Glenn didn't spot Josh tip-toeing to show that he too had a car with blue and yellow markings and a siren on top. Oliver would have noticed. I swallowed back the unbidden thought. It wasn't the same. Glenn was a police colleague I had no interest in, other than dealing with him about work.

Glenn nodded. He hung his arm out of the window, his fingers tapping the bodywork.

"We could only keep him overnight, until he got the alcohol out of his system."

"He's probably topped it up by now."

Tap-tap-tap went his nails on the paintwork. It set me on edge. I glanced behind, unnerved to realise that we stood in the firing line if the Flying Scotsman appeared with any missiles, which he might do if he saw me speaking to the police. I needed to get away from Glenn. I didn't want to go into Rachel's either – not with that man upstairs – but at least we'd be inside.

I lowered my voice. "Look, I've got to go, but I met with housing and they're doing all they can to speed things up. I'll email you on Monday."

He said something more, but I swung Josh into my arms – still holding his 'peace' car out – and hurried across the path to knock on Rachel's door. Through the glass her shadow moved closer until the safety catch rasped and the door clicked open.

"Whoa!" She stepped back as I shot inside with Josh. Frowning, she gazed out to Glenn in his police car. She looked from him to me. "Weren't you speaking to him yesterday?"

"Shut the door," I hissed.

She did as I asked before turning to me, looking puzzled. "Does he have a thing for you, or something?"

"Don't be silly. He's just looking out for his cousin, Janice."

Her eyes widened. "Janice from this block? Her cousin's in the police? No wonder she kept that quiet." She shook her head. "And no wonder the Flying Scotsman's got a problem with her."

Josh trotted back from his search to find Kieran and held out his cars. "Play cars, please."

"Of course, sweetie." Rachel ruffled his hair. "Just give us five minutes to get our drinks. I've got a lovely surprise for you too."

"Now you've done it," I said. "He won't want to wait."

Ne'er was a truer word spoken. Moments later Josh and I stood in the lounge watching Rachel hang over the back of the settee to drag out what appeared to be a thin rug. She unrolled it and placed it on the floor where it promptly curled back again, but not before I spotted what it was. A child's play rug with roads set within a town scene. I'd thought about getting him one, but had decided to wait until his birthday at the end of May.

"Wow, Rachel! It's brilliant. You won't be able to keep him away now."

"Kieran found it."

Josh knelt on one side of the mat, pulling his cars from his coat pocket. While he lined them up on the fabric road – the police car taking prime position at the front – Rachel used two metal dragon ornaments to pin down the opposite corners.

"They're unbreakable. Even if they weren't, I wouldn't care. I can't stand them." She got to her feet and gazed at Josh, her expression wistful.

In the kitchen, she returned to our earlier conversation. "This policeman then, he's just here to check on Janice, but he keeps bumping into you."

"He didn't know I lived here until last night." I didn't mention what he'd said about single-mum city. After all, he had apologised.

"Last night?" Rachel's eyes glimmered with interest.

"At the meeting. He was running it."

In silence, she poured boiling water into the mugs and bustled around the kitchen preparing Josh's blackcurrant squash. As she handed me my cup of tea and Josh's cup, finally she voiced what she'd been itching to ask.

"You don't fancy him then?"

I laughed. "Definitely not."

"Or this bloke Leah thinks would suit you? She reckons he's lovely."

"He's nice but not my type." An image of Oliver strolling away with his boyfriend crept into my thoughts. "Anyhow, why the questions?"

We went back into the lounge where we placed our hot drinks on the table away from Josh, although he was too engrossed in his game of cars to notice us.

"You seem preoccupied by something." She dropped to her knees by the car mat and I followed.

"Work, Josh, Dad, Will. I'll be shopping with Dad tomorrow, cleaning on Sunday, work the rest of the week. It's full on."

Not a lie. But not the truth.

I'd filled my time with everything but Oliver, leaving little room for him to squeeze into my thoughts more than a few times. But Rachel's questions about Glenn and Sean had drawn him to the forefront. Why had I fallen for a man who could never be more than a friend? I couldn't hide away from him to lick my wounds either, as I'd have to see him at Samson's Café this Wednesday and in meetings about the youth club.

"There was someone I liked." I didn't worry about speaking in front of Josh. He wouldn't understand. "We saw him when we came out of the restaurant on Saturday night and he set Leah's gaydar off."

"Aww, Maddie. Do you know for sure?" Rachel gave me a hug.

I fought back the tears that threatened to well. How stupid to get worked up about someone who'd never shown a jot of interest in me. All I had to go on was that his sister had said he liked me. But a busier than usual week of work, compounded by waking up early to get Josh dressed and fed before taking him to my cousin's or to nursery, and then doing it again in reverse order until Josh went to bed, had weakened my emotional barricade.

"When Leah said about him being gay, I just knew she was right. If you'd been there, you would have seen what she meant."

Rachel cuddled me tighter. "You'll find someone."

I dropped to my belly and grabbed the battered red car I'd driven around my lounge carpet half an hour earlier. I might have changed locations to do the same thing, but this time I had someone to chat to while we pushed brrmm-brrmms around the road.

"It's for the best." Then I fed her the line I used on myself. "I don't have time for a man."

♦

Saturday was shopping day. Josh and I arrived at Dad's house on the dot of ten, and Will answered the door, ushering us inside. He'd made more effort with his clothing. Gone was the usual sweater and jeans, replaced by a cream shirt and navy trousers. Puzzled, I assessed him.

"Going somewhere special?"

"Yes."

Astonished – he hadn't mentioned anything in our texts – I said, "Where?"

"Pizza with Christabel."

Oliver's sister had moved into first place in the running. "Crikey, Will. You're a fast mover. I thought you liked Erin."

"She asked me. As friends." He turned away, his cheeks crimson, and held his hand out to Josh. "Coming with me, little man?"

Leaving Josh with Will, I went through to the lounge where Dad sat on the settee, taking off his slippers. He held out his hand – an invitation to help him up – grunting with effort before he shuffled off, moaning about his creaking bones. I took in the coffee table – cleared of papers – and the windows, through which the sun dazzled. He'd taken down the nets. Now I thought about it, the house smelled different too. Of polish and detergent. The sound whistling came from whichever room Dad was in. I didn't know people still did that.

When Will came out, clutching his wallet, I nudged him with my elbow and jokingly said, "Dad seems a lot happier than usual."

"He's got a new friend next door."

"But Mrs Johnstone lives there."

"She died two months ago."

I frowned. "No one told me. She was lovely."

Will shrugged and moved away to the safety of the hallway. On reflection, I guessed why. The tone of my voice had made it sound as if I blamed him for not telling me about Mrs Johnstone, when Dad had probably mentioned it to me during one of our chats, when I'd been half-listening but not really focusing on his words.

I went in search of Dad to quiz him further then found Will in the hallway, holding his hands out, inviting Josh to punch his palms.

"Gentle, Josh," I said.

Will didn't look at me. "We're sparring like boxers."

He shouldn't be teaching Josh to hit people, but I didn't think he'd appreciate me moaning again.

"I wasn't having a go at you about Mrs Johnstone. I just didn't know."

Will kept his focus on Josh, clearly not interested in discussing his old neighbour. I changed tack. "What time are you meeting Christabel?"

"Lunchtime. After shopping."

"I'll drop you there. I can pick you up too if it makes it easier for you."

He paused to consider my offer, his hands dropping from their outstretched position. "Oomph!" He gripped his lower stomach, where Josh had scored a direct hit.

I shook my finger at Josh. "You weren't meant to punch him. That's bad."

Josh gazed at the floor but as I turned back to Will I glimpsed him sneak a look at Will's stomach. His expression betrayed more interest in the possible damage inflicted than contrition.

"He's getting strong." Will tensed his arm like a body builder and turned to Josh. "You'll be like me soon."

His muscles bulged beneath his shirt sleeves, but his stomach still clung to its seam of fat. Dad had called it puppy fat when we were younger, but it had really been the result of too many treats: people felt sorry for Will and insisted on feeding him. I'd benefited from this attention too, and my waistline hadn't thanked me. Since leaving home, I'd dropped pounds simply by not snacking.

Saying that, the extra layer had saved Will from the full effect of Josh's thump. I'd have to transfer Josh's energy to other pursuits, or I might have a lot of explaining to do at nursery.

Dad joined us in the hallway, straightening the sleeves on his thin jumper. A strange smell pervaded the air, bringing back childhood memories. Brut!

"Are you wearing aftershave?" I said, knowing full well he was.

He gazed at me, a picture of innocence. "And?"

"Will told me you have a new neighbour."

Dad shook his head at Will. "One Romeo is enough in this household."

Will flushed. "Alan, stop calling me that."

As I took in Will's reddening cheeks, I realised I'd missed the obvious. Will *had* transferred his affection from Erin. Good for him. At least his feelings would be reciprocated by the lovely Christabel, who'd told me at the park how much she'd liked Will. What a shame she'd got it so wrong about Oliver.

Chapter 21

WILL HAD BEEN ANIMATED on the journey to the supermarket and had seemed fine when we were inside, although he didn't squabble with Dad over their food purchases. Thanks to the pair of them bickering less than usual, we finished the shopping in record time. With the laden bags stashed in the boot, we drove in the direction of the town centre to drop Will off for his lunch date. The closer we got, the quieter Will became.

Two hundred yards from the drop-off point, we had stopped for some traffic lights. I moved the rear-view mirror so I could watch him. His fingers nipped the edges of his sleeve and he lifted his chin to rearrange his shirt collar. I'd be nervous too if I had the luck to be in his position.

"Have you got your money?" Dad asked.

Will patted his pocket.

"Isn't she paying?" I joked. "After all, she asked you."

"Don't tease him," Dad said.

I picked up the underlying message. Will could be a bit literal at times and if he thought she *should* pay, then it could cause a problem. An image of Will sitting there at the end of the meal with a wad of money, while Christabel struggled to stretch out her pennies, popped into my mind. Will wasn't tight but, when he knew right from wrong, he stuck to it.

"Point taken," I said. "Going halves never hurt anyone."

Dad glared at me and swivelled around in his seat to face Will. "Ignore your sister. Just do what you and Christabel think is best. If she wants you to pay, do it. The place isn't expensive. If she says

198

about going halves, that's fine too."

When I stopped the car near the taxi rank, Will gave Josh a flicker of a smile and jumped out. I leaned out through the car window.

"Have a lovely time, and text me when you're ready to come back." I glanced at Dad. "And ignore what I said. Dad's right."

"As usual," Dad muttered beside me.

Next we went to my flat, where I took my shopping inside and packed it away while Dad took Josh for a stroll around the estate, after agreeing to stay clear of the Flying Scotsman's place. Then we went back to Dad's to unload his bags.

After he'd finished, he surprised me by suggesting we go and sit in the garden as it was such a nice day. While Dad made the tea, Josh and I went outside to unstack the plastic chairs from beside the brick outbuilding and to wipe a winter's worth of grime from them. We lined them on the path beside a washing line strung with pegs. When we'd finished, Josh helped to take the blackened cloths indoors, dumping them in the washing machine before we went through to the bathroom – with just a sink and a bath – to wash our hands. Oddly, in their haste to move Dad and Will into this flat and release our old three-bedroomed house to a family, the council hadn't knocked down the wall that separated the toilet from the bathroom. The toilet stood alone next door, meaning you had to walk into the next room to wash your hands. Dad kept a pack of hand wipes in the loo, which half-filled the bin in the bathroom. I made a note to remind Dad to nag the council again about it. What suited people in the 1950s didn't necessarily work more than sixty years later.

The kettle hadn't boiled, but Dad had put a packet of biscuits and Josh's drink on the side. I took both into the garden, where I shielded my eyes while turning our chairs to face away from the low sun, which had appeared from behind a cotton-wool cloud. Josh refused the offer of a chair and crouched on the concrete path poking the weeds that crept through a crack until, defeated, he pulled his cars from his jacket and helped them achieve impossible stunts, accompanied by squeals.

Minutes later Dad joined us, shuffling down the path, taking care not to spill the two cups of tea. He handed one to me and sighed as he sat down.

His new neighbour had done a good job tidying her garden – unlike Mrs Johnstone, who had been too frail to deal with it. When Dad had moved in, Will or I had been let loose with the lawnmower and we'd dragged it around to hers, but mostly she and Dad had seemed to be in competition for the 'most unkempt lawn' award.

"Have you made plans for the garden?" My question was laden with more hope than he could have known.

To one side stretched a privet hedge that led to a wooden fence at the bottom, splotched with sage-coloured paint that dripped between the cracks, thanks to our neighbour's slapdash job. Better than the turquoise that had leached through when Dad first moved in but still annoying: we'd covered it with a timber stain the colour of creosote, which they'd spoiled by repainting their side again when we'd all had more important things to worry about with Dad. The fact that the splodges bothered me now showed me how far we'd moved on.

I turned away to the green chain-link fence that ran between his garden and the flat next door. The ceanothus bush had become unkempt, shading the surrounding bed, where weeds had beaten plants and slugs. Beneath its shadow the grass had become a crescent of hardened soil.

He shrugged. "A weed and a mow should sort it. And maybe a rose bush or two."

I chuckled at his underlying joke. He'd had two lovely rose bushes, which had been successfully transplanted from his old garden – until Will intervened. While Dad recuperated inside after the last of his chemotherapy sessions, he'd mentioned that the garden would need to be looked at come spring. Determined to do what he could to help Dad, Will found the keys to the outside shed and set about clearing the garden. It was a few days before Dad spotted the missing bushes. What Will had assumed were stubby thorn bushes had been thrown out with the rubbish, along with the snowdrops, which he'd ripped from the ground, thinking they were grass.

I couldn't say I would have done much better. Months later, Dad had come out to find me tending a perfect row of flowers in the bare patch left by Will. They were tall with delicate pink petals.

He'd scratched his head. "What I can't understand is how those weeds have grown exactly a foot apart."

"Weeds?" I'd blushed. "I thought they were the seeds I'd planted, so I thinned them into a line like the instructions said."

After that I'd chosen a book about flowers from the library and learned the names of plants but, to be honest, Will and I decided to leave the garden in Dad's safer hands, even though he was too exhausted to care much for it. But now he surveyed the 'flower' bed with interest.

"I think I will plant a few roses," he said. "And maybe get a few bedding plants too, when the frosts have finished."

He had no idea how much those words meant to me. He wasn't just showing an interest in his garden, but in the future. No one would buy flowers if they didn't plan to see them grow.

I downed the dregs of my tea, tucking the mug between my legs, before leaning across to give him a hug. "I love you," I whispered.

He squeezed my hand and we sat there, letting the peace settle upon us. Birdsong trilled in the air, an echo coming from distant trees, until it was drowned out by the yap of a nearby dog. When it quietened, we were left with the drone of a lawnmower. I breathed in the scent of freshly cut grass and shut my eyes. The sun burned orange through my closed lids.

My phone pinged. Leah.

R u in?

I typed a similarly brief response. *At Dad's.*

At the sound of the phone, Josh stopped playing and ambled over, holding his empty cup and a car. As Dad bent to ask him about his toy, my phone pinged again.

Wot time u back.

Waiting to pick up Will. Home by 3 or 4.

Her response fired back. *Okay. X*

Did that mean Leah would come around then or not? Should I ask, or just see what she chose to do later? I sighed to myself.

"Boyfriend trouble?" Then Dad chuckled. "Oh, I almost forgot. He fancies another man."

I pretended to punch his arm, stopping an inch away. Josh's eyes widened.

"I didn't touch him. That's important," I told Josh.

Again, my phone pinged. I glanced at it in annoyance. Was Leah aiming for a record with the most messages in a minute?

"Oh, it's Will." Surprised, I checked my watch. "He wants me to pick him up in half an hour."

"That's quick." A frown clouded Dad's face. "I hope it went well."

He'd echoed my thoughts. What could have happened to make them want to come back so soon? Did they have nothing to say to each other? Had they argued? Or – I shuddered – had they disagreed over the bill, thanks to what I'd said?

Dad looked worried too. He got up from the chair. "I'll come with you, if you don't mind."

Within five minutes we were in the car, Josh strapped in the rear car seat. It meant we'd arrive with ten minutes to spare, but I didn't care. The sooner we arrived, the quicker we'd know that Will was okay.

Exactly thirty minutes after he'd texted me, Will loped into view. Christabel was nowhere to be seen. His face was stern as he walked towards us, with not a glimmer of a smile, even though Josh called to him through the open car window. When he reached the car, he dropped into the rear seat.

"Where's Christabel?" I asked.

"Oliver picked her up," he said.

"Didn't he offer to take you home?"

"I told him you wanted to."

Dad butted in. "How did the meal go?"

Will shrugged. "I liked the meat feast pizza."

This was like pulling teeth. "You didn't spend long with Christabel. Did you have a good time? Come on, Will."

"I've told you. We had pizza and it was nice." He caught my eye and sighed. "I paid half the bill and then I texted you."

When Will turned to tickle Josh, making him giggle, Dad shrugged. "He had a nice time. Let's leave it there."

♦

I'd texted Leah to let her know I'd be home a bit earlier than planned. She promised to be at mine by three, but she was already in the car park outside my flat when I pulled up fifteen minutes early. Not spotting us, she gazed through the bramble-strewn fencing as a train clattered past. Strange that she hadn't gone around Rachel's to wait there, rather than stand outside a block of flats, I thought.

When I nudged the car into a parking space, forcing her to step aside, she grinned sheepishly, as if we'd uncovered her little secret. A closet train-spotter. I chuckled at the unlikely thought.

"Just watching the trains. Nothing else to do around here." She shrugged.

Why had she felt the need to explain? I gave her a mischievous look. "Don't worry. I won't tell anyone."

A metallic smell filled the air, as it did after each passing train, although some left the heavy stench of diesel. I opened the rear door and leaned across the seat to unclip Josh. He'd fallen asleep in the car but had woken up moments before we arrived. He swiped away my hands, determined to clamber out unaided, which meant us waiting for him. When he finally leapt from the car, Leah gave him a fist bump. He tugged her hand to pull her towards the flat, but she looked down the road.

"Coming inside?" I said.

She hesitated. "I was hoping we'd go for a walk."

I frowned. The words 'Leah' and 'walk' didn't usually go together.

"I could do with a chat." She squinted at the sun. "It's a nice day."

The sky was blue and dotted with puffy white clouds. Even where we stood, in the shade of the flats, it was warm. It wouldn't be long before it turned chilly, but we could head back before then. Although I'd changed him before leaving Dad's, I checked Josh's nappy. Thankfully dry, but I stuffed a nappy, baby wipes and his plastic cup into my bag, in case we had to stop and get him a drink.

"We'll have to go to the park, unless you want Josh interrupting us every two minutes."

"Let's go to Denefield. It's been years since I went there."

I frowned. Our usual park was miles better, and closer, but if Denefield had swings Josh would be happy.

We headed around the corner of our block – I didn't like taking Josh via the shortcut through the bin area – and along the road by Rachel's flat, avoiding the Flying Scotsman's missile zone. Kieran's car was outside, which explained why Leah hadn't asked Rachel to join us. He might offer to come along too and Leah needed to talk in private. Josh swerved towards Rachel's flat, but didn't argue when we kept walking. Instead, he called out to be swung between us while we walked, his high-pitched squeals of, "Higher, higher!" putting paid to any sensible discussion.

A lorry passed, buffeting us with fume-filled air. Then I noticed the speed of the cars flying past. They must be doing way more than 30 mph. I chuckled. Even on my days off, I couldn't escape from work.

We walked the length of the road towards the Denefield estate, our arms aching from swinging Josh. When I told him we needed a break, he agreed but slowed his pace to a crawl, until Leah suggested it would be quicker to swing him there.

"Remind me why you wanted to go to Denefield park?" I said.

"Look, let's go to The Cricketers instead. It's got this great beer garden with swings and stuff." She pointed across the road to an alleyway, which could be reached by a nearby pelican crossing. "If we cut down that alley, it's only five minutes." She bent down to Josh. "You could have pop and crisps. That's if your mummy says yes."

Josh jumped up and down, his puppy eyes pleading. I shot a furious look at Leah. What was she playing at? She knew that Josh operated on a finely honed system of cupboard love, and it would be all but impossible to get him back home without delivering the promised items. Her smug expression told me that, whatever her endgame was, she'd planned this master stroke.

"Looks like it's sorted." She held out her hand to Josh. "Come on. I'll let you push the button."

I hurried after them, punching her ear with a hissed, "What. Are. You. Doing?"

"This'll be miles better than Denefield park," she said in an amiable voice. "This way, we get to chat and Josh has fun too."

In other words, she wanted a drink. I sighed and gave her a look.

Grinning, she pointed to the 'WAIT' sign that lit the screen. "Patience is a virtue, you know."

Chapter 22

I GAZED IN DISMAY at the rough-looking pub. Banners strung across its fencing advertised various sports channels and a board showed the forthcoming football matches. But I allowed Leah to lead us around the side and through a gate, which scraped against the paving slabs when opened, where we found a pleasant rear garden with clean benches and empty ashtrays. Even better it had a wood-chipped area with a small adventure playground.

It was lovely sitting in a garden, sipping an orange juice and stealing the odd crisp from the huge bag in front of Josh. He eyed the wooden playground behind us, which included the mandatory – in Josh's view – swings.

"So, what do you want to talk about?" I'd tried broaching the subject earlier, after Leah had brought out the drinks, but she'd claimed she needed to use the toilet and shot off with her knees clamped together, as if to prove the point. I'd rolled my eyes, while Josh giggled and called her silly. He wasn't far wrong there.

But now she couldn't change tack. Or find another excuse.

"You." She held my gaze as she bent to sip her lemonade. (I'd nearly fallen off my bench when she came out with a tray laden with soft drinks, assuming she'd dragged me here because she wanted alcohol).

"*Me?*" My mouth fell open. "Why?"

"All work and no play isn't good, you know."

I glanced at Josh. "Well, I don't have much choice."

"'Course you do." She shrugged. "If you're talking about that gay bloke you fancy, there are others."

"I can't believe Rachel told you that!"

"Hang on to your knickers. Rach didn't give away your secret, although she should've. I saw you mooning after him, remember."

It was a bit of a coincidence that, within twenty-four hours of telling Rachel about my unrequited feelings for Oliver, Leah was haranguing me about my lack of love life.

We'd all planned to have a few drinks around mine the previous evening, but I'd cancelled because I'd been too tired. Instead, Leah must have taken her bottle round to Rachel's. While Rachel wasn't usually one for telling tales, after a few drinks she might have accidentally dropped a clue or two about my confession.

Leah waved her hand in front of my face. "Hello! You still there? See, you're mooning again and it's no good for you." She pursed her lips. "Rach and I can babysit at any time, but I can't do Saturdays." She knocked back her lemonade. "I mean it. Don't shut nice blokes out just because you think they're not your type."

I grinned. "Finished?"

"Just promise that you'll take what I said on board."

If it meant shutting her up... "Promise."

"Good." She pushed herself up from the bench. "You take Josh for a swing and I'll fetch us another drink."

"My round." I unzipped my purse and pulled out a tenner, which I stuffed into her hand.

With help from Leah and me, Josh had almost finished the bag of crisps. Salt and crumbs speckled his lips and his fingers shimmered with grease. I took a baby wipe from my bag and cleaned his hands and mouth, then I hefted him from the bench. When I put him on the grass, he took off, reaching the swing in seconds where he hung on to the seat, begging to be lifted.

I'd been pushing him for around five minutes when the back door of the pub opened and a tall man stepped out, carrying a tray. He had his head down, watching for the step. I turned back to Josh, who was pointing at a pigeon cooing on the fence.

The man put the tray on to the bench next to ours. When he looked up, I gasped. Sean! So that's what this was all about.

His stunned expression mirrored mine. He'd been set up too.

"Maddie." He said it as both a statement and a question.

"Hi." I grinned at him, but inside I cringed. Did he think I'd orchestrated this?

He came over to me. "Is this Josh?"

"Well remembered. Yes."

Josh gazed curiously at Sean. "Look!" He pointed to a squirrel gambolling along the top of the fence.

"A squirrel," Sean said, beating me to it. "And over there."

Josh tracked to where he indicated.

"I spotted a cat asleep under that bush."

"A cat?" Josh pushed himself from the swing seat.

"No, don't!" I grabbed the chain to bring the swing to a stop.

Sean helped me, holding the swing steady while I tugged Josh's legs from beneath the bars. "Sorry, I didn't think."

I shrugged. Why would he? That was my job. I kept a tight grip on Josh as we crossed the lawn to find the cat. The poor thing didn't need a wake-up prod. We knelt on the grass, and Sean whispered to Josh to take care not to frighten it. With one finger Sean lifted a trail of clematis that draped from where it entwined the bush above. A plump tabby cat with a shiny coat and pink paws surveyed us with unblinking eyes.

Once Josh had bored of looking at the cat, we moved on to

209

check the undergrowth for other creatures – where Sean pointed out beetles and worms – before going back to the playground. I admired his patience at answering Josh's incessant questions. With Josh tucked in the swing, our conversation turned to Leah, who hadn't reappeared.

"Did you know I was here?" I asked.

"She asked me to take her drinks out as she needed the loo. But I reckon it was a ploy. She's in there chatting with Paul."

"You reckon?" I laughed. Then I felt bad for him, being made to come outside when he could be in a warm bar, watching football. "You don't need to stay with us."

"If you don't mind, I'm happy out here with you both."

A glimmer of worry flitted through my mind – would he think this signalled the start of a grand romance? – but I shrugged it away. Leah might have plans for us, but we didn't need to play ball. Anyhow, it would be nice to talk to someone other than Josh.

When Leah came out twenty minutes later, she watched us from a distance before making her way across the grass. By this point, we'd enticed Josh back to the bench with the promise of lemonade. While he drove his cars over the table – using the glasses as obstacles – we chatted about the people we both knew. I found it easy to talk to Sean and soon relaxed. We were laughing about our schooldays and the rivalries between the local comprehensives – he'd gone to the one in Radley Heights where all the posh kids went – when Leah's arrival drew our conversation to a close.

I stood up. "I need to get back. It's getting cold."

"If I'd known you were coming, I would have driven," Sean said.

"We're fine, thanks anyway." I faced Leah. "Bit obvious,

wasn't it? Even for you."

She held out her hands, her face artfully innocent. "What's decided? Next date?"

Sean winked at me. "Marriage is definitely on the cards for both of us one day. But I have no idea who with."

◆

I paid for my relaxing Saturday when Josh woke up on the Sunday with rosy cheeks and grey smudges beneath his eyes. I checked his temperature, but it was normal. If he'd been ill, he might have lain on the settee, but instead he followed me around whining that he wanted to go to the swings, to Grandad's, to watch *The Simpsons*. I'd mastered the art of ironing and cleaning while looking like Jake the Peg with a clinging toddler as my third leg, but his grizzling tested my patience.

On Monday morning, I'd been about to call Emma and explain that I needed to work from home when Josh bounced into my bedroom, looking the picture of health. At nursery he tugged off his coat – turning the sleeves inside-out – and rushed off to the playroom without a goodbye. He was plainly feeling better.

Thanks to a broken-down car blocking the road a mile from the office, I arrived ten minutes late. I rushed into the meeting room, scattering apologies. Soon I wished I hadn't bothered. The meeting could easily have been conducted via a few emails. While pretending to type notes on my laptop, I checked my emails. Richard Lewes, of the Chartley library group, asked me to send documents to him ahead of our meeting. I did as requested before moving on to the next email, from Agnes Drew, who was

211

wondering how the meeting with property services had gone. In my haste to leave the office on Friday, I'd omitted to provide her with an update, which I hurriedly gave now. Then I remembered that the police sergeant, Glenn, would be wanting to hear what the housing team planned to do with the Flying Scotsman, so I emailed him, all the while making eye contact with the meeting attendees so they wouldn't suspect what I was doing.

Then I opened Kavita's email, which she had sent on Friday afternoon. Oliver's name leapt from the page. Her email started with an apology for the late notice, then moved on to explain that the flyers had been created and everything was in place for the youth club opening. The only workable date for the Samson's Café group was the coming Wednesday, so Oliver had sent an email asking for volunteers to distribute leaflets about the youth club opening session. According to Kavita, Oliver was sure the attendees would welcome the chance to do this, and he'd asked all the committee to be there too. Sure enough, my next email was from Oliver – blind-copied to the café-goers and, for a few of them, their carers – explaining that the café would be open, with Harry holding the fort, but those able to go leafleting would be welcomed.

It could be worse, I thought. With Will, Tariq, Erin and Christabel there, I wouldn't have to spend too much time with Oliver.

As the convenor brought the meeting to a close, I snapped my laptop shut, stuffed it into my bag and hurried out, checking my watch as I called a goodbye to everyone, so they knew I was too busy to chat.

My day improved when I found out that David had called in sick. When I offered to make drinks for the team, I discovered bags of doughnuts in the kitchen for my colleague, Theo's, birthday. I took one and carried it and a tray of hot drinks back to my desk. After wishing him a happy birthday and handing out the drinks, I settled into my chair and tucked in while my laptop whirred into life. To my dismay, a blob of jam splashed my cream blouse. No amount of attacking the stain with a wet cloth helped to get rid of the mark – all it did was make my top translucent, revealing my lacy bra. I sighed. At least David wasn't here to sneer at me, and I had a jacket for my afternoon meeting with the Chartley library group.

At one-thirty, I collected my papers and set off for Chartley. As I drove, I recalled Emma's frown when I'd mention Richard Lewes' name, and I felt a flare of anxiety.

When I arrived at Chartley town council office, Richard and his two companions greeted me. They led me through to a dingy room, where plastic chairs were set around a group of melamine desks that had been pushed together. Through the high windows I could see nothing but the grey sky. Richard made us all a cup of tea and even brought out biscuits, which I refused. I couldn't talk and eat. At that point, I remembered my stained blouse and wrapped my jacket more tightly around me.

The meeting seemed to go well. Unlike the Didlingbury group, the Chartley group weren't particularly concerned about their library staff. It was the second-largest library in Holdenwell Council's area, and one of the women pointed out that they'd be left with a library manager and another part-time member of staff, who'd be perfectly capable of dealing with volunteers. Uninvited, the phrase 'herding cats' popped into my mind. While it would be lovely for people to volunteer, they would need to be trained. Also, when most people thought of library work, they'd think about the fun side of it – handing out books and chatting to people – when there were plenty of less enjoyable roles that would need to be done.

When the meeting ended, Richard escorted me out past the clerk, who was taking a phone call. Outside, he shook my hand. "It's so nice to have such a conscientious person to deal with at the council. Thank you for emailing those documents. See you in a fortnight."

I had to raise my voice above the noise of the traffic. "Not a problem. Let me know what else you need."

I'd parked in the town centre car park, close to the library, not realising there was a small car park behind the council offices. At least the walk back meant I could stretch my legs. While Chartley had the usual Boots, Superdrug, a Sainsbury's Local, charity shops and a tiny WH Smith, it also had a wonderful range of independent shops. I couldn't help pausing to admire a stunning poppy print in the window of an art shop and some wooden carved ornaments in the gift shop next door. The smell of pastries and hot chocolate drifted from a café and I glanced through the window, marvelling at the array of cakes on offer. Something familiar about one of the customers made me pause. Yes, I'd been right. That was the same balding head with the closely cropped strawberry-blond hair I knew so well.

David must have felt my eyes on him – or else he'd been alerted by his acquaintance's puzzled glance in my direction – because he turned around. Our eyes locked. As always, I was the first to look away. Twice now I'd caught him elsewhere when he should be in the office. He wasn't sick. How many more times had he done this?

Back at my car, I put my laptop and bag into the boot, then slumped into the driver's seat and gripped the steering wheel. If it was David's neck, I'd sodding well wring it. At least then I wouldn't have to worry about what I should say to Emma about what I'd seen. That's if I should I say anything at all. Maybe silence would be better.

Chapter 23

DAVID BEAT EVERYONE INTO THE OFFICE the following morning. I didn't arrive until eight-thirty, when I found his possessions scattered over his desk, but no sign of him. My colleague Chrissie called me over.

"He was in before I got here at eight." Her eyebrows were raised in surprise. Then she leaned forward and hissed, "Something's up. When Emma came in, he rushed over and dragged her off."

I didn't mention that I'd seen him the previous day. After chatting for a minute, I switched on my laptop and went to make us both a cup of tea. Near the kitchen Emma and David sat on chairs around a small table, deep in conversation. No doubt he was feeding her a good story in case I told her I'd seen him the day before. At least it meant I no longer had to worry about it.

As I left the kitchen carrying two cups, Emma and David walked past. He threw me a look of jubilation, missed by Emma, who smiled. "Good morning." Then she uttered the words I'd come to associate with a mountain of work: "Can you spare a minute?" She checked her watch and held out her hand. "Which one's yours?"

She took the other cup from me and handed it to David, not noticing his scowl. "Give this to...."

"Chrissie," I said.

She ushered me back to the table where she and David had been a moment before. I lowered myself down and cringed. The chair was still warm from his body heat. She paused – a trick all bosses seemed to employ when they knew what they wanted to discuss but the other person had no idea. Was this about David? Or had something else happened?

She took a deep breath. "You were in Chartley yesterday?"

Why was she asking that? "Yes. At the library group."

"Did you get the sense that they were unhappy?"

The meeting had been nothing out of the ordinary. I'd answered most of their questions and promised to come back with responses to the ones I didn't know. When Richard had shown me out, he'd been complimentary about my work.

"Not particularly. They seemed eager to move forward. Before the meeting Richard asked for the financial documents and information on the book stock which I sent. They've raised a few other questions, but they seem straightforward enough."

"Who was at the meeting?"

I gave her the women's names. She frowned.

"Tread carefully. As you know, Mark Carradine is the councillor on this patch and there's a lot of politics involved."

I'd emailed him at the start of the discussions to invite him along, but he'd just asked me to keep him in the loop. At the time I'd wondered if that was because he hadn't forgiven me for telling him off in my first public meeting soon after I'd joined the council, but it was unlikely. With his job and his councillor duties, he'd be too busy to get involved at this very early stage. Once working parties were formalised in the relevant areas, there would be more to do.

"Mark was happy to be kept up to date."

Emma chuckled. "And at arm's length. But, seriously, make sure you're working closely with both him and the library service." With that she got to her feet, checked her watch and muttered apologies, leaving me confused. As I headed back to my desk I wondered if this had been a minor telling-off, which would be odd because I *was* working with the library service and they'd agreed that I would attend the initial meetings with the working group. And I *was* emailing the local councillor with all updates. Or was there a more sinister reason? Had Emma heard rumours that trouble lay ahead? Recalling her frown when I'd first mentioned Richard Lewes' name, I suspected the latter. But I couldn't tell for sure.

Wrapped up in my thoughts, I paid little attention to David as I wandered past, although I glimpsed him swivelling around in his chair, tracking me. I placed my tepid cup of tea on my desk, ready to make inroads into a stack of emails, which included sending Richard Lewes answers to his questions. It would be easier to call with the figures he wanted, but email would leave a record of our discussions. Thinking back to Emma's comments, I decided from now on that would be wise.

♦

I'd come to Dealsham for the youth club meetings but, other than parking beside the shops to go into the community centre, I hadn't seen much of the wider area. Like much of Holdenwell, this part of town had been built to accommodate people moving out of London. Rows of staggered terraces with wooden panelled frontages and flat-roofed porches lined the streets. Like Dad's estate, few houses had been bought from the council – or, if they had been, the residents hadn't changed the windows or roofs. But his estate was different: greener and more spacious. Here, car ports made of corrugated plastic in various stages of disrepair covered concrete drives while, behind the houses, alleyways shielded by high brick walls led to squat back gardens which barely fit a rotary line and a swing.

Nearby, a buzz of excitement filled the air. Will was looking forward to being let loose with leaflets. I'd wondered how Erin would take the news about his lunch with Christabel, but she was chatting with everyone, laughing as she prodded Tariq, who'd most likely told another bad joke.

Unable to face a walk at tortoise pace with Josh, I'd rediscovered the pushchair tucked into my car boot, but it had become the leaflet trolley as Josh refused to sit in it. Instead he clung to my leg, wary of all the people and our unfamiliar surroundings.

As expected, the youth club committee had come along, but just a few huddled together – while the others, including Kavita and Oliver, had peeled away to talk with other people. I glanced at the woman who always tried to insist I should take minutes at the committee meetings – believing that I was David's secretary – but, when our eyes met, she turned away. Unnerved, I shuffled closer to the Samson's Café crowd. While I hadn't expected us to become good friends, I hadn't done anything to make her dislike me either. Unless she thought I should give David credit for everything he hadn't done.

Kavita moved from where she'd been chatting with a cluster of young people – they lived on the estate and were keen to do what they could to help start the youth club – and came over to me.

"Thanks for speaking with your press people. Just another five minutes to wait until the local newspaper is here."

After I'd spoken to the press team about publicising the launch of the youth club, I'd mentioned the leafleting session and given the start time. They'd phoned later to say a photographer from the local paper would be there for six o'clock, which had surprised me. I guessed it must be a slow news week.

A sleek car pulled up – the photographer? – and someone I vaguely recognised stepped out. He didn't have a camera but wore a smart suit, as if he'd just come from work. I frowned, trying to place him.

As he strolled towards us, Kavita hissed, "I don't believe it."

Then it clicked. He was the local councillor. The one who hadn't wanted anything to do with Dealsham youth club. Until now.

"I wonder what's enticed Steve Lambourne here," Kavita said, her voice thick with sarcasm.

Usually, I'd be expected to go over and introduce myself to one of our councillors, but with a child strapped to my leg – I'd chosen to do the leafleting in my own time – it felt inappropriate. Apologising to Kavita, who understood my predicament but pulled a face about the one I'd put her in, I left her to welcome him.

Moments later the photographer arrived, met by Kavita and the councillor. I stepped aside while everyone lined up, and Erin asked to hold Josh for the photograph.

I doubted Josh would go, but shrugged. "If you can get him off my leg."

She shot me a gleeful grin when Josh allowed her to carry him. Grunting, she staggered off and I heard her say, "You're getting heavy."

Not one for photographs, I watched from a distance, taking joy in a beaming Will beside Christabel, who'd tucked her arm around him. My gaze travelled to the end of the row to Oliver, with his white-teethed smile. I glanced away to Erin, who was cuddling Josh. With a start, I realised that newspaper readers might assume she was a single mum with a child. And one with Down syndrome too. Stuff them if they did. I'd had enough of the Meadow Manor Daphnes of this world, with their bigoted and thoughtless remarks. Will and I had faced enough of those during our lifetime. While my decision to become a single parent had been a choice, of sorts, Will's Down syndrome hadn't.

At the park he'd been bullied by other children who'd noticed his different looks, the thickness of his glasses, and his health issues which, for him, included an inability to run more than a short distance. Thankfully, Dad had never been far from his side in those days. Even adults made ignorant comments. Dad had told me that, more than once, Mum had been told what a beautiful baby Will was and then, in the same breath, asked if she'd considered aborting him.

Will's laughter pulled me from my bitter thoughts. Something had tickled him and Christabel but, whatever it was, Tariq didn't share the joke. He towered behind them, beaming for the camera. Again, my gaze darted to Erin, who bounced Josh in her arms, untroubled by Christabel and Josh's new closeness. What had happened to make her so relaxed about it?

When the photographer stood up and thanked the group, they drifted into the small huddles of earlier.

Erin returned and dropped Josh to the ground. "Oomph." She straightened up. "He can come round with me."

"Great. I'll join your leafleting team too." No matter how lovely Erin was, I wouldn't be letting Josh out of my sight – he was in a clingy mood.

Oliver sauntered towards us, his hands tucked in his coat pocket. While Erin greeted him in delight, I managed a hello before dropping to my knees to fuss with Josh, keeping my head low to hide the self-consciousness that I knew must show in my face. But I could only re-button Josh's coat for so long, so I took a deep breath and stood up, to be met by his wide grin.

"You won't believe what I just heard."

"What?"

"That bloke over there was telling the photographer that he's been a big part of the work for this youth club and he's on the committee. Is he one of your councillors?"

I rolled my eyes. "For this area. We should invite him to come leafleting. That way there'd be a sliver of truth to what he's saying."

I hadn't met Steve Lambourne, other than in passing at work, but I had a good idea he'd say he had another obligation that would, sadly, prevent him from joining us. His Jaguar looked out of place on the estate. It would better fit a golf club. As he chatted to the photographer, his gaze strayed more than once to his car.

"Shame Dana isn't this area's councillor. She'd be up for it," Oliver said. "I work with her on another project and she's excellent."

"You'd never know she was in the same party as him. Talk about opposites. Have you come across Agnes Drew? She's really community-minded. Shame the ones like him, who do the least, make the loudest noise about what they've done, while the others, who actually do the work, just get on with it."

"Sounds like someone else we know." Oliver laughed.

David! I groaned. "He's quite something."

Then it struck me. Irked by the councillor's behaviour, I'd forgotten to fancy Oliver. Instead, we'd simply become colleagues having a moan about people taking credit for work they hadn't done.

Tariq joined us. He jerked his head towards Erin and Will. "They're boring tonight."

I grinned, unable to take offence. "I can imagine. It's not fun being a gooseberry."

He gave me a blank look but I was saved from any questions by Erin, who linked her arm through his. "You can come round with us, Tariq."

When Erin's offer didn't seem to perk him up, Oliver bent over to him, whispering, "You okay, Tariq?"

Tariq glanced across to Will, who had his arm around Christabel's shoulders. "I'd like a girlfriend," he said simply.

"You're not the only one." I spoke without thinking, and immediately wished I hadn't. Not only had I announced it in front of Oliver, but poor Tariq didn't need me feeling sorry for myself, especially when he'd just opened up about his feelings.

"I understand how difficult it is for you," I told Tariq in a motherly tone.

Erin tucked her arm through his. "My friend took me to another club the other day, where I met my boyfriend. You should come along. There's loads of people there. We play pool and there's a tennis table and other stuff."

So Erin had a boyfriend. Good for her. But no wonder Tariq felt out of sorts, with all his friends pairing up. I hadn't heard about this other group before. Even if Will was with Christabel, it would be nice for him to get out more.

Oliver turned to Tariq. "I heard about it starting up a few weeks ago. I was going to take Christabel and see if you all wanted to go too."

In the background, Kavita clapped her hands, calling for everyone's attention. We had an hour to leaflet our assigned roads.

Oliver rested his hand on my shoulder. "I'd better get back to Christabel and Will or they might forget they've come here to work." He walked away. His shirt had come loose and hung out over his jeans. I sighed. If only. I caught Erin watching me and blushed, even though she couldn't possibly have guessed my thoughts.

"Christabel said he liked you," she said.

"I know." I gave her a wry smile. "But, sadly, there's like and then there's *like*. And he just likes me."

I took Josh's hand, using my other to steer the buggy. "Come on. Let's get this leafleting done."

Chapter 24

THE FOLLOWING TWO WEEKS passed in a flurry of work, meetings and phone calls. The first night of the Dealsham youth club was a success, with sixty young people attending. Work moved forward on the proposals for Didlingbury library, with positive noises being made about the money that the council could make if the post office moved into the other building. We just needed to find a use for the additional space, but the postmaster seemed keen to be given the chance to develop a business plan for a shop.

Agnes Drew, the local councillor, frowned when I'd mentioned Derek being allocated some credit for the idea, then shrugged and said that community came first. In return, Derek suggested she was 'off her rocker' worrying about library staff, but he liked the savings shown in the report and the recognition that we had given him.

Another meeting with the Chartley library group committee passed uneventfully. This time it was also attended by colleagues in the library service. At the meeting we went through all the options. Everyone left smiling, after agreeing that we would work towards finalising an initial proposal by early June. The group were keen to press on, so we'd agreed to another meeting the following week.

Back in the office, David continued to ignore me, which made for a tense atmosphere at times, but didn't affect my work. Who knew what he might be up to when I turned my back? But I had more important things to deal with. I'd started working on a project to reduce social isolation, particularly for older men, in

Holdenwell. It chimed with me, knowing how tough it had been for Dad to make friends as a widower with young children, one with a disability.

My home life was as busy as usual. Will had just been on his third date with Christabel: a trip to the cinema, followed by pizza. On the Sunday I took Dad out to the garden centre and we fought the crowds to fill his trolley with two rose bushes, fertiliser and compost. I added a few trays of bedding plants, although Dad shook his head and warned me they wouldn't survive the last of the May frosts.

"At this rate it'll be autumn before they get planted," I'd moaned.

We'd spent a lovely afternoon digging the compost into the bed before planting the roses, along with the begonias, petunias and snapdragons I'd insisted he needed. Dad's energy and enthusiasm reminded me of the days before he got ill. When I couldn't get the fork past a large stone, he took it from me and stabbed it deep into the ground.

"Lightweight," he'd joked.

My gaze had turned to his neighbour's kitchen window, wondering if he was trying to impress her. But although I kept my eyes peeled, I didn't spot movement behind the nets. I couldn't wait to bump into the woman who'd somehow brought about this change in him.

Since we lived so close together, Rachel and I saw each other regularly. When Leah came around for drinks she mentioned Sean, but didn't push the point or suggest another meeting. Instead she told us about the short break Paul had booked for the following bank holiday weekend in Devon, her eyes sparkling. She made me envious – but thrilled for her – when she showed me pictures of her lovely B&B room and told me about the day trips they had planned. With her developing relationship came a change in her lifestyle. I had no idea Leah enjoyed visiting stately homes and walking around historic towns in preference to spending an afternoon in the pub. I wished we'd thought of doing such things before Josh came along.

The fortnightly Samson's Café meeting rolled around again. Will had been given a lift there. He'd also been offered one back, I found out later, but had turned it down; he'd told Oliver that I liked to pick him up.

When I hauled Josh out of the car that evening, I chuckled at how differently we saw things. While I considered picking Will up from Samson's as doing him a favour, he thought that the lifts helped me.

We'd arrived fifteen minutes early, so I didn't mind when Josh dawdled to the café. I feigned interest when he pointed to a piece of chewing gum embedded in the pavement which he said looked like a face. But we both stooped to gaze at a stag beetle clipping across our path, its black body iridescent in the evening sun. I hadn't seen one in ages and pointed out its antler pincers raised as if prepared for battle – then saved it from a swift poke by grabbing Josh's hand. We moved on after it had made its bumpy way over the grass verge and moved into the undergrowth.

A tinny sound reached us by the row of shops, growing louder until, two doors from Samson's Café, I could make out the words and the thumping beat. Curious to find out what lay behind the – strangely – closed blinds on the café windows, we picked up speed. I pulled open the door, to be hit by a blast of heat and noise and the smell of perspiration. Inside, the tables and chairs had been shunted to the edges of the room and a dozen or more bodies leapt around, holding aloft their mobile phones and torches so beams of light cut into the gloom.

Looking nervous, Josh lifted his arms up to be carried. I hefted him onto my hip and sidled past an unfamiliar man who was jabbing the air as he stood next to a small flashing speaker. Will, who'd perfected the art of dad dancing, gave me a wave but didn't stop bobbing to come and greet us. I stepped past a smiling helper, who stood, arms folded, by the door, and into the sanctuary of the back room, where Oliver and Harry leaned against a countertop.

"Bit lively out there!" I called. The noise swallowed my words, but they caught the gist.

Harry shook his head wearily but Oliver chuckled. He raised his voice over the din. "Erin brought her new boyfriend." He glanced up at the clock. "It's time they wound it down, though."

"The pleasure is all mine." Harry disappeared through to the main café area, and clapped his hands and shouted, "Okay, guys!" But either no one heard or they chose to ignore him, as the intensity of the music didn't change.

"Guys, that's enough now!"

Oliver and I grinned at each other. He opened a cupboard and pulled out a saucepan. When I handed him a dessert spoon, he pointed to the neighbouring drawer, which held an assortment of wooden spoons, among other objects.

Oliver mimed to Josh to cover his ears and went to stand beside Harry. I followed with Josh, backing away when the wall of heat hit us. I decided to watch from a distance.

Harry cupped his hands around his mouth and bellowed,

"That's en—" only to be cut off by Oliver bashing on the saucepan. As silence punched the air, he stopped. "Enough, guys. It's time to pack up."

Groans filled the room, but the ravers shuffled off to collect their coats and bags.

"Next time it won't be music. Sadly." Harry pulled a sorrowful face. "But hopefully it'll be sunny enough for a picnic and the legendary Pooh sticks. We'll meet at the park entrance. If anyone can't get there, let me know."

I chuckled at his ability to act crestfallen. While Harry had an excuse for not enjoying the music – I guessed he was in his early forties – Oliver and I weren't much older than the revellers. What was our excuse? My clubbing days were long gone. All I could think about was the kettle and armchair that awaited me at home.

A flushed Erin came over, dragging a red-faced man behind her. His fringe appeared to have been dipped in water, with a dark strip from which beads of sweat clung like decorations. She linked her arm through his and puffed out her chest, seeming to grow an inch taller in delight.

"This is my boyfriend. I met him at Monday club."

Oliver stood beside me, his arm brushing mine. Penned in by people barging past, I couldn't move. When the gentle scent of his aftershave enveloped me, it took all my willpower not to lean closer, but Erin moved away so I stepped into the space she had left. Josh chose that moment to grab hold of my hair and tug it. Wincing, I tried to disentangle his fingers, but it was difficult to carry him and pull my hair free. Oliver leaned across to unpick Josh's fingers from my hair, which defeated the point of me moving away. "I'm taking Will, Tariq and Christabel next week.

That's if Will doesn't insist on you driving him, like he did tonight."

It would be lovely to share the lifts, especially if it meant Will doing more activities. I understood why Tariq's parents couldn't take him – his mum had MS and his dad was her carer – and Erin's dad worked until nine on weekdays, which made it more difficult as her mum couldn't drive. So far, my Wednesday evening work meetings had fallen between the fortnightly Samson's Café sessions, but that wouldn't always be the case. If Oliver could help on the occasional Wednesday, I didn't mind sharing the Monday club drive when I could.

"I'll tell him it's that or he'll have to pay for a taxi. I know what his answer will be."

As Josh tried to wriggle from my arms, I glanced over to Will, who stood by the door clutching his anorak. "I'd better round everyone up."

"Just Will," Oliver said. "The others were happy to come with me."

"Here, have your nephew," I told Will. Both child and adult seemed to be surprised at the offloading, but I didn't care. My back ached and I longed to get home and slump in front of the TV. "Come on, let's go."

We stepped outside, to be greeted by a blue sky and a warm breeze. In the gloominess of the café with the blinds down, I'd forgotten it was a spring evening outside. I took a deep breath, letting the stifling clamminess drift away before following Will.

We'd gone no more than a dozen steps when Oliver caught up with us. "I forgot, I wanted to speak to you."

Intrigued, I gestured to Will to hold on.

"It's about David," Oliver said. "I heard on the grapevine that he's up to his old tricks at work. I don't know what, though."

He hadn't told me anything I didn't know already, so I went to thank him, but he continued. "It's just that he's good friends with one of the people linked to Chartley library. I don't think you've met them. To be honest, I wouldn't have made the connection, but I remembered you telling me when we were leafleting the other night that you were working with the group."

I frowned. "I am. We had a meeting a few days ago and it all seemed fine. I've got another next week."

He gazed back towards the café, where Christabel had stepped outside holding a broom.

"I'd better finish clearing up. Look, I don't mean to worry you, but the way I look at it, forewarned is forearmed."

Chapter 25

NOTHING I HAD SEEN OR HEARD in the week since I'd spoken with Oliver suggested David had anything up his sleeve. Ignoring me, he kept to his standard two positions: either hunched over his desk, bashing the keyboard with his index fingers or laid almost vertical in his chair while chatting on the phone. The only changes were that he was in the office every day and he'd been unusually subdued during that morning's team meeting, with none of his usual butting in or regaling us with his extensive knowledge. Even Emma had noticed, as she'd asked him if he wanted to add anything, but he'd declined.

Since then, the time had ticked by more slowly than usual, until just twenty minutes remained until I had to leave for Chartley. Unlike other library group meetings, this one was being held at six-thirty to accommodate the committee members who worked full-time. It meant I had more time to think about what Oliver had said. Several times I found myself turning to gaze at David, wondering whether I should try to find out whether Oliver's warning bore a glimmer of truth. But I couldn't. Any possible olive branch had withered months ago, taking with it the prospect of a civilised discussion.

I tried to talk sense to myself. What could David have done to cause mischief? Even if he told the group that I'd taken his job – which he still believed – any person with an ounce of intelligence would know it wasn't true. Maybe he planned on taking credit for the work I'd done at Chartley, just as he'd done with the grant for the youth club? But, apart from sending the group the necessary paperwork and liaising about their proposals for the library, there wasn't much in the way of progress to show yet.

Lost in thought, I packed up my laptop and paperwork. As I did so, Emma looked up. "This is has just come through, in case you missed it." She pointed towards her computer screen and an email from one of the library team. "Kim has just emailed to say that Mark Carradine is attending this evening's meeting."

Mark Carradine? Odd that he should want to come when I'd been told the Chartley group weren't fans of his. Richard Lewes, in particular. I glanced across at David, but he didn't appear to have heard Emma's comment.

"I don't think I can reschedule my plans for tonight." Emma frowned. "If I can, I'll be there, but I'm sure it'll be fine. You and Kim should be able to handle this."

I'd met Kim several times. She was leading the work around transferring libraries to the communities and was more than capable of dealing with Richard Lewes. But the fact that Emma was considering changing her plans unsettled me. She obviously thought there was a chance, however slim, we would need her help.

I gave her a confident smile. "I'm sure it'll be fine."

She mirrored my expression. "I'm sure it will."

♦

Usually I met with Richard Lewes and his fellow committee members in the back room of the parish council offices, but tonight he'd booked the large meeting room at Chartley library, which could be accessed from the outside when the library was closed. As I cut across the slabbed pavement, I bumped into Kim and we exchanged pleasantries. There were too many people around for me to mention the email she'd sent, although I itched to do so.

The group reached the door and one man held it open to his companions. He signalled for us to go through, but his friendly smile changed to a frown when he spotted my council lanyard and badge.

"One of them, are you?"

His tone didn't indicate whether he intended to make a joke or an observation, so I shrugged. "That seems to be the case."

A hubbub echoed into the hallway from the meeting room – at odds with the usual quiet of a committee meeting. Odd, I thought. When I stepped inside, I was taken aback by the number of people there. Beside me, Kim's face paled, but she straightened up and walked briskly into the room.

As expected, a table had been set out with a dozen chairs around it. But behind it lay four rows of chairs – no, make that five – filled with people. A buzz of anticipation filled the air. The audience looked as if they were waiting for a performance to start. My mind whirled. Why were they all here for a small committee meeting? Public meetings had already taken place with the library service, and more might be held. This wasn't the time or the place for one – not when the agenda focused on the paperwork and finances relating to the future community library.

I took the seat at the end of the row beside Kim. She caught my eye and looked across to the audience, her meaning clear. Did I know about this? Baffled, I raised my shoulders. I had no idea. Richard sat at the other end of the table, twiddling a biro while chatting to the committee chairman.

Then I spotted Mark Carradine in the doorway and a shiver ran down my spine. His shocked expression told me he hadn't expected this gathering either. Pursing his lips, he pulled out the chair opposite me, which banged against the metal table leg. Excitement rippled through the crowd.

The chairman called the meeting to order. Richard Lewes lowered his head to mask a smirk, which widened when the chairman began by explaining to Kim, Mark and me that many people in the town were interested in the work that was being undertaken and had come along to learn more. While Kim's tension palpably deflated, Mark Carradine's jaw tightened as his angry gaze roamed the rows. He scowled at Richard Lewes and crossed his arms. His posture made me prickle with unease. What was about to happen?

I didn't have to wait long to find out. After the usual apologies for absences and confirmation of the previous meeting's minutes, Richard Lewes stood up and cleared his throat. The other committee members settled back in their seats.

"A library is the lifeblood of a community. Without one, many people cannot afford to read. But it is more than a place of books. It is a community hub, where people can come together. The older members of this town…" – he paused to look at the audience behind me – "know how vital it is to have somewhere they can go to simply sit and read, to take their children and grandchildren, to use the computers, to learn technology. But…" He left the word hanging while his gaze travelled from me to Kim and finally Mark Carradine. Until now, I'd agreed with everything Richard had said but, from his darkening expression, I knew he'd prepared the noose from which we would swing. "These people want to take this all away from our fine community."

"Balderdash!" Mark Carradine exploded. He turned to Richard Lewes. "You know full well that's not the case."

But Richard Lewes pointed his pen at me.

"If that's not true, why won't Madeleine send me the financial information along with everything else I've asked for on countless occasions?"

What? Of course I'd sent him all the paperwork! He'd praised me for my prompt response to all his requests. Stunned, I said, "What do you m—"

Richard Lewes cut me off. "It's as if the council is deliberately trying to sabotage the process so they can close our library."

Gasps and jeers filled the room.

I gulped, unable to believe he'd lied to my face. "But I *have* given you everything."

"So you say!" a man hollered from just yards away. "But we know what you people are like."

Mark Carradine frowned. Did he think Richard Lewes was telling the truth? I had to make them see sense. Surely they'd believe me. What reason would I have to lie? My legs trembled as I got to my feet and turned to the audience, which blurred into a sea of angry mouths and indignation.

"That's not true. Richard has already confirmed by email that he's received everything he asked me for." I held out my phone, which held all the emails we'd exchanged. "It's all on here."

A man jumped up from his chair in the front row, stabbing his finger at me. "You're disgusting." He stepped closer.

Corralled between the table, chair and Kim, I couldn't back away. He'd moved to less than an arm's length from me, his weathered cheeks threaded by a network of purple veins, his eyes bloodshot, saliva stretching like bars between his lips when he snarled, "Look at you trying to save your job with your lies!" Spittle shot from his mouth and landed on my burning cheek. I wiped it away with my sleeve.

These were intelligent people. Why couldn't they see they were being manipulated for whatever ends Richard Lewes wished to achieve? I tried again.

"You've got it wrong. I've sent Richard everything. We don't want to close the library."

Mark Carradine stood up. "That's *enough*!" He turned to the chairman. "I don't know what's happening here, but it is *not* on to abuse council staff."

Sneering, the man moved back to his seat, to be patted on the back by others. I looked gratefully at Mark. He'd come full circle since the first public meeting I'd attended, when he'd held me out as bait to lure the residents away from him.

But any hope I might have had that he'd calm the situation died when someone else jumped up and bellowed, "So, Mr Councillor, you tell us. What are your plans for this library? And don't give us any baloney."

The heckles sounded like Question Time in Parliament, except the MPs had a speaker to keep order. Here the chairman refused to step in and quell the audience.

Agnes Drew and her kindly group of helpers at Didlingbury library popped to mind. They genuinely cared about their library staff and the community, whereas here much of the action seemed to be more about political point-scoring. Not one person had mentioned the library workers. I knew from what Richard Lewes had already told me that the staff weren't foremost in his thoughts, and I didn't know if he really cared about elderly and vulnerable residents either. But why had he joined the library committee if it was just to stir trouble?

"Come on, Richard. Many of us know the real reason behind this charade." Mark Carradine sounded bored, but the pulse beating in his jawline betrayed his calm exterior.

The meeting erupted. A few people sniggered, as if they knew something the rest of us didn't, while others leapt up, pointing and jabbing their fingers, fighting to be heard. Mr Spittle joined in, firing the stuff in all directions. I shuffled my chair closer to Kim's, wishing I hadn't chosen to sit nearest the audience. Scratch that! I wished I was anywhere but here.

The room closed in. My chest tightened. Desperate to get away from the furious man yards from me, who was bawling, "Sack the lot of them!", I pushed my chair away from the table, knocking my pen onto the floor. As I bent to pick it up, I saw one of the female committee members, who I'd met previously, nudge Richard Lewes's leg with her foot. When I sat back up, I found them smiling in delight at each other.

The chairman stood up, wearing a benevolent expression. He raised his arms, palms outstretched, as if in surrender. But it was clear that whatever battle plans had made this evening, the library committee had won.

"I think!" he shouted. Lowering his hands and his voice as the noise levels waned, he said, "I think we've shown the council how much Chartley values its library. I can assure you that the committee and I will strive to ensure it remains for another fifty years."

He paused to allow people to call, "Hear, hear" or "Too right."

and took a deep breath.

"Thank you for attending tonight. But now I propose that we take forward the rest of the meeting with the committee and the council. We will ensure that you are all kept abreast of proceedings, but rest assured your presence has strengthened our hand."

The audience stood up, chatting and laughing as they filed out, with the exception of the angry man, whose furious "Pah!" hit the back of my neck. I closed my eyes, longing to be able to step into the shower and wash him away.

When the door banged shut behind the last person, we watched them through the large windows. They gathered in righteous huddles, not realising they'd been fed the story they'd wanted to hear. But while I couldn't blame them for caring, I wished they'd spent a few moments to consider the human being behind the badge. The one who had to look after Josh tonight and tuck him into bed, when all I wanted to do was bawl my eyes out. I glanced down at my hands, which trembled.

Richard Lewes turned to me. "I expect you'll finally send the promised emails tomorrow, will you?"

Before I could respond, the woman opposite sighed. "Oh, belt up, Richard. There's no need to keep on with it. Everyone's gone now."

Chapter 26

BEFORE ANYONE COULD SAY another word, Mark Carradine got to his feet.

"This is the only time you will ever get to pull this stunt. Take this as a final warning. Try it again and see what happens."

I glanced at Kim, surprised to find her nodding. After thinking about it, I came to understand their position. If we were to form a working relationship, there had to be trust on all sides, including ours. How I would ever trust these people again, I didn't know.

Within half an hour the terse committee meeting broke up. Kim, Mark Carradine and I packed up in silence. As we filed out, leaving the committee members to discuss their next steps, Richard Lewes' gaze never left Mark. His eyes bored through the window when we stopped to chat outside, where the victorious spectators had stood earlier.

Every fibre of me trembled. I'd never had anyone shout at me like that before. In fact, I couldn't remember anyone other than Dad raising their voice to me – and I didn't blame him for the few times he'd got to the end of his tether when Will and I had played up as children. But the angry man at the meeting had been different: aggressive and scary. My cheek tingled where his saliva had landed. I longed to scour myself clean.

"Thank you for standing up for me. I did send Richard everything he asked for."

Mark swiped his hand through his hair. "That Richard Lewes is a bloody idiot. He's been waiting for this moment for years. He blames me for his estate agent's business going down the pan in the recession, but he did that all himself. He's a snake. It's not my fault people didn't trust him and sold through us instead."

"You're an estate agent?"

He scowled. "I ran the business until some idiot convinced me to become a councillor. My son is running it now. I keep my hand in, though."

He glanced through the window to where the committee members were standing up. "Fancy a drink in the Red Lion to get over that mullering?"

I shook my head. "I have to pick up my son from the childminder."

Kim checked the time on her phone and shrugged. "I've got twenty minutes until my husband arrives."

I walked with them to the High Street. As we reached the corner where we'd go in separate directions, Mark paused.

"It's odd, but a friend phoned me today to say something was up. He'd bumped into one of the committee members in the pub last night, and he told him to come along to the meeting today and have some fun." He put air quotes around the word 'fun'. "Shame he didn't think to ask what it would involve."

I stared at him. That explained Mark's decision to attend, but something else seemed to be bothering him. He rubbed his chin. "The thing is, my friend didn't think it was anything for us to worry about, as the committee member was with someone my friend recognised from the council. But that doesn't make sense. If it was a staff member, he should have warned us. I wonder if he knows this man's name."

Oliver had warned me that David was friends with someone on the committee! The council worker must be him. Who else could

241

it be? I didn't know whether to say this or leave Mark to find out for himself. I decided on the latter. Right now, I didn't need any more hassle. I just wanted to get home, wash, and give Josh a cuddle.

Goodbyes said, I walked away from them towards the car park behind the High Street. The last time I'd been in Chartley, I'd admired the wide array of shops, but now I didn't even glance through the windows. As I cut through the alleyway towards the car park, I tore my council lanyard from my neck and stuffed it into my bag, quickening my pace. I didn't want to bump into angry man or any of the committee members on their way home.

There was something familiar about the tall man who sauntered towards me, his head down as he rifled through the pocket of his jeans. A crumpled receipt tumbled to the ground and he stooped to pick it up. His blond fringe hid his face until he straightened, then his eyes widened with surprise.

"Maddie!"

"Hi, Sean." For some reason, my voice shook.

He frowned, his gaze boring into mine. "Are you okay?"

He couldn't have said anything worse. It took every ounce of willpower not to crumple into tears and wail about the awful experience I'd just endured.

"Fine." My attempted smile felt wonky, as if the corners of my mouth refused to lift. "A bit tired, that's all." I glanced away in case my welling eyes betrayed me. "I'd better go. My cousin's looking after Josh."

His hand rested on my shoulder and he bent down towards me. "If you're sure you're okay."

I pointed to the car park, where I'd parked in the bay beside the footpath. "My car's just there. It's the Fiesta."

"Next to mine."

A 4×4 sat a few spaces from my car. I couldn't help saying, "At least you can get in and out of that one without getting stuck."

He grinned. "You'd need a ladder, though."

I gave him a playful swipe. "Cheeky!"

As I walked away, I realised he'd made me forget the meeting for a moment. When I reached my car, I turned, to see him standing at the end of the alleyway making a phone call. He raised his arm to wave, and I waved back. When I pulled away, he was still there, but when I drove past the alleyway entrance in the High Street he had gone. I felt a strange jolt of disappointment.

♦

My first job the next morning at work involved forwarding all the members of the Chartley library committee a copy of every email Richard Lewes and I had exchanged, even though it was unnecessary. They knew I'd done so. The chairman confirmed this by emailing me to tell me there was no need to fill up his email box, but I didn't care, and pinged another five off to them all.

"You look a bit happier than I would have expected." Emma dropped her laptop bag onto the desk and dropped into her chair.

Kim had phoned me while I dropped Josh at nursery to ask how I was feeling. Before hanging up, she said she'd call Emma next.

"Have you spoken to Kim?"

Emma nodded. "And Mark Carradine, who is on the war path. He reckons one of this council's staff members was involved with last night's fiasco."

Instinctively, I glanced across to David, whose index fingers hovered above his keyboard. He couldn't bash away *and* eavesdrop on our conversation at the same time. His face was blotchy, his expression pinched. I turned back to Emma, who'd tracked my gaze. Her expression darkened. The last thing I needed was for David to think I'd told her. My job was becoming difficult enough without his friends and allies making it harder.

"I'd heard," I said. "But I don't know who."

"We'll find out soon enough. Mark Carradine has left a message for his friend to call him back."

Her ominous words must have reached David as he sprang out of his chair, clutching his phone and his coffee. In silence we watched him scurry between the rows of desks and into the kitchen where, no doubt, he would be phoning his friend to try to stop any mention of his name leaking out.

"Was it him?" Emma asked in a matter-of-fact tone.

I shrugged. "I can't say for sure."

She pursed her lips. "What did he hope to achieve, though?"

To make me leave my job, I thought, but I didn't say anything.

Emma opened her laptop and connected it to the main screen. "Did Kim tell you they've managed to relocate all but two of the library staff so far who didn't want to take voluntary redundancy? One of those is the Didlingbury librarian, who should be able to keep working there if we can get the building hire or sale through. Which you will."

Her words focused my mind. Stuff David. Jobs were at stake here. Volunteers were giving up their time to shore up their communities. And I had work to do to help them.

"The library group in Didlingbury is a lovely bunch. *All* the library groups are great." But then I remembered last night and the committee smirking as that awful man bawled at me. I couldn't help but add, "Except for Chartley."

"Don't take it to heart. It's politics at play. They don't dislike you, just what they think you represent."

I pulled a face. "Is that meant to make me feel better?"

About ten minutes later, a scowling David returned to his desk. As the morning progressed, the steady thump of his fingers on his keyboard began to sound like a shovel digging an ever-deepening pit around him. When Emma left for a meeting and David disappeared in the direction of the toilets, a few of the team sneaked over to me.

"Do you know what's up?"

"Do you think it is related to what happened last night, Madeleine?"

"I heard about that. Poor you. What a nightmare!"

As they spoke, they darted glances towards the double doors, clearly worried that David might appear and catch them being nosey. I gave a heavy sigh, leaving them in no doubt about my thoughts, without giving anything away.

"Who knows? This is David, after all."

They nodded, but their expressions told me my answer hadn't fed their appetite for gossip, but I was saved by the clang of doors behind us. My colleagues spun around in shock, guilt plastered on their faces, and took it as their cue to head back to their desks. It wasn't David, but a man carrying two boxes.

By three o'clock, David hadn't reappeared. His laptop remained open on his desk, the council's logo and strapline on his screensaver announcing our commitment to residents. Desperate to get away from my desk and the curious eyes of my colleagues, I checked my pocket for change and got to my feet.

"Would anyone like anything from the café?" I asked. They all shook their heads.

In the café most of the food had been cleared away, leaving a few cakes and a fruit bowl on display. Tariq stood behind the counter wiping the inside of the glass display units, but placed his cloth down when he spotted me.

"Hello, Maddie." He clamped his hand to his mouth. "Oh! Can I call you that?"

"You're an old friend, Tariq. You can call me whatever you like."

When a devious grin lit his face, I added, "Anything polite, that is."

"So not Mad, then?" He looked pleased with himself, until Elaine walked out of the office. He puffed out his chest and said in a formal voice, "How can I help you?"

Elaine threw me a smile and walked off to tidy the chairs and tables. I gazed at the small selection of cakes, not fancying anything stodgy. I plumped for an apple.

"50p." Tariq tapped the price into the till and held out his hand.

"Did you go to Monday club?" I asked him.

He glanced over to Elaine. "Oliver took us. It was great."

"Were there girls there?" I didn't mean to tease him, but I remembered how left out he'd felt when Will and Christabel had paired up and Erin had found her DJ boyfriend. It would be lovely for him to meet someone too.

He blushed and gave me a coy look. "Yes."

"You can tell me more when I see you next week," I said.

Again, he swung around to check Elaine's whereabouts. Seeing that she was emptying one of the bins, he beckoned me towards him. He must have found a girlfriend already. How exciting.

Leaning over the counter, he cupped his hands to his mouth. "What's worse than finding a worm in your apple?"

For a moment he had thrown me. But this was Tariq and he did love a joke, even if this one was on me. "I don't know – what's worse than finding a worm in my apple?"

"Finding half a worm."

He gave me a knowing look and went back to his cleaning duties, leaving me to turn the apple over in my hands to check for signs of a tell-tale hole. When I got back to my desk I put the apple to one side, feeling dubious about eating it in front of people. Did Tariq know something I didn't? Spitting out a mouthful of apple wasn't a good look in the office.

David's desk was as he'd left it three hours before, while Emma had returned from her meeting and sat at her desk, focused on her screen, her lips tight, her jaw clenched and her eyes too bright. Disquiet pervaded the atmosphere, as if no one knew what to make of David's disappearance or Emma's silent fury.

She swung around to face me. "What have you got on tomorrow?"

"Other than emails and finishing this report, just preparation for next week's workshop and the grant application for the men's group. I'm off tomorrow afternoon." I added the final sentence in case she'd forgotten I didn't work on Friday afternoons if I'd had evening meetings during the week.

"You can do that from home?"

For some reason, I felt it wasn't a question but a command. I hadn't planned to work from home as the workshop preparation was easier to do in the office, but I gave her the answer she wanted to hear.

"If I take the marker pens and flipchart paper with me."

"Good." She smiled, but it looked strained. Then she gave a deep sigh and her expression lightened. "Sorry, I've got a lot on. But there's no point you coming all the way into the office tomorrow for a half day when your work can be done at home. It'll give you a more time to enjoy the weekend with your lovely son too instead of travelling back and forth."

"I understand," I said, although I didn't.

She checked her watch. "Why don't you get everything you need together and go home a bit early?"

Something was definitely up. But what? Clearly it involved me. Had David been spreading more lies, or had I said or done something wrong? Didn't she want me in the office? Whichever it was, I wished she'd tell me rather than sending me home to worry alone. Before I could say any more, she jumped to her feet and strode out of the office, leaving the double doors to slam behind her.

Theo swivelled around and used his feet to roll his pedestal chair next to mine. His eyes glittered with excitement. A smear of yoghurt or something daubed his crimson tie. As he leaned forward, the smell of garlic wafted towards me.

"I heard on the grapevine that David had something to do with that rumpus last night."

"Did you? How?" I played innocent.

He shrugged. "Mark Carradine was giving David what-for in the corridor."

"No!" I gasped. Councillors weren't meant to get involved in matters relating to council officers. If he'd shouted at David or said anything inappropriate, he could be in trouble too. "Who told you?"

"It's all round the building. I'm surprised you haven't heard. It doesn't make our team look good."

It certainly didn't. I half-wished I'd told Mark about my concerns regarding David the previous night. At least that way I could have placated him before he found out for himself. But it still didn't explain why Emma wanted me out of the way. Did Mark Carradine think I was involved – even though I'd taken as much of a drubbing as him – and that I'd planned this with David? Surely not.

After thanking Theo, I turned back to my laptop. The words blurred on the screen. *Enjoy the weekend with your lovely son*, Emma had said. How would I do that now?

Chapter 27

IT WAS ALL VERY WELL taking workshop materials home, but it involved keeping a grip on a toddler while carrying rolled flipchart sheets, a laptop, a handbag and Josh's bags up two flights of stairs, then trying to locate a front door key from a handbag that kept slipping down each time I bent over. Thankfully, a passing train entertained Josh, who pressed his face between the green-painted bars to watch it while I rummaged through my bag.

As I stepped into the lounge, brushing my fingers through my hair, which had been tangled by the wind, my mobile rang. I dropped everything on the table, except the flipchart pad, which unfurled and crashed onto the floor, and pulled my phone from my pocket. Emma. Why would she be calling me at six-thirty?

Nerves burbling, I took a deep breath and answered. "Madeleine speaking."

She took an age to respond, which didn't help with my agitation.

"Sorry, I just had an email from Derek."

Was that the reason for her call, or why she'd taken so long to speak?

"Have you got a pen and paper handy?" She didn't sound angry. Just distracted.

"Hold on."

Josh had settled down by his garage, making happy *brmm-brmm* noises as he drove his cars down the ramp, which meant he wouldn't disturb me for a few minutes. I pulled out a chair and sat down, rifling through my bag to find a pen. Rather than undertake a further search for my pad, I bent down and ripped off a section of flipchart sheet.

"I'm ready."

"Your priority job tomorrow morning is to give me a statement on what happened at the library meeting. Word for word. I don't care about office politics or how this affects you or the team – just be honest. I also want you to provide a full and accurate statement on your previous dealings with David and the grant funding. And…" she hesitated. "This is to be kept separate. I'd like you to explain why you thought that David might have had something to do with last night's meeting. I saw the way you looked at him."

"I can do that, but any suggestion that David was behind last night would be hearsay."

She sighed. "I think it's gone beyond that. But please don't speak to any of your colleagues about this. It is a serious matter."

When she ended the call I sat in silence for a moment, trying to absorb everything she'd said. I wasn't in trouble, but I couldn't see how this would bode well. If David saw my statement, he'd really have the knives out for me.

The sound of the doorbell cut into my thoughts, and I got up to answer it. An unfamiliar silhouette stood on the other side of the opaque glass. Too tall for Rachel or Leah – my usual visitors. It might be the gas or electricity man here to read the meter, but they'd never been this late before. A terrible thought struck me. What if the Flying Scotsman had discovered that I had reported him to the council? I tucked the thought aside. Battering the door down would be more his style, not ringing the bell. I slipped on the safety chain and pulled the door ajar.

"Sean! What are you doing here?"

He flushed at my obvious shock.

As I pushed the door shut so I could unclip the safety chain, it occurred to me that it looked like I was shutting him out. "Hold on," I called.

When I unlatched the door, he was glancing down the walkway, as if about to leave. Behind him an empty crisp packet twirled, whipped high by the wind, and the treetops beyond the train line bowed.

"I'm sorry, I shouldn't have come."

A gust of wind blew through the open door, drawing with it the faint scent of his aftershave. A nice smell. Strange how he didn't seem to tower over me in the way I remembered either, but he seemed a nice height. Once a teacher had told our class never to use the word 'nice' as it was meaningless. What was nice, other than something inoffensive? Sean would be hurt if he knew that's how I felt about him.

He held a bouquet of freesias and irises. Blues and pinks. Beautiful.

"I shouldn't have brought these either, but…" His voice trailed off and the colour heightened on his cheeks. "I was worried about you yesterday."

Now I felt bad. He'd gone out of his way to check on me, even buying a gorgeous bunch of flowers – just the kind I liked. I took them from him and lifted them to my nose, admiring their gentle fragrance.

"Come inside." I stepped back to usher him through.

He followed me into the kitchen, where I took a pint glass from the cupboard and filled it with water.

"Do you fancy a cup of tea or coffee?"

"Coffee would be great, thanks."

While I bustled about making the drinks and snipping the ends off the flowers, he stood by the door. He didn't say a word or raise his eyebrows when I put the flowers in the glass and rearranged them, but I felt I had to explain.

"I don't have a vase. I never have flowers."

"Please don't tell me you have hay fever," he said.

"Just a lack of admirers." Then I cringed. "I'm not saying that's what you are."

He laughed. "We'll be apologising all night if we worry too much about what we say. Think of me as a friend who's just making sure you're okay."

I handed him his coffee and showed him through to the lounge. Josh spun around in surprise and leapt to his feet, clutching a car.

"Hello, little man." He used the same expression Will did with Josh. Without being asked, Sean put his mug on a coaster on the mantelpiece, out of Josh's reach. "What's that on your cheek?"

He picked off a flake of green paint and showed it to me.

"That's from the balcony railings. He was watching a train go past earlier."

"I loved cars and trains as a child. What I wouldn't have done to become a mechanic, but my parents wanted me to join the firm."

We'd never spoken about his job – or mine, for that matter. But then – schooling aside – we'd never had a one-to-one conversation before that strayed too far into our personal lives.

"What is the firm?"

"We have a small chain of supermarkets. Don't you hail from the Roundel Way estate? We have one near that."

"By the pizza place? My friend Erin works there!"

"Erin? She's amazing, isn't she?" He grinned. "She puts me in my place if I do or say anything that doesn't follow the rules on running a supermarket."

I chuckled, remembering how Will had gone to ask Erin out but she wouldn't speak to him as she was working. Poor Will had been so dejected – but look at him now, happy with Christabel.

The conversation moved on. Before I knew it, I'd told Sean about the previous night, about the wider issues at work, Dad and Will, and he'd told me about his parents and many sisters.

Then he raised his hazel eyes to mine and a flush crept over his cheeks. "I'm meeting my sister and my niece at Potterham model village on Saturday afternoon. Would you join us?"

I swallowed. Would that be too much like a date?

He seemed to sense my hesitation and held up his hands. "Just as friends."

Last year, when I'd taken Josh to Potterham model village, he'd been too young to take much of an interest in the trains, model houses and figures. This time he'd enjoy it more, although he'd probably run me ragged by bolting here and there, trying to touch everything he shouldn't.

"I don't finish shopping with Dad and Will until twelve or so."

"Great. I could pick you up at one."

Josh sat on the floor crashing two cars together, before driving his police car around making *nee-naw* noises, even though most police cars nowadays don't make that sound. Sean had never seen him being anything other than good. What if he decided to have a tantrum if he couldn't touch the trains?

"You may live to regret this," I said. "Josh can be a handful at times."

"What, that little angel?" Sean said with a straight face. Then he grinned at me. "Only joking. I have seen the terrible twos in action. Don't worry."

♦

After we'd said goodbye to Sean, I went through to the kitchen. Josh had been given his tea at nursery, but my stomach rumbled in angry waves. The last embarrassing one had been the catalyst for Sean leaving – he realised I hadn't eaten and he was keeping me from my dinner.

I settled on a speedy meal of baked beans on toast and popped an extra slice in the toaster for Josh, knowing he'd drool like a dog over my food if I didn't.

"Come on, little man." I beckoned for Josh to follow me through to the lounge and chuckled. Now I was calling him that too.

Usually we took our seats at the table, but all my work and Josh's bag lay strewn across it from where I'd dumped them to take Emma's call, so instead we sat on the settee. Josh sat with outstretched legs and his plate balanced on his lap. I curled my legs up under me, taking pleasure in the naughtiness of eating while watching TV. That is, until Josh wiped his buttery fingers on my favourite cushion.

From then, our evening followed the standard routine: a short break before bath and bed for Josh, while I had the luxury of a few hours to watch TV in peace before clambering into bed.

The next morning, I decided to leave the workshop materials on the table and get on with the statements I'd promised Emma. I'd cancelled Josh's morning at nursery, so he played with his cars while I stretched along the settee with the laptop resting against my bent legs. It felt decadent but, in reality, saved straining my neck by looking down at the screen for too long.

The statements and emails took longer than I'd expected, not leaving me time to sort out the workshop materials. I made a start on the grant application, although it wasn't easy to concentrate with CBeebies blaring from the TV. Understandably, Josh had tired of his cars after a few hours. When the clock ticked around to one o'clock, I made our sandwiches, refilled Josh's bag in case he needed a drink and nappy change while we were out, and headed for the park. Grey clouds hung ominously in the distance, so I packed his coat too.

As we walked through the estate, with the flat windows draped with assorted nets and curtains, clothes hanging from lines on the rear balconies, verges churned from where cars parked on the grass, I realised that I hadn't worried about what Sean would think when he'd arrived at my door the previous night. If it had been Oliver, I would have panicked, seeing my home through his eyes. Was that because I felt more comfortable with Sean than I'd ever felt with Oliver? Or simply because I didn't care what Sean thought? While I mulled this over, Josh stooped to admire worms and ants, making our ten-minute journey last forty-five minutes.

At the park I pushed Josh on the swing and monitored the clouds rolling towards us. Perhaps if I cut short our trip to the park, we could go shopping today. Josh and I could then take Dad and Will in the morning and help them pick what they needed, which meant I would get home earlier and give myself more time to make myself presentable for Sean.

Stunned by the thought, I almost forgot that Josh's swing was flying towards me. Just in time I caught it and gave it a hard shove, sending him flying back with a "Wheeee!"

There. I had it.

I *did* care what Sean thought of me.

How very odd.

Chapter 28

SHOPPING DONE AND JOSH FED, bathed and put to bed, I made a start on clearing the table. Rachel had a new board game she wanted to play later. (We lived the high life.) Since there was little space in the lounge, I took the flipcharts, sheets and pens upstairs and stashed them at the bottom of the wardrobe, along with my laptop, which lived there at evenings and weekends.

When Rachel and Leah arrived, each holding a bottle, I pulled out the wine glasses and settled down to figure out the game instructions with Rachel, while Leah tapped the side of her glass.

"So you're seeing Sean tomorrow," she said.

I glanced up to find her wearing a mischievous grin. Rachel didn't raise her eyebrows, which told me they must have discussed my potential romance on the way over.

"As friends."

"Why've you gone red, then?" She held her hands to my face as if to warm them.

I pushed them away and turned back to the instructions. "Don't be silly. Let me make sense of this in peace. It's like a Mensa test."

But then it struck me. What had Sean said to her?

"How do you know, anyhow?" I tried to keep my tone nonchalant.

She grinned. "Don't worry. Seany Babe hasn't been shooting his mouth off. His sister told me."

"His sister? Why?"

"She wanted to check out the nutter who was dating her beloved brother."

Rachel slapped her arm. "Don't tease her." She'd taken her glasses off to wipe them on the hem of her shirt, leaving a sharp indent on each side of her nose. "When Sean told his sister that you'd be joining them, she did the usual thing and called Leah to get the low-down on you."

"That's what I said." Leah opened a bag of crisps and stuffed a handful into her mouth.

I felt uncomfortable at the thought of his sister checking up on me. Maybe I should text him and cancel? But I didn't have his number. I eyed Leah's phone. It would be on hers. She must have read my thoughts, as she slid the phone off the table and tucked it between her legs.

Pointing to her mouth, she crunched her crisps noisily. Then, wincing, she swallowed the lot in one go. "Don't think you're getting out of going, missus. Anyhow, even if you don't have fun, Josh will."

♦

I woke before my alarm went off to find Josh gazing at me, his lips black.

Eh?

Blinking, I tried to focus. What on earth had he done? Then I spotted the wall behind him, covered in black scribbles, and I shot out of bed. As I did, I realised the sheet and pillowcase had become his canvas too.

"Josh! What have you done?"

Grinning, he held up his weapon – a marker pen he must have found at the bottom of the wardrobe. I couldn't have closed the door properly when I stuffed everything inside. I snatched it from his inky hands, horrified to see it was a red pen. Where was the black? Then I slumped back onto the bed. My bedside table, the radiator, even the carpet were covered in scrawls in black, blue and red indelible ink. What else would I find if I left the bedroom? Luckily the stairgate meant he couldn't get downstairs.

Without another word, I picked him up and carried him through to the bathroom, where I caught sight of my face in the mirror and squealed in shock.

"Josh! I can't believe it!"

He giggled and prodded my face, but I wasn't in the mood for jokes. I dumped him on the floor, shutting the door behind us so he couldn't run away.

"This is ridiculous. You know you're not allowed to use pens. You're a very naughty boy!" I shouted.

I turned back to I examine my face, which he'd artfully covered in zebra stripes on one side, including my chin and forehead. Thankfully – if it could be classed as a mercy – the other half had been protected by being embedded in the pillow.

How had he managed to do all this without waking me? Leah and Rachel had left by eleven o'clock and I'd gone straight to bed. I'd had just two small glasses of wine throughout the evening – not enough to make me comatose. I must have been exhausted after my difficult week at work. But, while my body had decided I needed to rest, Josh hadn't agreed.

"What am I going to do?"

As Josh sobbed, I grabbed his hands and turned them palm upwards. They were covered in pen marks. Horrified at the amount of scrubbing that would be needed to get us both clean, let alone the bedroom, I turned on the taps and glugged bubble bath into the tub as if it was free. Josh decided he needed to raise his decibels above the noise of the gushing water. As his howls echoed through the small bathroom, firing through my shattered nerves, I ripped off his ruined pyjamas, ignoring his furious fists as he fought me off.

When the bath had reached a few inches deep, I checked the temperature and dumped him in the water. He wouldn't sit, so I left him standing while I grabbed the hair-washing bowl and the flannel – a lovely white one with an embroidered Thomas the Tank Engine at the corner.

"Sorry, flannel. It's time to die," I muttered, and soaped it. Holding the back of Josh's head so he wouldn't smash into the tiled wall trying to evade me, I rubbed the ink from his mouth.

Although it seemed mean, it felt like an apt punishment for him, since I'd have to spend the morning scrubbing myself, the paintwork and the carpets. But as I rubbed first his face then his hands, dyeing the flannel charcoal, I realised that no matter how hard I rubbed, an imprint remained on Josh's skin. The black might have gone, but it had been replaced by a faint slate-coloured tattoo.

Half an hour later we emerged from the steaming bathroom, wrapped in towels. My face felt raw, the skin tingling where I'd tried to scour the black lines, but the faint grey blemishes wouldn't shift. From my bedroom came the sound of the alarm on my mobile phone. How long it had been playing, I had no idea. I kept the alarm on at weekends so I would wake around the same time as Josh. It hadn't worked this morning.

I hurried over to my bedside table, to find the alarm had started just five minutes earlier. Although I'd spent ages attempting to scrub myself and Josh clean, it was just past seven o'clock. But there was a silver lining to this morning's dark cloud. The extra-early start gave me a few hours to clean my bedroom and make Josh's breakfast before driving over to Dad's.

♦

A hanging basket hung on a shiny bracket by the door – further evidence that Dad had regained his interest in gardening and flowers. I pressed the doorbell and stepped back to admire the purple surfinias, red geraniums and the other dainty blue and white flowers that crept through holes in the moss. More of the basket than flowers could be seen, but it wouldn't be long until the blooms had filled the spaces.

Muttering filtered through the door, then it was opened. Without so much as a hello, Will turned and trundled back to his room.

"Alan's in the lounge," he called over his shoulder.

"Aren't you coming shopping, Will?" I said to his retreating back.

He wore a new grey hoodie and dark jeans, although he'd put on odd socks, one striped, the other black with a pink band across the toe and heel.

"Yeah. I need my shoes."

I gave a silent victory jig. He hadn't noticed my face: proof that the double layer of foundation had worked. I carried Josh through to the lounge, where I found Dad tying his shoelaces. He gazed at Josh and frowned.

"Has he been eating liquorice?"

"Marker pen." I hadn't plastered Josh in make-up, so his lips still had a grey tinge.

Dad nodded, as if a child eating a marker pen was the most natural thing in the world. Perhaps it was. I'd heard some of his stories about our childhood. We must have been nightmare children to look after, particularly with Dad being on his own. I remembered bus journeys to the hospital for appointments relating to complications causes by Will's Down syndrome – we'd spent the journeys spent bickering and fighting, while Dad pleaded with us to behave. No wonder he'd aged so much in comparison to his peers, and even more so after his cancer treatment.

When Dad bent down to tie his other lace, I spotted a letter on the coffee table, and picked it up to read it. The logo showed a tree and the name of the local garden centre. Not the usual hospital or rejection letter. My heart leapt.

"You've got an interview!"

"Have you ever thought about joining MI5?"

I chuckled. "Have you got interview gear?"

"Gear? Like Will.i.am in there? He's gone all down with the hood, as he keeps telling me."

At that moment, Will came into the room sporting a pair of trainers and dark sunglasses, his hood pulled up. He folded his arms and looked over the rim of his glasses. "You can call me Will.i.am."

"I heard," I said. "Except you've gone up-with-the-hood."

Will frowned. "No, it's down, not up."

I'd learned not to try to explain my bad jokes. "Come on, you two. I need to hurry. I have places to be this afternoon."

Dad raised his eyebrows in interest. "And where's that?"

"Potterham model village. We're going with a friend."

"That sounds nice."

He turned to watch the postman walking down the path holding a bundle of letters, his trolley abandoned by the gate. But when the postman moved on to the next house, Dad's gaze didn't shift from the window.

"What's the matter?"

"I used to take you two there. I was just thinking how lovely it would be to go back again one day."

When I'd gone with Josh the previous year, I thought it had been my first trip, so it was a surprise to hear Dad say I'd been before. I didn't probe further, though. From what I recalled, it was a lovely place. If he wanted to go, it wouldn't do any harm to take him.

"There's nothing stopping us going after shopping next week."

I led the way through the gloom of the hallway, where I shuffled the scattered circulars into a pile that I handed to Dad. Blinking, I stepped into the dazzling sunshine. Josh squinted and shielded his eyes, while Will looked about without difficulty, his sunglasses now having a purpose.

A lawnmower droned nearby, wafting the aroma of freshly cut grass in our direction. I breathed in the smell, hoping the beautiful morning would stretch into the afternoon. Behind me, Dad patted his pocket to check he had his keys and stuffed a roll of carrier bags under his arm before shutting the door. Then he turned and stared at me, open-mouthed.

"What on earth are those marks on your face?"

♦

If I'd had Sean's number, I would have cancelled our trip on the grounds that Josh had been naughty and didn't deserve a trip out to Potterham model village – an excuse also known as 'I don't want to be seen out looking like this'. He turned up on the dot of one o'clock and tapped on the front door. Not wishing to be melodramatic – although I was – I made him stand well back from the half-open door until he'd heard my explanation.

"You have to be honest. How bad do I look?" I said.

His eyes searched my face and he shrugged. "There's nothing to see."

I turned to give him a profile view of the graffitied side. He peered intently at it.

"You can see a few marks, but not enough to worry about."

Mollified, I grabbed the bag I'd packed with nappies, drinks and our rain macs – although we wore T-shirts – and ushered Josh out of the door. We strolled at his pace along the walkway and down the steps to where, unable to find a space, Sean had abandoned his huge car in front of mine.

When I opened the boot to get the buggy, I said, "I need to get the car seat too."

"No need. I had one properly fitted for my niece. Josh is the same age."

"A good look for a single man." I sniggered.

He shrugged. "Who cares?"

Once I'd strapped Josh into the child seat, I jumped into the front. Sean's dashboard looked more spaceship than car, and nothing like mine, which had plastic knobs for the radio and round dials for the speedometer, with the only digital item a tiny clock.

To think I'd been proud to have electric windows on my two-door car, although the passenger one sometimes jammed and needed a bit of levering to get it open. I preferred it that way to refusing to close.

This car gave the option of different temperatures for the front seats. Mine was set to 17°C, which meant cold air blasted out from the vents, giving me goosebumps, but I didn't mind. It tempered the heat of the sun through the windscreen.

"I'm looking forward to seeing the model village again," I said. "Dad was gutted he couldn't join us."

Sean shrugged. "Why doesn't he? We've got room."

I laughed. "That would be fun for you."

We'd reached the junction for the main road, where Sean brought the car to a halt. "I mean it. It's a gorgeous day. Why leave your dad inside when he could be out enjoying it with his grandson?" Then he grinned. "And it would be another body to look after the two terrors. Believe me, we'll need all the help we can get if Josh is anything like my niece."

I thought of Dad's wistful face. Apart from regular trips to the supermarket, we'd gone to the bank, hospital and once to the garden centre this year. Hardly exciting. Occasionally, we went for a walk to the local rec, but I couldn't remember ever popping by to drag him off for a walk in the woods, to feed the ducks in Holdenwell's main park, or for a drive to the lovely Didlingbury, even though I'd thought he'd like it. I'd invited him to come to London during the Easter holidays, but that had been a step too far for him at the time.

But a trip to the model village would be perfect, especially on a beautiful day like this.

"It would mean bringing Will too."

Sean shrugged. "As I said, the more help the merrier. Give your dad a call. We'll be with him in ten minutes."

Chapter 29

DAVID'S DESK WAS EMPTY apart from the monitor, its wires trailing along the top, the phone, and a paperclip, its end bent out of shape. Was that the one I'd seen him using to pick his teeth the other day? I cringed at the memory: his face contorting as he dug the implement deeper into his teeth, then extracting it to examine whatever he'd drawn out.

Emma had emailed me to say that David was off sick this week and asking me to assign his work among the team. I'd read this on my phone, while waiting for my laptop to start up, but it seemed to have got stuck on updating the system.

At a loss what to do in the meantime – I'd finished the workshop sheets at home the previous day – I made hot drinks for the team and settled down to flick through my photographs from Saturday: Josh trying to climb over the rocks to reach a passing train, rescued by a laughing Sean, who had spun him around like a whirligig and put him down elsewhere; Will examining the quirky shop names and bending down with Josh to peer inside windows and through the parted church doors; Dad stunned by the size of the real-life fish in the ponds and the beautiful plants and hedging, but complaining – in a joking tone – that the zoo animals weren't to scale. I'd tried to remember what the model village had looked like when we'd been children and whether Mum had visited with us. But both remained a blank. Memory could be an elusive thing, refusing to yield even under the most desperate longing.

Sean's sister, Casey, had arrived an hour late after her daughter had thrown the most awful tantrum – her words, not mine – and refused to leave the house. She hadn't wanted to let Sean down, so she'd come as soon as she could. When we decamped to the café for ice creams and drinks, Casey's little one sat at the end of the bench, arms folded, lips jutting, refusing to join in. She made Josh look saintly, except for the tell-tale signs of his earlier mischief, which stained our faces. Thankfully, the photographs were kind to me – either taken from my unmarked side or making the lines look like shadows cast by nearby branches.

On the desk beside me my work phone buzzed. Oliver. Usually, I'd feel a flutter of excitement at the thought of talking to him, but they didn't appear.

He sounded his usual relaxed self. "Hi. I hope you don't mind me asking, but can you pick up Christabel, Tariq and Will and take them to the Monday club tonight around five-thirty?"

"That's fine. I could bring them back too if that helps," I said.

"No need. I'll be out of my meeting well before then. How are you doing, though?"

My laptop finally installed its updates and whirred into life, requesting my password. I needed to finish the grant application ahead of this afternoon's workshop, so I kept my response polite but brief.

"Good, thanks."

Then I felt bad. He was a friend. Just because I had work to do, it didn't mean I should be curt. "How are you and Christabel?"

"Love's young dream?" He laughed. "You'll have to ask Will. He sees more of her than I do."

I didn't say that the last thing Will would discuss with me was his love life. During our trip to the model village, Dad had teased him about going out for Sunday lunch with Christabel the following day, but Will had responded by pointing out that at least *he* had a girlfriend, which had caused the conversation to grind to a halt.

"And you?" I could ask without feeling wistful or forcing myself to sound cheerful.

"Good, thanks. Tom and I went to London at the weekend to see *Idomeneus*."

The way he said it suggested I should know what he was talking about. "That sounds great!" then I hesitated. Was this Idomeneus a person, a band or something else? Not wanting to sound stupid, I said, "Hold on, I've dropped something."

It would take too long to open Outlook on the laptop, so I grabbed my personal phone and typed 'Idomeneus London' into the search engine, hoping I'd spelled it correctly. The results showed it was a theatre production. I had a vague recollection of reading something about it.

"Did you enjoy the production? The critics say it's good." At least, the one I'd found did. An extraordinary reworking of a Greek myth, apparently.

He chuckled. Did he know what I'd done? "Excellent, thanks. What did you get up to?"

"We went to Potterham model village."

"Nice," he said, using the meaningless word.

Then it hit me. Not a sledgehammer-type whack, but a tap-tap that had been trying to make itself felt. Even if Oliver hadn't been gay – which was an impossible 'if' – we would have had no chance together. He might be a lovely man, good-looking and kind, but he and I were very different people, only linked by work and our siblings.

"It was fun, but probably not your thing, unless you like being surrounded by a horde of screeching children."

He shuddered audibly down the phone. "I'll stick with young people. They're easier."

He wasn't wrong there. We said goodbye and I put my phone down. Through the dusty office window, a plane cut across the sky leaving a twisting white trail, while below someone honked their car horn. I let the noise wash over me, enjoying the natural beauty: the birds flitting between the buildings, the pigeons nestling on nearby window ledges, the leaves shimmering in the sun. Gone was my longing for something I couldn't have. Instead I felt a sense of calm.

Finally, I was free to move forward.

My phone pinged. Sean – we'd exchanged numbers on Saturday.

Are you around Wednesday evening?

Smiling, I typed: *Not until eight, I'm afraid. Got to pick up Will from Samson's. What about Thursday evening?*

I could ask Oliver to do it, but I'd rather save his help for another day. Also, Dad had his job interview on Wednesday and I wanted to see him to find out how it went.

Moments later my phone pinged again.

Great. Say 7? I'll shout a takeaway. Will Josh join us?

He'll probably be in bed, I typed. At least, I hoped he would.

◆

Less than an hour before I was due to leave the office on Wednesday, Emma slid into her seat beside me, clasping her laptop to her chest and holding a takeaway drink from the café.

"Do you have a minute?" she hissed.

"I need to leave by a quarter to five latest."

Her 'minute' never equalled mine – or adhered to the laws of physics.

Smiling, she checked the time. "This won't take long."

She put her laptop on the desk and nodded towards the meeting area by the kitchen. When I'd saved my work, I followed her over, choosing the chair that faced the office, so I could see anyone walking towards us. I'd formed that habit thanks to David, who could often be found lurking in the kitchen on the pretext of making a drink while spying on people in the meeting area. I sat and gazed expectantly at Emma.

"I'd like you to keep this confidential for now, but David has chosen to hand in his notice rather than go through the disciplinary process."

The jubilation I'd expected at the thought of never having to confront David again in the office or at a meeting didn't materialise.

"Poor David."

She raised her eyebrows. "Not quite my sentiments. His actions to foment trouble with the library group were nothing short of stupid. It's incredible that he would risk irreparable damage to Chartley library's future – and that of our team – because of his ego. Thank goodness Mark Carradine is aware that David was a lone wolf."

We fell silent. I could see what he'd hoped to achieve. If I'd had to face many more meetings like that one, I would have found another job, freeing up the neighbourhood manager role for him (or another person).

But she was right. While David had made his feelings clear about me taking his coveted position – there was no excuse for what he'd done. It wouldn't be plain sailing now he'd moved on though. He could turn up at a residents' meeting or as part of a local action group, able to stir trouble without the constraints of his role to hold him back. If he'd felt upset before, I dreaded to think about how his fury would build over the coming days and weeks.

Emma crossed her legs and shifted in her chair. "His position won't be filled. We need to absorb staff losses while we can."

I'd been lucky to be taken on at a time when most areas were cutting staff, not recruiting them. But her words were a stark reminder that the scythe that felled the youth service and library staff wasn't far from our door. Although this job hadn't been quite what I'd expected, I didn't want to go back to my old boss to beg for my old one back – or to any sales role, for that matter. With David on the loose, would it mean that other meetings could go the same way as Chartley? I shuddered. I couldn't bear to be shouted at like that again.

Spotting my gloom, Emma gave me a warm smile. "But you're doing well with Didlingbury. When does the report go to committee?"

"Next week. Fingers crossed they approve it – it would be fantastic for that small community to keep their librarian."

"And they'll get a shop," she said. "A win for them. And you're working on that project around social isolation for vulnerable men. How's that going?"

Emma had a way of showing the positives among the negatives. I settled down to tell her. Before I knew it the time had flown by. I glanced at my watch and jumped up.

"I have to go! It's twenty to five."

She laughed. "So it is! My minutes do seem to be elastic."

♦

Tariq and Will jumped out of the car, throwing 'thank yous' in their wake. At least Tariq shut his door – making the car shudder – whereas Will raced off, barging into Samson's like a love-struck bull. They'd both been in a state of excitement since receiving a text from Christabel which mentioned a chocolate cake she'd made. Christabel and cake: two of Will's favourite words. I had a feeling that 'pizza' still ranked first.

Sighing, I leaned across the front passenger seat to pull the door shut. As I drove off to collect Josh from nursery, I remembered Dad's job interview. When I'd swung by to pick up Will, I'd been in such a rush that I'd forgotten to ask how it had gone. I tried to recall Dad's expression – had he seemed more happy or sad than usual? – but there had been no clues in his countenance. He'd just seemed glad to see the back of Will for a few hours, particularly when Will's midweek day off fell on the one day all his friends worked.

Once I'd picked up Josh, we headed over to Dad's house. The earlier blue sky had been replaced by a drizzle the weather forecasters promised would turn to heavy rain by nightfall. I hoped it would wait until we made it back to Samson's Café or, even better, home.

My wish didn't come true. We arrived at Dad's to heavy rain and just one parking space halfway down the road. I unstrapped

Josh, who slowed the process by wanting to do it himself. Once out, I swung him onto my hip and, squinting in the pelting rain, dashed along the road. His bag cut into my shoulder, his bouncing feet pummelled my stomach.

"Next time, remind me just to phone Dad," I hissed more to myself than him.

But when I reached the door and Dad opened it, I didn't care about my soggy top or the drips trickling down my back. I simply wanted him to have good news for once. He stood back to let us in, still in his interview shirt and trousers, although he'd discarded the jacket and tie.

"Has Will forgotten something?" He sounded worried.

As I stepped inside, the warmth buffeted me, thick with the smell of cooked food. "We came to see you. To find out how today went."

Without answering, he headed through to the lounge. The BBC news blasted out, making it difficult to chat.

"You've got that a bit loud."

He punched the volume down on the remote and eased himself onto the settee. A navy tie lay over the arm rest, creased where he'd knotted it earlier.

"So, are you going to tell me or is it top-secret?" I settled down beside him, tucking Josh on my knee, but he wriggled free and knelt to pull one of Dad's TV listing magazines from the shelf beneath the coffee table.

Dad chuckled. "With your MI5 skills, I was expecting you to tell me."

I rolled my eyes. "Just answer. Please! Do you think you did well?"

He rubbed his chin and gazed heavenward. "Think? That's a relative term. I might think I did well, but others may not."

I slapped his arm playfully. "Dad!"

Josh looked confused to see me telling Grandad off. He got to his feet and tapped Dad's leg. "Naughty Granda."

"See," I said. "Even Josh thinks you're being a pain."

Dad took a deep breath and grinned. "They offered me the job."

"Dad!" I squealed and gave him a tight hug, feeling the warmth of his body, the sound of him breathing. Something I hadn't done since his cancer treatment, when he'd seemed too fragile for more than a gentle cuddle.

Laughing, he pushed me away. "I didn't say I accepted it, though."

"Did you?" Surely he was joking.

"I did! I start a week on Monday. It's on the tills, but I could do more in time."

I threw my arms around his middle again, this time giving him the tightest bear hug I could manage: a bone-crushing hug that wrung away all the worries and stress we'd gone through over the past few years. He had a job. Money of his own. A reason to leave the house each day. Best of all, it would give him the chance to meet people. I gave him a big sloppy kiss, ignoring the face he pulled as he used the back of his hand to wipe it away.

"Well done, Dad. I'm so chuffed for you. Josh, give your grandad a high five!"

Chapter 30

THURSDAY WAS A LOVELY EVENING. Sadly, an excited Josh – unused to having male visitors – decided to make regular appearances, so Sean and I didn't a chance to have a proper conversation. The way I looked at it, if a boomerang toddler refusing to go to bed didn't put him off, that was another thing ticked off the list. No doubt there would be many more hurdles in our growing friendship. And, yes, we were still more friends than anything, although I found myself hoping that our relationship would blossom into a romance.

No longer did Sean appear too tall. Instead, he seemed a good height – a nice one, even. Inoffensive. At least he'd be able to reach the upper shelves in supermarkets, whereas I had to climb up the shelving, praying that it would hold my weight. He had strong hands too, able to twist the lid off an unco-operative jam jar. I could have done it myself by banging it on the counter to release the air lock, but sometimes it's nice to be able to resolve an issue without risk of injury to myself or the house.

Often my heart gave a little jolt when I gazed into his hazel eyes. He was such a wonderful man, what could he possibly see in me?

Sean couldn't come around at the weekend, having agreed to visit his friend who'd recently moved to Brighton for work, but we texted each other and he sent a photo of the beach and, a few minutes later, the view from the pub.

On Tuesday he phoned me at work during what he hoped was my lunch hour. That was unheard of in my current team – and even in my old job. Laughing, I choked on my sandwich, spitting soggy crumbs onto my laptop.

"A working lunch," I corrected him, using a wipe to clean the keyboard.

"I have to work both days this weekend, but have you got this Friday afternoon off?"

I stopped myself from taking another bite of my cheese sandwich. "Yes, but Josh won't be at nursery."

"How about we all go to the park? And then…" He paused, the silence stretching into what felt like an age. "I-I don't know how you feel about it, but would you like to go out for dinner with me on the Friday night? Leah has said that she and Paul will babysit."

"Leah!" Thank goodness I didn't have food in my mouth, or it would have splattered the screen. But when he didn't say anything, I realised I hadn't answered his question. The usual anxiety about money crept to mind, but I pushed it away. He might offer to pay, but I had a bit saved up and could go halves. "I'd really like that, but are you sure Leah would be happy to babysit?"

He sounded relieved. Had he thought I'd say no and remind him that I wanted to be friends?

"Apparently, she and Paul helped his sister out the other day and she's a demon babysitter. Her words, not mine."

"I can imagine." I left him to decide what that meant but I felt ridiculously pleased when he laughed at my dry sense of humour.

We chatted for a few minutes more, neither of us wanting to end the call, but both knowing we had to get back to work.

Down the line I heard someone call to him and he apologised. "I have to go. I'll call later."

As I said goodbye an email notification popping up on my laptop screen. Property services. The one I'd been waiting for.

I hung up and clicked on the email. *Please let it be a yes to the report's proposal.*

It was! They'd copied Agnes Drew into the message, but I decided to give her a ring. She and her band of villagers had worked so hard with me to make this happen. Now, instead of losing a library and their librarian, they'd gained space for a village store alongside the soon-to-be-moved post office.

♦

It was with a happy heart that I strolled with Josh to Rachel's house that evening. As we passed the parking area by her block, a police car headed our way, slowing to let us cross the road at Josh's pace. The policeman leaned out of the driver's window and called out to me.

Smiling, I went over. "Hello, Glenn. I didn't recognise you for a moment. How are you?"

He lifted his sunglasses. "Madeleine." As usual, his voice carried an edge of sarcasm, even when being friendly. Now I'd got to know him better, I'd come to understand that it wasn't intentional. "Better now I've got the news. Janice is well chuffed."

"News?" I frowned.

"Haven't you heard?" He seemed delighted that I hadn't. "Your council has kicked him out."

I didn't need to ask who, as Glenn jerked his head towards the Flying Scotsman's flat above. I stole a glance at the windows, praying he wasn't spying on us. I couldn't spot a shadow behind the nets, but he might be lurking unseen. Once he'd topped himself up with beer or whisky, he might decide to come looking for someone to blame. That would be Janice and anyone else he'd seen associating with the police, which might include me. Hopefully, he'd never know the part I'd really played.

"But where will he go?"

Glenn sniggered. "That's the best part. They're putting him in a hostel in my old patch. He'll be the new sarge's problem."

"Chartley? What have they done to deserve him?"

A serious expression crossed Glenn's face. "I don't envy anyone living near the likes of him but at least he won't be near Janice."

I had a thought – wouldn't it be wonderful if the Flying Scotsman ended up next to Richard Lewes? – but I shoved it aside. Even he didn't deserve that and, anyhow, the likes of Richard wouldn't live near a hostel.

Glenn and I said our goodbyes and I walked over to Rachel's flat.

"Have you heard the good news?" I asked Rachel after she'd let us in. Josh had zoomed off, making plane noises, in search of Kieran. An "Oof!" told me he'd found his landing pad.

Rachel smiled. "About you and Sean?"

"Not that! About the Flying Scotsman. He's being evicted."

We went through to the kitchen where she switched on the kettle and I relayed the little I knew from what Glenn had told me.

"Chartley." Her breath whistled between her teeth. "I hope that flaming idiot, the one who stitched you up, ends up living next to him."

"He won't. They never do."

"No, it'll be some poor sod like us," she said. "Give me a min."

She went through to the lounge and came back a moment later, putting a finger to her lips as she reached into the bread bin past the loaf to bring out a packet of cigarettes and a lighter. I didn't say a word. Giving up smoking was a battle she'd have to win by herself.

We stepped outside. Thankfully, Glenn's car had gone and the Flying Scotsman's flat remained silent. Rachel ushered me around the side of the block, where she leaned against the wall and lit her cigarette. A decade ago we would have been hiding our cigarettes or alcohol from our parents or teachers, but she'd simply moved on to concealing her smoking habit from her husband. I didn't believe Kieran had no idea what she got up to. If the smell of stale cigarettes didn't give the game away, the random nicotine patches she wore every few months or so should.

Behind Rachel's block stood a row of tall leylandii trees that hid the business park behind – or, rather, obscured their view of our estate. A small beech hedge neighboured us, fronting a path beside the main road. The drone of passing cars forced Rachel to raise her voice.

"So Leah's babysitting your Josh on Friday night, then?"

"Do you think she'll be all right?"

Rachel gave me a playful shove. "What do you think she'll do? Leave him while she goes to the pub?"

"No, but…" I fought to form the words. "She's great, but she's not the babysitting type."

"She might not have been a few months ago, but you should see her and Paul now. I reckon they're close to settling down."

"Really? Already?"

"Since when has Leah lasted more than a few weeks with anyone? This is *the* great romance. And they're well suited. He's steadied her right down. Old dogs can change their spots, you know."

Although I doubted Leah would like being called an old dog, I didn't remark on Rachel's mixed-up expression. Instead, I considered her point. Leah's drinking *had* noticeably decreased in the past months. She'd told me about trips she and Paul had taken to Warwick Castle and Hampton Court Palace and the wonderful walks they'd done by the Grand Union Canal and nearby rivers. My ditzy, tipsy, man-loving friend had joined the world of boring adults.

"You're right," I said.

"Kieran and I can pop around to see them on Friday night and say hello. That way you'll have your mind set at rest." She took a drag on her cigarette and blew the smoke out in a horizontal stream. "And we can be there to find out how your date went."

"If Josh hears Kieran's voice, you'll have him for company too," I warned.

She took no notice. "I'm so pleased you've gone for Sean. He's wonderful, and he's got money."

"That's not important," I said.

"But it helps." She screwed the tip of her cigarette into the wall, but didn't drop the butt. "There's nothing glamorous about not running out of food or not being able to top up the electricity meter."

We strolled back in silence. Words weren't needed. We'd had similar upbringings and knew how hard life could be when money was tight. While it was lovely that Sean had a good income of his own, I'd come to like him for other reasons – not least his kindness and empathy with the most important people in my life: Josh, Will and my dad.

But it was more than that.

Unlike Oliver, who I'd been immediately attracted to – for all the wrong reasons – Sean had been a very slow burn, but he'd lit a candle in my heart that brightened each time I thought of him.

While I waited outside in the fresh air, Rachel stopped by the bins and scraped her cigarette against the wall to check it was out before tossing it away. She took a bottle of perfume from her bag and gave herself half a dozen squirts before pulling out a packet of chewing gum and folding a piece into her mouth.

"Want one?"

I pulled one from the pack. The stench of her perfume hit the back of my throat and made my eyes water. At least the spearmint flavour might help.

"I told Kieran I was getting the latest gossip on you, but I knew it all, really." She linked her arm through mine, overwhelming me with her scent. "I never thought I'd see the day when you and Leah had partners, but here we are."

"Hold on a minute," I said. "We haven't even had our first date yet."

♦

I'd spent the afternoon with Sean and Josh at the park wearing jeans and a top, although it was more like a smart work top than a T-shirt, but when it came to dressing for a meal in a restaurant with someone I wanted to impress, I found myself standing in front of the wardrobe, at a loss. I gazed at my palm, remembering my happiness when Sean had slipped his hand into mine as we walked to and from the swings. Excitement had spread through every part of me. This was happening, this was real. It had been so long since I'd held an adult man's hand, it had seemed strange. After Sean left, Rachel came round to look after Josh until Leah arrived, leaving me with too much time to get dressed. I couldn't wait for tonight.

Last time we'd gone out for a meal with Sean, Leah had worn a sparkly black dress and heels, but I didn't feel comfortable looking too showy. I pulled three dresses from the wardrobe, which I hadn't worn since my pregnancy, and laid them on the bed. None of them would do. When Rachel came upstairs a moment later, she found me in my towel, sitting on the small patch of bed that didn't contain a dress, and staring out of the window.

"Nothing's right," I said. "I should have bought a new dress or something. These are like nightclub outfits. No good for a meal in a restaurant."

"I've got something that might work."

She scurried back to her house, returning with a lemon and white shift dress. I was dubious but when Rachel urged me to try it on, I realised how lovely it was, although I didn't have a pair of co-ordinating shoes. Would black heels work?

"I'd lend you my sandals, but my feet are two sizes bigger than yours. Anyhow, your feet will be hidden under the table and he'll be too busy looking at your face to care."

Within five minutes of Leah and Paul arriving, the doorbell rang. I was pushed outside with barely time to give Josh a swift kiss – not that he cared, as Rachel had brought her play mat round so he could drive the cars around the roads.

Sean stood on the walkway, looking handsome in a well-fitting suit, the same coy smile on his face as he'd worn when he'd brought me flowers. But now he held out nothing but his arm. Grinning, I linked mine through his and we sauntered away, in full view of the trio craning to watch us. We drove away but, after he turned the corner, he pulled over.

"Before we go anywhere, let me do this." He leaned over and gave me a gentle kiss. When he went to move away, I drew him closer, needing more.

A pair of young lads strolled past, jeering, and we broke apart, grinning. He steered the car back onto the road but rested his hand on my thigh until we reached the junction. The warmth left a tingling imprint through the fabric of my dress.

I hadn't thought to ask where we were going. The name of a restaurant would be meaningless to me, since I'd been to so few. But when he pulled into a car park filled with shiny Range Rovers and BMWs, I raised my eyebrows and fingered my handbag, which held a precious fifty pounds. More than Josh and I spent on food and nappies some weeks. Knowing my luck, it wouldn't cover the cost of half a bottle of wine here. I tried to tuck the worry to the back of my mind.

Sean turned off the ignition and swung around in his seat to face me. His eyes searched mine and he reached out and took both of my hands in his. "I can see what you're thinking. But, please don't. Let this be my treat."

When I went to protest, he stopped me. "I could have chosen somewhere different, but I wanted this to be special. You have no idea how much I've waited for tonight. Ever since I saw you at Rachel's party in March. And now, I get my wish."

I slipped from the car and he took my hand to lead me towards the restaurant. I felt the familiar burble of nerves building. Would the posh people in the restaurant look up from their meals and spot the council-house girl in a borrowed dress and mock me? I held my head high as we followed the maître d' through the dimly lit restaurant to our table, but no one gave us more than a passing glance.

A candle flickered on the table between us, casting shadows across Sean's face, its light shimmering in his soft hazel eyes. He reached for my hand and I held it gladly, basking in the warmth of his gaze.

"I love your humour, our easy chats, your intelligence. In fact, just being with you."

I glanced down at the table, embarrassed by his scrutiny but he squeezed my hand, drawing me back.

"The thing is, Maddie, you deserve this. And you mustn't forget it. This life…" He looked at the tables around us, where women – and men – flashed jewellery worth more than I could imagine. "Should belong to you as much as anyone here. Don't define yourself by where you live. It's a building, not a person. People like you who work hard, are loyal to your friends, loving to your family, caring to others – you deserve the world."

I opened my mouth to disagree, but my voice caught in my throat and I swallowed. Until now, the phrase 'people like you' had always been used as a put-down by Derek and people like him who couldn't see past the house to the person inside. But Sean was right. I didn't always have to choose which world I lived in. People like me could have both.

Chapter 31

I CLASPED MY COFFEE and allowed myself to melt into the memories of the previous weekend. What wouldn't I do to relive it? But, like a rainbow, my dreams moved further away with every step. I'd found my treasure though: Sean, who'd entwined his fingers through mine, gazed into my eyes as we ate, and made such interesting conversation I hadn't noticed the time passing.

"He's gorgeous. He came around last night and we watched a film."

It happened again. The tightness in my chest each time I thought about him, leaving me breathless with anticipation.

Rachel smiled fondly. "Is he coming on Sunday?"

I nodded. "Dad and Will are coming too. We're getting the party bits when we do the shopping tomorrow."

"What? They're coming to yours? I thought the steps were too much for your dad."

"He says he'll risk them." I chuckled. "He's got so much more energy now. He's happy in his job too. I can't believe the change in him."

Rachel sipped her tea and murmured, "Ditto for you with Sean."

She gazed over to the kitchen window, which she'd put it on the latch moments earlier after complaining about how stuffy it was. Her nets billowed in the breeze, drawing in the strains of Josh's voice as he helped Kieran to clean their car. No longer did we have to worry about burning cigarette butts and other missiles being launched by the Flying Scotsman. Now daisies and dandelions covered the grass in front of Rachel's flat, although if the distant sound of the lawnmower was anything to go by, the council's ground maintenance team were heading this way.

"So you're not dumping us for Sean, then?" Rachel said.

I raised my eyebrows then realised what she meant. Tonight was our girls' night in, where we played daft games and gossiped, aided by Prosecco.

"I'm not going to drop my mates. Anyhow, he's coming round tomorrow when he finishes work."

Again, my heart twisted in delight at the thought of seeing Sean. I'd never felt this way before. Not about Josh's father, Scott, or Oliver, who'd been nothing more than a crush. If I added up my feelings for every man I'd ever dated or fancied, it couldn't touch the way I felt now. I let my pent-up breath hiss out between my teeth. If I didn't, I would surely burst with longing.

Twenty-six hours before I saw Sean again.

"I feel like a blooming teenager."

"Make the most of it. Soon you'll be up to your ears in nappies." She grinned. "Whoops. You did that one already."

♦

Sean arrived on the dot of ten o'clock on Sunday morning. I spotted his car pull up and waited by the open front door, hoping for a moment alone with him. Smiling, he strolled towards me, carrying a brightly wrapped parcel. He radiated summer in a pair of cotton trousers and a short-sleeved cream shirt, undone at the collar, looking so suave and sexy it took everything I had not to race over and throw myself in his arms.

"Long time no see." He grinned and I smiled back. It was just twelve hours since we'd kissed goodnight after he'd spent the evening here.

He leaned down, enveloping me in the scent of his aftershave. As his lips met mine, Josh raced out, screeching, "Sean! Sean!" and bound his arms around Sean's leg.

"Happy birthday, little man. Or should I say 'big man' now you're the grand age of three?" Sean laughed. "I can't walk with you attached to me like that."

Duly released, we went through to the lounge where Josh pointed out his new wooden railway track, where he'd lined up Thomas beside two new carriages, his old police car and assorted other cars.

While Sean put the box on the floor and helped Josh to rip the paper into shreds, I took on the role of litter picker. I knew what Sean had brought, so I watched Josh's face as he pulled out a turntable, a tunnel, and a suspension bridge with red plastic towers.

Beaming, he lifted out a red engine, then a green engine. "Percy *and* James!" he whooped.

It seemed a shame to take him away from his new toys, so Sean and I settled down for an hour on the carpet before going out to feed the ducks. I'd wanted to take Josh to the zoo as a birthday treat, but it would have been impossible to cram everything into the weekend. Instead, we would all go the following Saturday, along with Dad and Will.

Sean had brought proper duck seed from the pet shop and I'd made us each a roll so we could sit on the riverbank and watch the world go by, but Josh had other plans. He raced among the Canada geese, pretending to be a dinosaur – which had the unexpected bonus of a geese-free duck-feeding session, until he accidentally tossed his roll at the ducks instead of the seed. As an Exocet goose bombed into the water to lift the dripping roll in its beak, wave after wave of its comrades followed, splashing down to battle for pieces of the roll.

Tears welled in Josh's eyes and he pointed at the flapping, squawking geese. "Naughty birds."

Sean patted Josh on the shoulder. "Sadly, that's called karma. They didn't like being chased, so this is their payback. But—" He picked Josh up and swung him around. "You get to eat cake later and they don't. Tell you what, why don't we start with ice cream?" He rifled through his pocket. "My treat."

I folded up the blanket and stuffed it into my bag and we ambled over to the ice-cream stall at the edge of the park. As Josh toddled in between us, holding our hands, Sean looked across to me and smiled, making my insides churn. We chose a table beneath the shade of a horse chestnut to eat our ice cream. When I scooped the melting drips off Josh's cone with my thumb, Sean caught me and grinned.

"You've got a bit here."

He wiped the smear from my cheek and popped his finger into his mouth. Not to be outdone, Josh dabbed my bare arm with his ice cream and leaned over to lick it. Romance would never be plain sailing with a son on board, but it wouldn't be boring either.

Later, Sean lit the candles on the cake and I carried it in to the lounge to an enthusiastic but out-of-tune rendition of 'Happy Birthday'. Josh, who had abandoned his toys to sit on Dad's lap for the cake, clapped in delight with everyone. Next to him Will and Christabel had squished onto the settee. He'd strung his arm around her neck while she'd spread her lovely dress over his lap so it didn't get crushed. She'd have to move it when we shared the cake.

Across from them, Leah and Paul were crammed into an armchair while, on the carpet, my cousin Chelsea and her family had re-laid the train track so it ran across the lounge and over to where Rachel and Kieran knelt beside the play mat they'd bought Josh. Now he could drive his cars – and trains – from the station on one side of the room to the town's roads and beneath the viaduct bridge he insisted should be in the town square.

After the cake had been eaten and Christabel's dress had been wiped clean after Josh had smeared it with blue icing, we attempted a game of pass the parcel. Christabel won the whoopie cushion. Josh shifted his affection from Dad to Christabel until she handed the cushion over to the birthday boy, who insisted on holding a competition to see who could make the loudest farting noises.

"I can see you're teaching him well," Dad said. But he allowed Josh to place the cushion under his seat and obliged us with a thundering trump.

All the time Sean was there, working with me, helping me, handing out drinks, making sure no one wanted for anything. Least of all me. When I stood to one side to survey the happy scene, I found his hand reaching for mine and he pulled me closer. As he wrapped me in his warmth, a bubble of happiness grew inside me, so huge it must surely burst.

When Josh rubbed his ears and yawned, Dad shifted to the edge of his seat and signalled for me to come over.

"Are you okay to take us back now? It's getting late."

I glanced at the time. Seven-thirty. Josh needed to get to bed, especially as he had nursery the next day. "Of course."

"I'll take you all," Sean said. He turned back to me. "Are you okay for me to come back after?"

I gave his hand a tight squeeze. There was no need to ask. I'd love it.

Sean returned to an empty house, cleared of mess thanks to my wonderful friends, who'd insisted on tidying up while I put Josh to bed. I made him a cup of coffee and myself a hot chocolate which we took through to the lounge and settled down to watch TV. I lay with him tucked behind me on the settee, although he couldn't have been comfortable with his legs hanging off the end.

The programme rolled on, but I couldn't concentrate, aware of his warm breath against my ear, his fingertips travelling up and down my arm, sending shivers down my spine. I shifted around to gaze into his gorgeous eyes. His lips met mine, sending shards of excitement through me.

I wanted him so much. Needed him.

"Stay tonight," I whispered.

"Are you sure?" He caressed my cheek.

I thought about Josh asleep upstairs. He liked Sean and I'd never met a boyfriend I trusted more. But I'd make sure to close my bedroom door and to set my alarm clock an hour earlier, so I'd be up before Josh.

I was sure. This felt right.

My fingers entwined with his and he allowed me to lead him up the stairs, leaving our drinks to go cold on the coffee table.

◆

In the morning Josh woke up to find Sean and I sitting in the lounge chatting. He acted as it was the most normal thing in the world and

– after insisting Sean sat at the breakfast table and joined us for a bowl of cornflakes – brushed his teeth and got dressed quickly so he could spend five minutes playing trains with us before we took him to nursery.

As Sean had the day off, he offered to drive me to work and Josh to nursery. Then later he'd pick us up and take us to his flat for dinner. I hadn't been there before, but he warned me it was a typical bachelor pad, except – and he'd grinned at Josh at this point – it did have a huge box of toys, thanks to his niece's frequent visits.

As I clambered back into his car after taking Josh into nursery, Sean's hand strayed to my thigh and he gave it a gentle squeeze. Was he remembering last night? I'd never forget it. Or the early hours of the morning. Enclosed by a flood of delicious happiness, I smiled to myself and rested my hand on his, feeling the warmth of his body. I couldn't wait for tonight.

He pulled up outside the council offices and leaned across to give me a lingering kiss, only to be interrupted by a tap on the window. Derek, of all people! When Sean wound the window down, Derek stretched his arm into the car. I thought he meant to shake Sean's hand but instead he gripped his shoulder.

"Sean! What a surprise." He glanced over to me and his eyes widened behind his glasses. "Madeleine!" He turned back to Sean. "I thought it was you coming out of Court Place yesterday. But I thought it couldn't possibly be, or I would have tooted."

"You live at Court Place?" Sean said in a voice loaded with humour.

"Goodness, no!" Derek took his glasses off his purple nose and pointed the stem at Sean. "Driving past. Wouldn't catch me within fifty feet of the place." He pulled out his handkerchief and flapped it.

"He was visiting me," I called from the passenger seat.

Derek frowned. I could tell he couldn't decide whether to guffaw at another of my jokes or believe what I'd said. Instead he busied himself by wiping his glasses with his hankie.

Sean rested his elbow on the car door. "I'm moving in with Maddie. She's got a lovely place there."

I didn't know what to say. I liked him, but there was no need to rush to the next stage. But I kept my face serene and fought to hide the turbulence I felt inside.

"That's nice." Derek smoothed his frown. But he couldn't hide the crimson flush that engulfed the thread veins on his cheeks. He held out his hand to Sean. "Great to see you again. Please give my best to your father." He glanced at me and nodded. "Madeleine."

In his haste to get away, he almost tripped over the kerb. Laughing, I got out of the car then retrieved my laptop bag from the footwell. When I went to say goodbye to Sean, I found he'd got out too. He took me in his arms and kissed me.

"That one's for Derek and all the idiots like him. And don't worry, I'm not moving in tomorrow." He shrugged. "I just couldn't bear the thought of him looking down on you for all the wrong reasons. Just be yourself with him, Maddie. People like him are not worth the effort." He bent to give me another kiss. "My dad can't stand him, you know. Calls him a stuck-up twerp. And quite a bit more. Thankfully, Dad taught me the value of people, not money."

He glanced up, caught Derek peering at us through the glass wall that fronted the reception area, and waved. I giggled as Derek scuttled away.

"Dad's family knew his well. Derek's parents got their money thanks to an inheritance from an aunt, not from their extraordinary business acumen, as he likes to tell people. If he ever puts you down again, ask old Del Boy where he lived as a child. Not that it should matter, but he chose to make it that way." He bent to whisper in my ear. "The answer is Court Place. Where my favourite people live."

While I gasped, he pursed his lips, his gaze straying to the foyer where Derek had stood moments earlier. "I don't know why he tries so hard to hide it. Who cares about his childhood home? Just think what good he could have done if he'd accepted his past and worked to make people's lives better. Instead he hides behind a wall of pretence."

I, too, had built a wall between my worlds, furnishing them with different names, speech and friends. Thank goodness I hadn't been able to keep them apart or I could have found myself walking alone on a cold marble path, like the one Derek had chosen, rather than my sometimes haphazard life filled with friendship, love and laughter.

Sean tilted my chin to give me the final of a hat-trick of kisses. Stunned by the revelation about Derek – and myself – I hurried away, crossing the concourse and dashing up the steps. At the top, the glass doors yawned open and I paused to blow him a kiss. Giggling, I turned to find a bemused Emma standing by the reception desk. Still in the heady whirl of romance, I hurried over to her, treating her like a friend rather than a boss.

"I've had the most amazing weekend. And guess what?"

She obliged me with a "What?"

It's unbelievable, but you know Derek's always mocked people who live at Court Place?"

I didn't wait for her to answer before I blurted out, "He and his family lived there when he was young." Then it occurred to me that she might not like me gossiping about our Portfolio Holder. "I'll keep it quiet, though. But I had to tell someone."

"Was that your boyfriend?"

Her question puzzled me, but I nodded.

"He knows Derek, I see. Well, I can't imagine Derek will be mentioning Court Place again in a hurry, but if he does..." She gave me a sly look. "I've always found that a little bit of knowledge gives you a lot of power when you're dealing with people like him." She checked her watch. "My meeting attendee is running late. Have you got a—"

"Minute?" I laughed. "I've got ten, if your minute stretches that long."

I turned to face the window, to gaze out to where Sean's car had been moments earlier. Usually, I enjoyed work, but today I was impatient for it to end so I could be in Sean's arms again. As I smiled to myself, I saw a figure reflected in the window, and I turned to find Derek scurrying past. Looking like a startled rabbit, he caught sight of me, checked his watch, and gave me the briefest nod before bounding away through the doors.

No doubt he was late for a meeting, but his flustered expression made me want to burst into laughter. Instead I muttered a silent 'thank you' to my lovely boyfriend, who had brought so much to my life: joy, kindness, passion – and a bit of gossip that meant Derek was unlikely to mention Court Place in my earshot again. In turn, I would no longer care what people who didn't matter thought about me.

I hugged myself in delight. If Sean had given me all this in a few short weeks, I couldn't wait to see what our future would bring.

The Two Faces of
Maddie Meadows

The Two Faces of Maddie Meadows is a fictional account. I was raised on a lovely council estate similar to Alan and Will's one. Later, I lived for a while in a block of flats which had a poor reputation but where the vast majority of those living there – including myself – were trying to do our best for ourselves and our families. My son's behaviour as a toddler did inspire a few scenes. Toddlers are useful in that respect.

When I started writing this book, I looked forward to showing it to my dad as I thought he would enjoy reading this story. Alan's quiet but dry sense of humour is very much like his. Sadly, my dad didn't get to see this book. Instead, I have dedicated this to him, who – like so many single parents – worked so hard to raise his children the best he could.

If you enjoyed reading The Two Lives of Maddie Meadows, it would be really appreciated if you could take the time to review it on Amazon. Reviews are extremely helpful to authors.

The next book in this series: **The Gift of a Rose** is out in late summer 2020.

Other books by Sharley Scott

Bedlam & Breakfast at a
Devon seaside guesthouse

Katie is desperate to leave her stressful job, so she doesn't think too hard about moving to Devon to run a B&B, even if it means uprooting her family. She is certain she and Jason have a strong and loving relationship that can weather any storm.

Hooked by the beauty of Torringham with its quaint harbour and stunning coastline, they purchase Flotsam Guesthouse which needs more than a lick of paint to keep it afloat. Soon, Katie finds that renovating and running a guesthouse is taking its toll, especially when dealing with challenging guests and madcap neighbours, Shona and Kim. Katie comes to learn that trouble is afoot whenever Shona begs a favour.

However, when her adored daughter moves back to their old hometown, she wonders if they've made a huge mistake, especially when cracks begin to show in her marriage.

Her seaside idyll is crumbling along with her relationship. Should she let Flotsam Guesthouse founder while she salvages her marriage? Katie needs to decide where her priorities lie. The only issue is, she doesn't know.

B&Bers Behaving Madly at a
Devon seaside guesthouse

Running a guesthouse is never plain sailing, as Katie can testify. Eccentric or challenging guests are the usual order of the day. But when a sinister man moves in across the road, the first ripples of unease appear.

Katie has learned the hard way that a seaside idyll is never what it seems. She and Jason have worked hard at their marriage, but now she has other issues to tackle.

While her new cleaner has proved to be a godsend, she comes with a complicated love life. Then there's Katie and Jason's daughters, Emily and Lucy, whose boomerang visits definitely have an ulterior motive.

And what about the threatening man opposite who has taken an intense dislike to Shona, the madcap owner of the adjoining B&B. Shona's life has always been chaotic, but now it's verging on disaster.

As the season moves on and guests come and go, Katie fears her daughters have been keeping secrets of their own, while Shona's troubles come to a head.

When the B&Bers are behaving madly, anything can happen. Can Katie weather the storm?

Printed in Great Britain
by Amazon

55392054R00180